FOOL
STAR

FOOL STAR

James A. Landry

Fool Star

This book is written to provide information and motivation to readers. Its purpose is not to render any type of psychological, legal, or professional advice of any kind. The content is the sole opinion and expression of the author, and not necessarily that of the publisher.

Copyright © 2020 by James A. Landry.

Printed in the United States of America.

ISBN   978-1-951913-17-5   (Paperback)
ISBN   978-1-951913-18-2   (Digital)

Lettra Press books may be ordered through booksellers or by contacting:

Lettra Press LLC
30 N Gould St. Suite 4753
Sheridan, WY 82801, USA
1 303-586-1431 | info@lettrapress.com
www.lettrapress.com

"You know I was born to travel,

Can't be sorry I'm not home.

Rand McNally wrote my Bible,

Willie Nelson sings my song."

PART I

MEET TONY ==
THE FOOL STAR

CHAPTER ONE

The waxing gibbous moon is fat. Bulged and swelled in the midnight, it is hanging too low to the Southeast, like a bag of waters ready to burst. The Fool Star. It evokes anxiety, as Tony sits there inside sister Jean's screened-in sun porch, letting the chill in the air on this holiday evening cool his unease. Looking up at the moon, he feels like his own penumbra had gone a bit dim.

A lot can happen within the mind as one spends the time to recoup, recover and otherwise amp back up. To clean-up and get straight, as Tony tries this Christmastime, isn't easy, either. In Tony's case, *this* well-deserved time off, as have countless times before, hijacks the inviolable moment and forces him down. Down on a vivid excursion, another journey inward, to explore the lanes, ditches and gutters that run through the labyrinth of his memory.

Oh God, I'm on my way to a lesson.

There behind him, hidden so well it's obvious, appears the headstrong trail that Tony alone blazed. He realizes his aspirations and dreams had all fallen, thus far, sadly, short. This trip never fails to take a turn, by offering a glimpse of what the future might bring. It's a sometimes warm or sometimes terrifying, always powerful look into the shoulder blade of the illustrated man: Tony almost feels enchanted now. He sees before him times that look more like chores than a challenge. No longer could he view his life as he once did so confidently. The larger picture, once wholly constituted by all of the smaller portions of Tony's existence, was no longer sufficiently substantial. His colors, he feels, were running, like a flag in the hands of an enemy.

Some call it soul searching, others, confusion, or even mental illness. But, there's nothing mysterious about it, really. It boils down to what his conscience is asking the mind it oversees, and over which the soul passes judgment, the classically philosophical and rudimentary questions: who, what, when, where, how and why?

Yeah, how did it come to this?

Tony remembers… waking slowly, sure, it's Big D's annual Christmas party! The noise outside his door, however, droned afternoon. How many afternoons following the party? Tony cannot be sure. It's familiar territory.

I know I don't always wake up before the sunrise, which means I cannot be sure that sleep lasted the course of a single night.

Scared once again and compelled, many similar vows before, he can change his ways. His innards hurt, as if he swallowed a sword. Moreover, the directives in his head are loud and clear, like cannon balls bashing from wall to wall.

A vow to me… yet again… I shall! I SHALL wake daily… Before the sunrise… And, while the rest of my sick society slaves a Gregorian watch, I will simply watch the sun and the moon… Celebrate solstice and equinox… Always on time… All ways.

It sounds heavenly, but Tony easily reasons doing so reduces pure celestial events to mere timekeepers, nonetheless.

Hey, I am still a slave…

This has to be the worst hangover.

Never mind.

The auditory delay of the words formed by Pression's mouth wears off in a moment. Tony involuntarily jerks forward, realizing he's in the middle of a conversation, without knowing how or when he arrived.

"He shut me off, so I told him off," Tony tells Pression, stretching. Pression looks and sounds quite spirited for day's first words. She is slow in the morning, though not nearly as inherently sluggish as Tony.

"Like some creepy redneck, you told Big Daddy he could just *you-know-what your you-know-what*," corrects Pression. "But, from what I understand, it sounded more like '… jezz sugg mah digg…'" She's clearly incensed, but giggles at the very thought of having to utter the phrase, even in mere repetition.

Pression, at the same time, shoots Tony an uncommon hairy eyeball to stress her relative disgust. A look askance at him; a look of disdain and skepticism.

"You yelled at Big Daddy, Tony," she continues, "In front of his guests, and you really pissed him off."

In his mind's eye, Tony vaguely sees his bad little self, standing up to the grand, red man in the huge, green suit. Big D's Irish and Latino entourage surround them. It was later but not *that* late, and everyone else was still drinking as far as Tony could see. He too wanted another, Tony's mind spoon-feeding the information back now.

What else but a drink could have possibly mattered to a special guest at Big D's Christmas party - at the premier club in Miami - a town renowned for intemperance? Tony stumbles through justice, his own.

"You were turned away by the bartender," Pression fills in the gaps, "then you went right back to the bar, straight up to Big D."

Echoes of laughter and the beautifully ugly faces bring with the rejection belligerent intolerance. Tony's hearty barter for an adult beverage turned into a trip over the edge of decent.

"I'm glad I wasn't there to witness it," Pression says. All glamorization of what was already a low-life situation dwindles away as Tony imagines himself, eyes afloat, glazed and unfocused. His body sways rotationally, like Baum's Tin Man during the intoxicative middle break of his: *"If I Only Had a Heart."*

Tony isn't standing in the middle of the yellow brick road, though. Oh, no. Tony is standing in the middle of a human gauntlet of deep, dark Miami sludge, and his words actually sound more like "jezyoooszszsugmahdig… eyooo…

muthafug!" Humorously, Tony hides his ride on the guilt donkey again.

"Someday," he begins, "they'll say I am lucky to be alive."

"They already are!"

Pression is not impressed with the branded humor. This particular incident could have easily turned worse. Things can *most times* be better, Pression rationalizes, but things can *always* be worse.

"I have a headache, Presh." Tony murmurs. "But," he adds, "I don't feel too awful bad… considering." He reaches for Pression's rear end to round out his resolution.

"Jesus, Tony!" Pression uncharacteristically spits, "Go look in the effing mirror." She's crying now, into a flat, yellowing hotel pillow. Nonetheless, the incident pumps Tony up, to some degree, and the more he took in of his wounds, the better he felt. Queued male ego, beast-like, await release.

The boys in the crew must be extremely impressed. Oh, but what about the boys in the band? They may be a little pissed.

After all, it's not every day some displaced Yankee – a hot wire at that - walks up to, and tells the original Southern Big Dawg - Big Daddy - right up in his face, in the name of defiance, to "just... <u>SUCK</u> <u>MY</u> <u>DICK</u>!"

"I accept this whole thing as pure comedy, not much more, Presh," Tony believes what he is saying. "And, I expect the same reaction from the group."

No real harm done, Tony rationalizes, it was simply a hazard of the business. Nothing more than an extra bit of good, free press for the band. Maybe not so undesirable press for the Big Daddy's chain, either. Media and ratings are hunger-driven, and people down Miami are hungry for trouble.

We'll share an odd bit of humiliation, Tony justifies, and then the press will have been all but dead within a week. Big D is humiliated at having - against his own better judgment - invited a rock band to his finest and favorite gala of the year in the first place. He is most embarrassed, however, for having put-up with the cocky drummer's last-call nonsense in the second.

Tony's humiliation shown plain on the ass he made of himself in over indulgence. Beginning by then to desensitize, notwithstanding Big D's brand of punishment and discipline, that's what bothers Tony most. He's glad Presh was spared till the aftermath. Public humiliation, of course, makes Big D hurt worse.

...Always does, a mobster ego...

Tony, however, is used to all that. Traveling with a personal roady spoiled him somewhat, but Tony had eaten his share of knuckle sandwiches. The policy reads the crew not step in, until or unless, the talent is hit, or hits the ground first. This is not a group favorite, but agreed upon lawfully by all, as arising at all after hitting the ground can somehow build character. How long must talent lay still before the crew assumes there will be no ascension? The jury's still out.

Tony doesn't believe the oily, little grunt that slammed him in the face posed that much of a threat, but Presh cut short his explanation.

"He hit you hard enough to send you backward eight feet," she interrupts, "over the brass fence rail." All of Big Daddy's clubs have those maze-like entries in the foyers that lead to the action. Stereotypically true to theme, getting into a Florida Big Daddy's is reminiscent of a line for a Disney World attraction.

"Or, like a cow to slaughter," Pression says, "if you're a girl."

"Or, maybe a good milking," Tony forces a laugh.

Pression's still not laughing.

"Sawn," she puts on her best Farmer Brown impersonation, "in the shape you were in, boy, I do believe that a one-armed, rubber-breasted, Johnson City fem coulda done just as good a job, pinkie extended and all!"

"I consider myself lucky that Big D didn't haul off and hit me in his *own* defense," Tony replies, "Or offense, if you will."

Big Daddy is an easy six foot five and two hundred-eighty pounds of solid, Irish bruiser. He was the larger threat – the body of the guarded, not the bodyguard. Known on the circuit as a hot little Yankee, Tony stands five-feet-eight in his boots, maybe nine with his hair blown Lyle Lovitt high. A toned one-hundred-sixty-five pounds, born of northern Maine farmers, French-Irish, and Blackfoot-Indian boxers, Tony is full of Semtex and keg powder without an ounce of sissy. Mix all *that* up with a little alcohol and self-medication. Make that a lot of alcohol and medication.

"Early morning reports suggest," Pression continues, "you sailed backward, failed to regain your footing, and before you knew it, had a gut full of brass rail." She isn't finished. "You scored a ten from the crowd after doing a good-old-fashioned somersault over the damn thing."

With a crack and a splat, Tony hit those fucking Big-Daddy-green ceramic tiles, dead weight and face first. Mixing it up with kamikaze, pure white, and a head full of Ludes – as was the unfortunate norm – Tony was high, not hot. Higher than a Georgia Pine he was, until he hit the floor. From there, he's no higher than fresh cut timber, down, red sap running, ready to roll. He only need wait for the truck, like a log to the mill.

Instead of unconditionally calling it a night, Tony numbly shakes it off. He's blind to the splatters of blood on the walls surrounding him, as he shakes his head for clarity, like a chair-bashed wrestler. The crowd had already written him off for the night, and turned back toward the bar. While they were busy slapping each other on the back, Tony gets up again. There's no crew member in sight as he takes a token look around for support, so Tony stalks on. He swaggers over to Big Daddy with nary a thought, grabs a bulky, suited bicep, and with all his might spins the big man around. Bleeding all over the boss's lapels, Tony forgives the thrashing, and barters on for the night cap.

Tony, landing in the parking lot this time, isn't sure who knocked him senseless, and no longer cares. He can feel the ache in the seat of his pants; the kick off the tip of a polished Puerto Rican fence climber. He manages one eye open just in time to see Pression pulling around with the RV. Tony falls up the step and collapses on the deck with Hogweed cursing and grunting from behind. Dolphin sits at the cabin table ingesting a late night dose of the flake off the back of his '59 Telecaster. He's alert, all right, but doesn't bother looking up. Tony's wordless thought in a moment delivers him, finally, from brownout to black.

CHAPTER TWO

The land lay across some two-hundred-sixty acres in Portsmouth, New Hampshire, opposite the forty-four where Tony lives. The only access to the massive expanse is through a hidden trail a mile in from the roadway, along the woods that line the utility road beside the railroad tracks. The tracks of the old Boston-Maine Line run right behind the family property, known as Homeport, and intersect the road in front. The trains run twice a day, first heading north through town into Maine, and back South to Hampton, on return to Massachusetts: The old Bangor to Boston line.

The unmarked entrance to the old, long abandoned farming town is secret, known only to Tony and but a few of his close friends. The hike through is demanding, but once subjugated, arrival is rewarding. The pathway opens to the beauty of colorful, rolling hills. Delicate meadows slowly turn to thicket on the fringe. Surrounding forests, tall, thick, and lush, provide more cushion than enclosure.

The gaping stone foundations, still firmly set in ground, call out reminders of a much simpler existence past. A smattering of old posts, beams and trusses lay with intermittent clusters of toppled and leaning gravestones, a reminder to obsolescence. Sheathing and roofs, long collapsed or blown over, shelter legless legions of near survivors here and there. The oldest and mightiest hardwoods still stand, and the elder evergreens stand taller still. Otherwise, living among the second and third generation acreage, the gorgeously strong trees seem oblivious to time. The passive landscape long ago replaced the active, yet peace seems to outweigh sadness. There are no more working farms anywhere near. No one bothers to hay the fields anymore in the summer.

Nowadays, when a farmer says we gotta make hay while it's still summer, it means we better get whatever this is, done, before we all die.

Over the dead and under the sky, Tony imagines pent-up energy channeling through. He spends hours, sometimes days at a time out there, sad, curious, and awash in relief from an otherwise delusional life. The journeys fantastic, provided Tony by confessional cries from the willowed farm, bring that relief. The notion that power defies logic never occurred to him, or to his recruits.

The energy expounds, no matter queer, and is all the more evident by experiential testament by all who spend a night at the Ghost Farm. Tony's world, devoid of time, slowly turns with his every action. Under a favorite maple, grand and full, Tony stares out at the vastitude. When he sleeps there, he flies. Awake, he wanders induced by mellow conductivity.

He occasionally invites his clan to join the cultivating experience. The farm seems to promote an atmosphere that fosters freedom, spirit and growth, which evolve easily to sexploitation and mind-bending excursion among the tight circle of teenage friends that constitute his populous clan. Boundless vision toward peace, love and joy commingle laterally with getting high, frivolous sexual encounters and irresponsible rebellion. Rarely a mere preprocess to a harmless hangover, Tony knows time in the Ghost Farm could bring people together, but could also, he reasons, tear them apart.

*

Tony remembers clearly the warmth he felt the first time he met Pression. As early as elementary school, she held a certain power and prepotency, which is even stronger as a teen, over boys, girls, and adults alike. An instant first glance between Presh and Tony turned to a shared, locked-in stare. It was a gaze dissimilar to any Tony encountered as a child, and remains forever a defining and unforgettable moment.

Ascendancy over witchcraft, Pression was in complete control by junior high. She seemed to rise, intellectually, courageously to every new occasion. It isn't magic, but is seductively magical to share space with her, as if to know is to belong. Without an abusive cell in her body or a frayed thread in her spirit, Pression's mind is open and free, ideas the map, and the goodness in her heart, the key. Aura does all the work.

Growing up next door to each other kept Pression and Tony close. Much to their parents' dismay, they shared flavorful events, overlaid with mutual respect, as they saw and helped each other grow through puberty. They walked. They talked. They sang together. They bathed together. They were each other's first. If only the parents knew – Tony's dad a World War II veteran, Presh's a German man. As they grow, discussions frequent and deep kindle correlativity, despite earlier, slightly awkward years. They never made it a point to let-on they knew each other that well, but they subliminally and softly let each other believe in the soul kinship they share.

*

"A little too quiet for Vonegan," Tony shares with Drew. "Makes me nervous."

Tony and Drew snicker at the improbability. Vonegan is typically the first over-intoxicated, loudest and most lewd individual at the party. He now sits quietly at the end of a row, and appears a dite standoffish. This clan would never disallow Vonegan from, or kick him out of their party. There have been times however, with Vonegan at his worst; they premeditatedly rid themselves of him, somehow. They try one prank or another, and if all else fails, they merely feed his head until he passes out. Count on Vonegan to devour until it's gone, or until he's incapacitated, whichever happens first.

The faraway gaze is not typical of Vonegan. Indeed, Tony feels it unusual to the point of discomfort. Von's persona, usually so obnoxious, doesn't fly with the pseudo-spiritual, harmless pranksters'.

"I'm not feeling very well Tony," Pression says. He notes the faint burble of saliva in her slurred speech. This is unlike her, indeed, Tony thinks, but even Presh, in all her unpronounced perfection, must occasionally enjoy a buzz now and then, right along with the rest.

"Excuse me," Pression whispers. "I think I'm going to be sick." The recipe this night proves too much for the tiny frame and innards of her body to endure. Pression stumbles away toward the wood line, as Tony second-guesses himself out of following.

If Pression needed help, she'd ask me for it.

Vonegan, leaning against a boulder protruding from the foot of the hill at which they gathered, feels a spark of mischievous excitement ripple through his midsection. He can't quite hear Tony and Pression, but easily recognizes the scene. Calculation of benefit and feeding ruthlessness are natural responses. Part predator, Von's preying on misfortune comes easy, his immediate thought is how. Deep inside, he addresses why.

Why, she couldn't be as good a girl as they say she is. The smiles thrown my way surely mean more than friendliness. She commands a little too much respect, in fact. Seems like she has always had her smooth and lovely Elwyn Park life wrapped around every boy and girl in school.

Pression is obviously intoxicated. She is just sober enough to utter in Tony's ear a few unconvincing words of reassurance before treading heavily away. Her objective is to drag herself away from the party unnoticed.

The tents and sleeping bags that pepper the hillside do not make it easy. Once over the crest and headed downhill, Pression feels like she is flying on her way to woods. After a short period of discomfort and nausea, she feels better. Gathering the wherewithal to complete the return trip Pression yawns. Within seconds, she's fast asleep under a massive oak.

Most of the campers are participating in a little exercise, loosely called romping. Inhibitions to the breeze and disrobed to the flesh, the group gazelles all together through the moonlit field. Standing naked before God, world and each other, the celebration culminates in dance. Around the fat discovery tree, beneath which they would eventually sleep, they dance and sing quietly. An hour passes before they fall together, rolling in the tall grass, hugging, giggling, kissing and teasing. A yelp like that of a puppy dog drifts over the hill.

*

Von finds Pression lying among the brush just off the trail that leads from the tracks to the farm. He stands there listening to her lightly. It isn't the snore of an inebriated fat man; it is the delicate, whispered snore of an infant. The purring sound brings a smile to his face, remodeling a time gone past. Awakening from a nap to see his mommy looking lovingly down upon him, little Dickey Vonegan wonders why she is crying. Mom smiles down at him as he wakes from his nap in the day bed. She watches, and listens to the cute snores of her little baby boy. Tears stream down her cheeks and her chest heaves and catches, as she struggles to subside.

My poor child...

He doesn't understand, of course.

As the young child reaches for her, she extends her own hand, but then stops and turns away before running from the room. Hysterical sobbing fills Little Dickey's ears as he watches his mother rummage wildly through her bedroom. Saddened, he begins to wail too. He hears hers over his own as she strides down the hall and through the kitchen. The kitchen door creeks and slams shut. Two seconds later, he hears the car door close and the motor start. He can still hear wails of sorrow, and see the creased, distorted look of pain on her face, as she sped away. The painful ring of her boy's confused cries fills Mrs. V's head as she struggles to make it to the stop sign at the end of the road. Once quiet, Von drifts back to sleep.

Pression wakes suddenly, still incapacitated

and unable to utter a word, let alone an objection. Nevertheless, she somehow manages one long, raspy, high-pitched howl before passing back out. It was more the sound of a wounded animal than the near unconscious dismay of a young, disoriented girl. Within seconds, she's back asleep. The long howl of a cold and lonely prairie dog fills Pression's dream. Nose to the moon he bays. Head in her dreams, she succumbs.

*

She went to the White Mountains to camp-out on Wilderness Trail. It is an intermediate hike, right off the Kancamagus Highway, and includes a natural flume about two-thirds of the way up. As the sky threatens precipitation, she and her friends decide to use one of the riverside lean-tos. Fortunately, they found a vacancy right near the flume! Sliding down the flume provided chilly, exhilarating and exhausting late afternoon fun. Lying still in her sleeping bag that night, Pression can hear the water rushing down the flume and splashing into the cold, deep spring below. Thoughts of bears eating rations off picnic tables run through her mind. In the midst of that passing, volatile moment between wakefulness and sleep, that subconscious space without time, where one is able to hear but not listen, to feel but not move, Pression falls asleep.

The skirt, Vonegan brusquely hikes up to her waist. He quickly yanks the front of her blouse and tee shirt up and pulls them over her breasts. He lay there on his side next to her, as if he were cuddling a spouse. The middle two fingers of his right hand repeatedly plunge into and out of her pudendum, as he suckles her right nipple. He frees enough of his left arm from underneath his waist to reach his own intromitting organ, and busily dry-glides himself with it.

And then, she felt it. Down it went and back up it came. Then, down again… It was *in*, not *on* her sleeping bag; of that, she is fearfully certain. The rodent slows as Pression stills, and quickens as she fidgets. With a scratch to the thigh and a pinch to the ankle, it spasmodically burrows and scurries. Reaching down into her bag, truth hits Pression like a migraine.

"Mouse!" she thought she heard herself scream.

Or, was that a wolf she heard, or a dog, howling?

*

The noise, barely audible, was clear enough to alert the boys, and keen the girls. Romping complete, the party huddles once more around the base of the great Maple. The creepy sound has everyone wondering aloud. A secondary glance around invoked from Tony a sickly groan:

"Vonegan!"

Overcome by nauseous agita, with Vonegan's absence more than apparent, Tony tries it again, this time near screaming:

"Vonegan!"

Tony has the undivided attention of every boy and girl around the tree. So conditioned to Von, this group shared the same sad vibe before even looking to notice he was no longer among them. Collectively, they know right away that Vonegan has something, perhaps everything to do with the lonesome wail they'd just heard. The sound by itself wasn't recognizable, but together with Vonegan's disappearance, rang true enough for action.

"It's Pression!" Tony urgently cries.

The memory of that romantic, dramatic sound of a lone wolf bay, a cur puppy in the night, turns to a sad, shorter burst of disgust: blind helplessness crying from over the hill. Without a word, Tony jumps up, grabs the blanket he was sitting on, and tosses it to Drew. Literally diving over three bodies to get to his duffel, Tony tears through the contents. The blanket – Navy issue circa 1941 – is one of many Tony's family had tucked away in various closets around the house and garage. While packing, Tony grabbed – for no obvious reason – a baseball bat and golf club out of the garage. The old bats and Dad's golf clubs had until this night fallen long dormant, but he took one each without question. Shear synchronicity, Tony thought, and tucked them into his bag.

Tony wasn't the only boy in Portsmouth who

might even kill for Pression, so it was no trouble recruiting and organizing a posse. Vonegan, thus far in the course of his sorry life, made more enemies than friends. A gang of four marches over the hill instinctively directed toward the outcry. His three mates feel as anxious as Tony does, but no one charges full bore. Knowing not what they're bound to find, cautiously yet surely they trod. Knowing Vonegan well enough by now, inside each they can't help but have sickened ideas.

CHAPTER THREE

Vonegan sits at the edge of the pines painstakingly packing thousands of mini-gelatin capsules with Sweet 'N Low. Tony dealt speed, weed and LSD typically, but jumped at the buy-in on two thousand Genes for one thousand dollars. He could sell them at $3.00 a piece or 2-fer-5, and more than double his money, not to mention spread some laid back joy around old Po-town at the same time! Partners Drew and Neil went in on them, too.

Tony discovered he had been taken in short time. He also discovered soon after the rip-off that Vonegan had moved to Jamaica with the money he took. Vonegan is the type of guy who easily makes enemies, wherever he goes. He could be entertaining, but inevitably never fails to betray, adulterate, rip-off or piss-off someone at the party. Being in the islands would make no difference: Tony gave him five weeks to make as many enemies there.

Sure enough and lucky enough, Von saved just enough of his loot to get himself back to Portsmouth before an unavoidable lynching by a rough bunch of Rastafarians. He laid low for a while once back in Portsmouth but couldn't hide forever. It didn't help Von any that his sister was going out with Drew, either. Everyone heard all about the angry islanders literally chasing the Yankee scum through the streets, and their pursuit all the way to the airport. Vonegan managed to steal two kilos of herb from the very man who had given him a job and a room. He also managed to cause a fight in a local bar that cost the proprietor over thirty-five-hundred dollars to clean-up. Last, but not least, he even managed to be caught drunkenly propositioning his dealer's wife!

Welcome home, Von.

*

Neil lives with his grandmother out on Rye Beach. She runs a private nursing home and he helps her out with, among other things, dinners and clean-up. Typically, he was the only person in the big old place capable of lifting the invalids in and out of the tub, or back into place after a tumble or fall. Neil didn't like it much, but having his own key to the medicine cabinet made it worthwhile. It wasn't uncommon for Neil to come calling with a pint of liquid Demerol, liquid Valium or Morphine. Neil, Drew, John and Tony are, essentially, a pod group of Merry Pranksters, and casual users, but Vonegan was a regular drug-puppy. That played well into a prank that bordered the best, made up one night out on Witchatrot Road. It was quite simple, as long as they could save at least one bottle of liquid morphine just for the occasion.

Booking a one-way flight for one of the old ladies from Neil's Grandmother's nursing home would be easy. Dosing Vonegan down would be easy, but dressing him in a robe, shawl and veil, and wheel chairing him onto the plane themselves more a challenge. Tony plans, in due time, to arrange a pick-up at the Jamaica airport with a couple of Vonegan's old foes.

"He'll be down to Rosa's on Friday," Susan Vonegan says.

"We just want to talk to him about arranging some kind of pay-back," Neil says. All Tony wants is a fair square all around. Forgiveness will follow.

"He's safe as long as he agrees to meet with us in public," Tony says. "Right?"

They would have to warm Vonegan up a bit first - maybe spend a night or two partying with him - displaying good faith and intentions. Luring him with the promise of a brand new set of works and a bottle of hospital Morphine was an easy accomplishment, the thought of it all too much to resist. Once in Neil's van, Von was as good as theirs. He already had a good buzz by the time they met him earlier, in Rosa's, so it took less than expected to loosen him up enough to agree to taking a ride. With a cooler full of Tuborg, a bottle of Cuervo, and, as always, a stash of weed, pranksters and victim ride.

"You know Von," Tony says. "There're no hard feelings about the money."

This night could at least stand as a warm-up, to show Vonegan that they could laugh about it, after all.

"Pull into the park, Neil." Tony says.

Neil parks the van off South Street in a small parking lot near the South Pond.

"Good," Tony approves. "Let's break out the dope."

They let Vonegan have at it. Bulldog that he is, he went through three syringes, puking between each one before passing out.

"Let's de-pants him!"

Without a bit of perturbation at having not gone ahead with the big plan, all promise that next time they would. Of course, because it's Vonegan, it's safe to assume there will indeed be a next time.

"Besides," Tony pleads. "Look at those fucking socks!"

Silence.

"The scarf!" he adds. "Come on!"

With that, they could not resist.

The van drives slowly up Pleasant Street, toward the North Church. Turning left in the middle of Market Square, it stops just long enough to unload a passenger. Eased out of the vehicle, Von immediately sits on the sidewalk, and then tries to get up. Neil sped up Congress Street, the side door slammed by inertia, and all four laughed without looking back.

The morning paper reported that at about half past midnight the police picked-up a disoriented young man seen stumbling aimlessly through town, without his pants. He wore only a Boston Gene Sox cap on his head, a red scarf around his neck, and a pair of bright red knee socks.

"Genes" being the theme.

Small crowds of tourists and locals lined the square calling and cheering, laughing and throwing money. Finally, the owner of River Styx called the authorities in an attempt to get the crowd back in to his bar, where they belonged.

*

Four young men stand silently still, utterly amazed. For a shocking moment, they watch. As if on cue, Vonegan slowly rolls to his right, freeing all hold on Pression. He grabbed his own nipple with his left hand and his penis with his right. His legs straightened, as if he were trying to stiffen them as much as possible, as though he were in a body-shaping contest. The toes of his shoes slowly started to point outward, straight out, like his feet had been planted into the ends of his legs at the ankle, heel first.

Von's little pecker was about the size of a large peanut, poor guy. He was lying there, inexpensively jerking, by using only the index finger and thumb. Like a flying Okay. He gave his nipple a hard twist and quickened the pace of the beater. The spasm hit all four brigadiers at the same time. Von was ready to go, and the sickening, grotesque sight compelled them to unified action. They jumped. The blanket was over Vonegan before he could ejaculate, the four hunters rolling him deeper into the fold in a second. Vonegan had no idea what hit him, of course, he was near drunk as Presh. He was so entirely involved in the fantasy; it took him until this moment to voice even a sound. They dragged Von, folded into the blanket, down the path and out to the tracks. The blanket kicked and punched along the way. It reminded Tony of a sack full of stray cats rolling down a hill at a rivers edge… You know it's alive… It's moving… It's noisy… Yet you wonder if it's worth saving.

Leaving the lesson to the others, Tony jogs back to where Pression lay. She appeared to have slept through the whole thing. He gently replaced her clothing, and then sat with her until she woke up, about thirty minutes later. During that lull, the boys came back through returning to the camp. They had with them the bat and the club, but not the blanket. Tony needn't ask why.

Tony could only tell Pression what his four in legion encountered, but spared her details that took the bastard out to the tracks, and away from her. Presh recalled nothing, other than having a bad dream. The very incident helped convince Pression to, from that point on, live a substance free life. A simply complex step in life, one many never make.

*

Von came away with a fractured jaw, four broken ribs and two broken arms. He still had his teeth. When Tony thought how he took her forcibly… He felt humiliated for her… and disgusted with him. Tony could not help but dwell. Struggling at one point, he questioned whether his actions reflected some dark, secret, jealous rage. Just the thought of Vonegan's hands down her panties and his fingers groping for vulnerability, made Tony mad enough to want to kill him. Madness at the thoughts took hold, but instead of reacting, Tony waited. He waited until Vonegan recovered completely, then, one night not long after, followed him from Rosa's Tavern walking toward home, and hit him again.

*

Vonegan is drunk. Not thinking clearly, but wondering as usual about his father telling Dickey - in his own scuttled way - why he had kicked that no-good, cheating bitch out of his life. Out of <u>their</u> lives! The boy had been five or six at the time, but daddy told the story as though the boy had not been there at all. Von senior told it as though the child were a peer instead. Little Dickey was there. He was always there, and would never, ever forget.

His old man thought it strange that the wife continued to breast-feed her first son beyond his fourth year. In fact, he would never have been sure about that if not for that one strange and mournful day, when quite by accident he actually caught them in the act. He came home early from work with the aches, pains and symptoms of the flu. Expecting to find his wife washing the clothes, ironing, or performing some menial chore or another, he'd take some elixir and aspirin, and lay down on the couch with a Schaefer. Maybe she would rub the back of his neck for him.

Mr. V had to that point been worried about his son's bottle and the thumb sucking. It never occurred to him that his wife had been pumping and bottling her breast milk. Walking in to his home felt a little eerie. It was the silence, broken only by a beautiful humming sound. Stopped just inside the kitchen, he hears ever faintly, a favorite lullaby, breathy and perfectly pitched. Taken aback, he realizes he hadn't heard the sound of her voice like this since the boy was just a few months old.

Stepping slowly through the kitchen, then through the archway into living room, he saw nothing, but the song sounded notably louder. The hallway led from the living room to the master bedroom on the right, a laundry center on the left, and a closet further down on the right and the bathroom, straight ahead. He treads it. He dreads it.

He was just outside the bedroom door, but up the hall just far enough to be left unseen himself. The door was half-ajar and when he leaned just slightly forward, without even taking a step, he could see his wife there sitting on the edge of the bed. He stops suddenly, stands still and stares in disbelief. Her head tilts down and to the left as she looks lovingly at her son. He feeds gently and easily from her left breast. Her right arm hoists his left shoulder, her hand stroking the hair on the side of his head. She tugs and caresses the boy's right ear lobe as he continues to suckle. She sings on, oblivious to the heat coming in from the hallway.

So this is what they do every day after school, huh?!

As hot as his blood was at all of that, his head was full of the malady that sent him home in the first place. He hadn't felt this way in years: he was actually dizzy. Turning, tears in his eyes, he went to the couch and lay down… No elixir, no aspirin and no Schaefer.

The young father tried to understand, but later on that night, after she put the boy down to sleep the ensuing argument turned nasty. That alone could have ended things for the Vonegans right there, but a promise from the missus to desist led the discussion toward forgiveness and sympathetic understanding. He thought he could see, understand, that Sarah was merely a confused and dismayed young mother, reluctant to let go of her only child. Her little boy grew up so fast. Less than a year later, Susan was born, and life felt better in the Vonegan home. A year afterward, came Gregg.

Indeed, it did, however; the shots and beer after work every night had in short order completely desensitized the man. He hadn't made love to his wife since the birth of their daughter. He hadn't even thought about making love to his wife since shortly after Sarah had given birth to Susan. Physical love had always been uncomfortable for him. He grew up a gentle boy and teenager; he was popular in school and a decent, all-around athlete.

As early as junior high, he noticed that his LBJ, his Little Brother Johnson, wasn't growing with the rest of him.

Wasn't that normal? It doesn't get big until you're sixteen or seventeen, does it?

By high school, however, the answer became quite clear. When the junior varsity high school team hit the showers after their first practice that year, Dickey's shortcomings appeared suddenly validated. Over the course of the summer and half a semester it seemed everybody's underarm, chest, leg and pubic hair grew thicker, and penises noticeably larger. He did his best to hide the sight of his own member nonchalantly, pretending not to glance about in reconciliation.

He sees that his is the only penis that still stood straight out, like a mini torpedo, perpetually stiff and red in the head. It's the penis of a ten year old! The fact that he did have a fair amount of pubic hair by then did nothing but offer an additional place for what little he had down there to hide. Although Dickey couldn't quit the team, he did put-off seeing girls for a long, long time.

He met his wife later on in high school. Sarah was a local girl from an Irish-Catholic family. Most of Portsmouth was Catholic back then, either French or Irish. She attended Saint Sally's through elementary school and junior high, and then switched to the public high school. Dick went to public school all his life, which is one reason why they hadn't met previously. She led a sort of sheltered life, thanks to her parents and their pastor. She never dated until high school, when she started seeing her future husband their junior year.

Three weeks into it, Dick and Sarah knew they were right in love. He courted her and her family fabulously. He always had her home on time, and he kept impeccable manners at their supper table. Sarah's father liked to have Dick say grace on Friday nights, and special occasions. Though it was something Dick never did at home, he tried to accommodate Sarah's dad courteously and mellifluously.

Dick never saw it, but Sarah's room was all pink and white lace. The focal point besides the ruffled bed was a chunky, wooden crucifix hanging over its headboard. Porcelain dolls, Barbies, stuffed animals, and religious statuettes filled her shelves. Penis size did not matter to her. Sex is merely a means to impregnation and procreation.

Big Dick had been small, but following his own father's teachings, performed his manly duty nonetheless, just fine. Sarah went without the experience of orgasm even after years of marriage, but she believed in other levels of love. Moreover, she remains convinced, Catholic woman and all, that soft love could fulfill her just the same. Never the less, she was quite distressed when her husband seemed to lose nearly all interest in her following little Susan's birth.

She didn't mind his size, although she could never tell him so. Sarah just wants to be loved. Depriving her of both - physical love and emotional love - turned her wondering about the eventuality of consolation elsewhere. She exclusively bottle fed Susan (and Gregg thereafter), after she was born, that being a direct order from her husband. She could not have brought herself to do it any way. Every evening brings with it the sullenness of mood, blue with sadness, and yellow with guilt.

This night was no different than any of the others. The television line up varied by night but not much by week. The Newlywed Game, Beverly Hillbillies, Hogan's Heroes, Ed

Sullivan, The Dating Game, I Dream of Jeannie, Bewitched, Green Acres. They laughed together and argued about which shows to watch. The arguments are all in fun, of course, because Daddy always won. Daddy was always in charge.

The uneasy feeling of mischievousness that had accompanied toddler Susan had vanished some. Her rummaging through the drawers and under the sink in the laundry room, a place into which she had never wandered before, gave her little heart a quickened beat. She had no idea what it was she found inside a box in the bottom drawer, but she swung it back and forth, and round and round, giggling as she did. It made her feel good. It had a fun look about it, and it felt funny, too.

Down the hall she skipped, happy now she was out of the forbidden place, and as happy as any kid with a new toy would be. She was on her way to that familiar place where the rest of her family gathered, almost nightly, to watch their television. Heading toward the living room, safe ground and out of danger, she could hardly hold back the excitement of showing off the newfound toy.

She stood in the archway between the hall and the living room a little disappointed, because no one seemed to pay any mind to her, or to it.

"Hey!" Susan yells aloud. "Look what *I* found!"

It took a moment for the family to realize what it was she was playing with. In fact, her older brother didn't have any idea at all what it was, though it did look vaguely similar to something he had seen before.

Maybe something he had. Had she been in his room again?

"Hey!" Little Dickey yells back. "What's that?" He asks with envy. "Where'd you get it?"

At first, the object, the shape, is foreign to almost everyone there. Then, Sarah screams, and shrieking, jumps out of her seat as fast as an athlete in training, grabbed it from her daughter, and ran down the hall. Susan cries instantly at the loss, confused by the reaction, and at her Dad, who is yelling incoherently as he jumps out of his own seat striding assiduously toward his wife.

Big Dick wants to know just what-dah-kryst that thing was, and what it was doing...

"...*in my house*"!

Little Dickey sits there in shock, mouth open wide. He is in awe of the quick turn of events, witnessing the emotional explosion, and, of the queer object itself, which was now the center of everyone's attention.

The dildo was huge, grand almost to the point of ridiculousness. The veined anatomic monstrosity measured fourteen inches in length and had a tapered circumference of eight inches at the base to six at the bulbous head. Her father's disgust and anger at the forefront, Susan ran to her older brother, huddling with him in the corner of the couch. From there they watch, shivering with fright, as their parents fight fiercely for the peachy, rubber thing that Vonegan finally recognizes is a big, fat, fake dink.

By the time Susan was a year old the neighbor's wife had become close enough with Mrs. Vonegan to share her own sexual frustrations. Their conversations soon turned to deviations and solutions, as well. And it was she responsible for delivering the paraphernalia to Mrs. V. Through one of many sexually charged conversations they regularly shared, Sarah had just once shared her husband's anatomical measurements with her neighbor. Nevertheless, that was all it took. After witnessing the sincere disbelief, and accepting the condolences from the good neighbor's wife, she accepted the big guy into her life. Learning how to masturbate herself to orgasm and to fantasize changed her life forever. Sarah continued to get her fill, guiltily, yet absolutely, and that's what kept her marital relationship together as long as it lasted. Found out and confronted, Sarah is embarrassed beyond repair and deeply shamed. All the joy that the piece had given her over the last few years was obliterated in a matter of the last few moments.

He was beating her with it now. He was crying and whining hysterically, and she was curled up on the floor in the hallway whimpering like a mother dog giving birth. Genuflecting, as if in worship over her, Dick shook Sarah violently by the front her blouse fisted in his left hand, while he continued to bludgeon her with the rubber meat in his right. The back of her head and her shoulders were alternately pounding into the hall carpet. The dildo was making a slapping sound as it hit against the skin of her arm, shoulder, neck and face.

Hearing the children's screams and sobs, Dick suddenly stops. His crying, his carrying on, his beating-up his wife with the rubber penis, everything, just stopped. Disgusted as ever, he looks at the thing incredulously for a very brief moment, spit on it, spit on her, and then threw the dork down at her with all the force he could might. He meant to pitch it right down into her crotch, but missed his mark in all the insanity, hitting her shoulder instead, where it rolled off to the floor coming itself to a well-deserved rest.

The man was exhausted. Three scotch, three beers and one big dildo was about all he could stand in a single night. He yelled for the kids to go to their rooms. They went. As Dick cried silently, Sarah cried just slightly louder. Threatening to tell everyone, including her family, if she didn't agree to his terms, Dad got his way. She left with the girl, no questions asked, and he stayed in the house and kept the boys. Women should know their place, and keep sexuality out of it, gwod-damn-ut.

*

Alone for the follow-up, Tony used his favorite bat, the one signed by his godfather - Jimmy Piersall - and caught up with Vonegan just after the drunkard's route home took him down the tracks behind Atherton's Furniture. It's almost romantic, Tony picturing Anthony Perkins as Jimmy in "Fear Strikes Out," wailing with that 36-Louisville, smashing everything that got in his way. But Tony was going berserk all over this poor sod of a boy, not the water cooler in the dugout.

Von was found the next morning by a young girl taking her usual shortcut on her way into town. She said a dog had been sitting right there, whining faintly, and licking the man's blood as it dripped from, and dried on him. Vonegan's dog, left alone in the back yard the night before, sensed something had gone awry. Spawned by that keen sense of intuition, Sport jumped the fence and let his nose lead the way. A half a mile up the tracks, the old faithful mutt found his master. He stayed the rest of the night whining, panting and licking.

Tony sincerely hopes there is some kind of lesson to be learned. Pression hurt a little when she heard about Vonegan's mishap, but calls it Karma.

Just call me Dr. "K".

CHAPTER FOUR

Life can be colorfully full of humiliation and flavored with darker embarrassment. Those disappointments can range from the mere petty, to the catastrophic. Two rudimentary groups generally tend to represent most everyone dealing with bruised ego and wounded spirit. The first group takes all to heart, like a blow to an empire. The second group just wants to get on with their lives.

Some tend to dwell on, until their own self-critique drives them eventually to some degree of madness. A small blotch of blackness in a soul full of grace can feel punishment.

Punishment causes anger, derangement can take hold, and there's no telling where that may lead. Watch out for those who keep it inside, where it grinds and twists, dissects itself, repeatedly, like a cell, taking on a life of its own. In the brain, it squirms; until the day it bores itself insanely from within the mind back out. Regurgitated, unleashed, that humiliation having changed form, constituted by angry violence, sedates and massages the mind into clear, grievance akin to a sociopath. Acting, no longer re-acting, the victim marches on to some self-justified vengeance. No more pleasant as time goes on, that humiliation having turned into sickening, vocal disorder that fills the mind with ammo… at which point we can only hope there will have been a witness, with a camera.

Then, there is the second group. Embarrassed laughter at first may only serve as a lubricant, but then, before long, replaced by mutual, unabashed and guttural laughing. This group manages to shake the embarrassment and humiliation off, little by little, like shit off a shoe with a stick, or a stubborn nose scab from a finger. We stand tall, hoping that no one saw that low place into which we inadvertently entrenched ourselves, or heard about what we'd done. Everyone has felt at the least that level of paranoia, of course, but as long as the mishap remains unmentioned, the cool fantasy lives. As long as the fantasy lives, the comfort level rises. As long as the comfort level rises, so does the confidence, forming the pivotal point in life where freedom actually rings.

Big D has the best of all worlds. The son of a bitch didn't even have to say a word. He didn't even have to nod! It was no more a cosmetic grimace, an abdominal knot of pang, only a flicker from his eye that told that little beaner of his to take the stance and floor the now unwanted guest. He is indeed a man empowered, filthy rich and all-powerful.

Tony doesn't feel he should be looking over his shoulder over the incident. After all, why bother? Sure, Big D keeps sloppy help, but Tony was the sloppiest of all in Miami Beach that night. To bleed all over that Big Daddy white, green and red Christmas suit is what drove Tony back up to Big D in the first place. Tony wanted to make sure the man wore *something,* even superficially over the fine fabric, for all his efforts.

How well they really didn't know each other fed opposing views to both men. Outside a close-knit circle of acquaintances, no one really knows what capabilities Big Daddy resources. Like Gotti, Daddy is Teflon. Big D is aware of the power resident in entertainment, but doesn't know Tony at all. The more Big D demands background information on Tony, the less he receives, because no one at all has anything to offer. Big D rests assured, however, with no reason whatsoever to care.

*

Tony will sometimes lean toward headier an approach, rather than physical altercation, yet knows there is nothing like pain to stress a point unmistakably clear. Teach his lessons. Pass his judgments. Set his mind at ease. Justice serves, be it from the church of the mind, temple of soul, or beating on the street. Seeing both sides, coming from both sides, and understanding both sides make Tony, in the classic sense, a textbook diplomat (and Libra).

...When he is sober...

That multi-faceted view sometimes crazes the Libran. Condition and action has always felt this way, Tony reflects. He has stepped between and neutralized heated debate, if not hostility, between friends, families, strangers, man and animal. He has put himself into, and then brought himself back out of countless situations, good, bad, indifferent and ugly. He is good… Tony knows he's good.

…and he is sometimes bad.

From within that temple of mind, his church of soul, he tends also to try, decide, and sentence those who happened to get by on fate the first time around. Tony knows he can sometimes hurt people – very badly. Those deserving, he maintains. Few, excluding even mate Pression, are aware of that third, darkest side. Others have certainly seen or felt the derivative, though the source of that force remains a mystery.

…like that Vonegan creep who took my Pression that summer night…

Vonegan never knew what hit him, and he never stood a chance. Tony's first swing came without introduction, and landed with a crack up back Vonegan's head. Vonegan kept himself in perpetual trouble, seemed, his face in the way of many a fist, and his head just under many a hard object or trajectory. The beatings earned from Tony were neither the first nor the last Vonegan would receive in his pitiful life. Those from Tony might well have been two of the worse, but certainly not the only.

*

So, for as well-balanced and level-headed Tony thinks he is, and as good a boy as he is known to have been as a younger lad, there is an outrageous, unconscionable brood inside. Through self-analysis, his life reviews, he has narrowed the actors down to a trinity. His normal operative disposition is entitled

"The Correct and Tall"; his default mechanism of defense rightly named "The Catholicized Martyr"; and his non-compromising offensive, "The Fronted Schemer." The first two are essentially harmless, swinging from both sides of the pendulum - upswings and down – but the third may be, depending on the situation, considered dangerous.

*

The earliest recollection of his behavioral patterns is when Tony was six years old. Marie, his older sister by seven years, had lately been making it a practice to deliberately persecute, and pick at him until she had him in tears. Then, she would secretly tape record the little boy's sobbing, using her new portable cassette machine. Tony was never an easy crier, but, as little Tony saw it, Marie had a knack for driving everybody in the family nearly insane, anyhow. She constantly argues and fights with her older sister, Jean, manipulates and spins anguish into mother, and disappoints to no end, father. Although Tony is in the usual correct and tall posture, Marie had little trouble calling a storm of tears from his blue eyes sometimes. …His strongest side falling to her worst.

One typical Saturday afternoon, Tony is there at home with several friends over to play. The group is engaged in a severe game of ARMY. That was the unofficial pastime of all American boys, then. He brought onto the porch and tossed down into the yard nearly all of his hundreds of miniature green and khaki army men. Half of the boys choose the Americans and the other, well, the Japs, or maybe the Krauts. Essentially, whether it's ARMY or Cowboys and Indians, all they need for an afternoon of imaginative and excitement-filled fun were "The Good Guys" against "The Bad Guys," whomever they happen to be, or whatever the boys decide to name them. Tony is the only kid who happily volunteers to be "The Bad Guys." It's not that he really likes to be them; he is the only kid not afraid of welcoming inevitable death.

All of a sudden, mid-battle, they hear a loud, hysterical and babyish sobbing. It's coming from the front door. There is sister, Marie…

…but the crying sounded distant. It sounded tinny and muffled.

It wasn't live. It was… Memorex! Metallic and shrill.

Marie stands there, with her portable tape recorder held-out in her hands, smiling. Tony is already shattered, but senses there'll be more to come.

"You know who this is crying like a baby? It's him." She tells no one in particular.

Nevertheless, she had every boy at full attention.

"It's little Tony," she laughs.

"Do you hear that? That's Antonio, crying like the little baby he is."

Tony didn't blame his buddies for what happened next, but all the crying and calling for Mom was all of a sudden, obliterated by a large disharmonious burst of laughter. It didn't come and go quickly, though. Uh-uh. It seemed to roll on, repeatedly. Sometimes, he still hears it.

Into the house and up to his room Tony runs and there he stays until Dad came home from work that night. His friends rode home on their bikes, laughing and giggling all the way, deep down individually thanking God they'd been blessed not having the curse of a big sister like Marie. She seemed like a cross between the Wicked Witch of the West and Sweet Baby Jane. They had seen her in action before, but not anything quite as hateful as this.

Tony was still humiliated at midnight, but he wasn't up in his room pouting all night. He wasn't up there feeling sorry for himself. He realized that he would have to face the boys next school day, and face all told of the incident, as well, which, of course, will have been everyone. Yet, he wasn't up there wasting time. He knows that Marie had well planned her little coup against his realm, provoking, then secretly tape recording his bouts of tears. He fills with anger and frustration, realizing the breadth of the carefully conjured-up plan. To play the tape, at just the right moment, in front of his friends, was unforgivable and punishable. Tony knows in moments Marie wasn't going to get away with it. He'll make a plan of his own, and until he decides to carry out the initiative, he will pose as The Catholicized Martyr, and yet live as The Fronted Schemer. Absorbing admonishment and strength from father, and sympathy from mother and oldest sister Jean, Tony all the while weaves a web-like tapestry, custom made special, just for Marie. Humiliation, this time, indeed turned into a sort of lunacy.

*

Just like all the girls near her age in Cape May, Marie is madly in love with a local boy named Sally McGaye. She queries her Magic 8-Ball multiple times daily, on who the object of Sally's affections might be, and if she may someday be the chosen one. She even has a small handful of beach sand in a baggy that had once been his footprint. It was Cape May beach sand, stepped-on by Patrick McGaye, and now hangs off her bedroom bulletin board.

She had written his name, with hers, all over every book and binder she owned. Different variations of her name written in its married form, like "Mrs. Sally McGaye", or "Mr. and Mrs. P. McGaye," or "Marie James-McGaye." It was an obsession obvious enough for Tony to realize that the mere mention of Sally's name alone could, and would, cause her blood pressure to rise.

Two days later, Tony is downstairs in the kitchen and Marie is upstairs in her room. The James's have one telephone, in the kitchen, and one in the master bedroom, which only dad and mom are allowed to use. Invariably, whenever Marie had a phone call, she would come charging down the east wing stairs, round the corner at the bottom, and jump over the last three steps, through the open doorway into the kitchen to grab the phone off the counter, or out of the hand of whoever answered it. For this very reason,

Tony knows the family, at all times, keeps open the kitchen door at the bottom of this back flight of stairs.

Using that special number that causes your own phone to ring, he dials. After one ring, he immediately picks-up. He doesn't even bother with an "I'VE GOT IT!", although he did hear both sisters start to yell that same, ever so familiar phrase in almost perfect unison. And he's sure they are both ready to fight for gain in the hallway, and subsequently the receiver, but all he hears come out before he picks up mid-ring was an, "I'VE G…".

He pauses suitably, knowing there are two pair of ears throbbing with the anticipation of hearing their respective owner's name next being called. After mouthing to himself what would have been the script if the call had actually come, and counting a one-Mississippi, Tony yells up the stairs:

"MARIE,…PHONE! IT'S PAT… McGaye! MARIE! PHONE! Pat McGaye."

He hears, ever so faintly, a throaty gasp from both Jean and Marie. It's the kind of sound that all women make, by sharply and quickly inhaling through the mouth. The same sound mother used to make every time she thought toddler Tony was about to hurt himself, or whenever she is in the passenger seat of the car and father's trying to merge into traffic, or take a left off of a busy roadway. …Like a backwards "huh!"

Then, here comes Marie, barreling down that long flight of Victorian stairs. Just as she took that eighth double stride, with just one more to go before having to round the corner and jump through the threshold into the kitchen…

Tony slams that fucking door.

CHAPTER FIVE

Yeah, therapeutically, Tony guesses, it's good to identify them – the soul players. He just wishes he had been born with the wisdom to understand their movements, or that he could have learned how to thirty years or so ago.

Maybe I could have spared a little heartache along the way.

In twenty years, Big D never invited to his gatherings any lowly band that serviced his little empire, let alone to his famed Christmas party. One of his regional managers in North Miami was the executive producer of the band's latest single. The record was getting a good bit of air play, so old Big D, after hearing a lot of noise, in the end, relented. He invited the band and crew to his favorite annual event. He even made it a point to introduce, earlier in the evening, Tony and Dolphin to some of his other special guests. He almost seemed proud at the time, but the night was yet to end by the time he regretted his decision.

Tony thought it might be worth the effort and that it might be a good time for him, in writing, to extend sincere apologies to Big Daddy for the raucous incident. He offered to write a letter, but management thwarted that idea, citing Tone had already said (and done) quite enough to Big Daddy, thank you. This band was not only the first, but also the last of a band to ever gain entrance to any event that Daddy personally sponsored.

*

Resurfacing is probably the only way to describe coming out of a black out. Some folks tend to assume that a black out means passing out unconscious - cold. This is a fair assumption, of course, and may be a common course for those who tend to way-over indulge, but it is simply not the case every time. One way to think of it is by imagining the loss of a time span where you have no idea what you have done or where you have done it, or who with. But you know you were awake. The others tell you so.

It's very sad. The difference between passing out and blacking out is that when you black-out someone else can provide anchor by relating to you just what you had done, said, and where you had been. When you pass-out, you're down for the count. There is simply nothing more than that to tell.

So really, passing out is better.

There are no excuses, either. There can't be: only explanations. That should not even be plural. The only explanation available is that one has quite periphrastically over-done it. No glamour necessary. If you don't know what you are doing, what is the sense in excusing yourself for it? Sadly, for a while there, for Tony and the rest the group, that existence seemed a rolling fact of life, coined before and forever true:

Rock and Roll…

No excuse.

No apologies.

*

Rock musicians of every color turn to drug induced recreation, because at the subconscious level they know they haven't lived nearly enough of the blues to justify their playing it. It's eventually all blues. So, they create the blues through manifestations conjured-up by drugs and alcohol. With the exception of a few, most do not realize, or realize far too late, something very, very simple. Life is full of the blues, anyway. You just have to wait for it. It'll come.

The other reason is plain and simple: Boredom with accessibility.

*

Tony's first conscious, inner vision on this day was in fact the ugly account of himself verbally abusing some big, red faced, red-haired hoss, and of course a partial chain of events that followed, in slow-mo no less.

As if he needed a replay.

But this thought right away gave in to the now...

…atop her…

…within her…

His Pression. The woman remains as nice as nice could be in every kind of way that any one woman could possibly ever be.

He gets tongue-tied even now…

Like most women must, she wore a little history in the lines on her face, the scars on her body, but hers you had to look real hard to find, and once noticed, only added to her being, creature she is. Her manner never gave anything away. Tony and she practically traded their families for each other.

The missionary thing was feeling so good, Tony knew there was something extraordinary happening. He felt he had never been bigger, or harder. She was waterfall wet and they were both bathed in sweat. It wasn't about speed. It wasn't slow. It was slick, but just a tiny bit rough.

Then, through the clamor, the sweat, the haze of that crazy Christmas weeknight, and through the glazed look of total abandonment in Pression's eyes – his own feeling of recklessness and passion driven animosity – what it was they were so immensely enjoying.

"It's never felt so good there," Pression gasps

"You feel so nice," Tony manages.

He was in her rear-end and they were both engaged in and enjoying the most awesome ride down that old dirt road they could ever hope for. His heart was pounding so loud that it filled his head with reverberation that muted the perpetual ringing that normally courses through it.

"Wha...wha...what...?"

He can't even fuckin' speak!

"What's that pounding?"

"Mmm…sorry."

"No. It's not us."

"No, No... Uh-uh."

The booming sounds insane now. Pression is actually frightened and shivering all over. Tony is sweating profusely, and all he can do is apologize repeatedly to Pression.

"I'm sorry. I'm so, so sorry. …Sorry," Tony is lost.

"No… it's the door, Tone." Pression practices patience.

"It's pounding," Tony stupidly reports.

"Yes, Sweetie. It's the door. Someone is beating the door down." Pression had the kind of heart a woman really had to have to forever love a rock musician. The no-nonsense assault on the hotel room door finally brought him completely out. The violent nature of the moment brought them both out of that world they alone created moments prior, and within which, until now they thrived. They are suddenly delivered back into the harsh reality of just another air conditioned, mid-afternoon in Miami.

After all, Christmas time is a state of mind that is impossible to reach when you're a New England boy, breaking a sweat on Miami Beach in the third week of December. He remains too numb to realize that anything much out of the ordinary had taken place, anyway. Let it be just another wake-up call.

"Not this time, Tone."

Dolphin, along with a cop and two Latinos, stood there telling Tony and Pression that the call no one wanted to receive (but almost knew would eventually come), had indeed just come through. It was from their manager, and he is not happy. Their agent is not happy, either, and not least of all, Big Daddy is not happy…at all. The unofficial mayor of Miami and Irish under-boss of Florida had issued an underground statement that generally equated to telling the group that if they weren't out of Miami ("his town," he had said), by six that evening, life would become very tough for him and the rest of them.

They weren't too awful interested, management said, in playing any games, bluffs, or curious at all to find out exactly what the consequences may be. After all, we are talking about the fucking Westies here, people, as it was repeatedly noted.

The bloody Irish mob.

"Don't tell me we're having a fucking band meeting," Tony says facetiously to Dolphin. "Not at this hour."

"It's one in the afternoon," Dolphin begins. "And, yes, we have to have a Band Meeting. Gene's in five."

Fanfare, applause and drum roll, please.

It's another fucking Band Meeting...

It was decided without much deliberation that, the boys should go ahead and take that year-end vacation upon which they had always, after all, dreamed.

"Thanks due to Tony, and no one else, of course," Scar sneered.

You are all very welcome.

*

Pression and Tony head up to New England with the road crew. Droid and Hog, like Pression and Tony, were from Portsmouth. Stump and T.L. came along for the ride. They're from Georgia, but they passed going home to their folks' places to visit New England with Tony and the gang. The rest of the band spent the holidays at their homes in Panama City. Actually, Big D could just as well have kicked them all the way out of Florida, not just out of Miami.

Then, where would the band mates have gone?

The Fool Star's band happened to have a little bargaining power, what with the Governor of Florida being the brother-in-law of the President of Studio Center: the studio that the Fool Star contracted while in Miami, and he was definitely on the band's side.

Small universe.

See? Things can always be worse.

*

Sitting at Jean's table for that Christmas dinner, everyone was so happy to see Tony. His

Mom was there with his other sister Marie. He hadn't seen them in over three years, and it had been even longer since they spent Christmas as family. It was a great time, even though the only part of that dinner Tony could successfully and comfortably ingest was his sister's special, home-made pumpkin soup.

It was a little too gross to share over dinner, but the story of why Tony could not enjoy more of that delicious looking dinner, and how he came to have over forty something stitches in his face made for great after dinner conversation, though.

"Oh, Mon Dieux, mon petite garçon, Antoine!" Tony's Mom… She still breaks into her native French language whenever she gets excited. They reminisced over the old times, including the time little Tony broke Marie's nose and knocked out a couple of her front teeth by slamming the kitchen door in her face as she ran for a bogus phone call from a fantasy boyfriend. (A fantasy that would be shattered for every girl from Cape May a year and a half later, when Private First Class Sally McGaye died overseas, in some kind of freak service related accident, about which nobody would ever learn the details.) When Tony heard the news way back then, he remembers thinking to himself, though not hatefully, Gee, fate kind of tied it all up tight in a little, ugly, knotted package for me then didn't it?

*

So many unknowing souls downright refuse to believe that anyone who has blacked-out may not be passed-out, in fact, may even be up and functioning no less, and yet be in the middle of a time that will never be anything more than a null value. It's not that these non-believers are that much of a sheltered people; it is just that blacking out has never happened to them. God bless them, one and all. Personally, Tony came out of the Big Daddy's Christmas Party incident not unscathed, but in one piece anyhow. After Hogweed and Pression picked Tony up from, or shall we say off of the parking lot that infamous night, they and Dolphin took Tony straight to the Miami General Hospital ER. Tony argued the whole way there and beyond, but they realized he had no idea that he was losing a fair amount of blood. Most of that gore was running down from his mouth and chin, filtering through his beard, and then down the front of his shirt, stomach, and into the front of his pants. Tony hadn't yet realized that his ever faithful and protective crew, save for the Hog, at the last moment and not a moment too soon, had already abandoned him. Nor had he realized that the host had probably every right to shut him right off when he did. Tony was in the dark more ways than one.

After several ER staff tried, it took Pression and Hogweed to hold Tony down long enough for the physician to shave that part of his beard off and stitch up the gash under Tony's chin. They considered knocking him out with some liquid Valium, but along with what they knew was already flowing through his veins, thought the better of it. Even so, it was mighty tempting to them. They managed to jam the Novocain into the wounds, but only after a painful (and noisy) cleansing, then, everything and everyone were once again, just fine.

The landed punch of that little Columbian greaser had reopened an old scar that dated back to a fall off of a motorcycle several years before. But, the damage that is his and his alone is the stitching installed to replace Tony's lower lip to where it had originally been: attached to the rest of his face.

When it was all over, the only one who had the power to calm Tony down, and keep him that way, was Pression. His Pression, with whom he was grateful to find himself this afternoon. She stayed with him throughout the entire aftermath, as she had always, for what was now fifteen years. She had even passed on an audition for a new Burger King commercial the next morning, which is unheard of for an artist, even an aspiring actress like Pression, to do for anybody. Self-centered she'd never been.

After all, that is why the big Hollywood marriages fail, is it not? That, and over-accessibility. Any swelling had soon burst when notification to the band and their management arrived that the host for that celebratory evening had been far less than impressed. Any feeling, no matter what, is squelched by the thought of being hunted by a leg of the South Westies.

Gee. All I wanted was one more Kamikaze.

"I lost you ten years ago

Chelsea your last stop

The blade of a surgeon slipped
and it killed you

Time itself bled from the clock."

PART II

CHAPTER SIX

Though not the specificity of which, those are the garden variety of question philosophers and physicists alike, on a more or less profound level (and still unable to answer after all these years), have been asking themselves and each other for centuries. How did we get here? Why are we here? What's next?

"No big deal"

At times, Tony finds himself pleading ignorance, just hoping for some kind of transparent aggression. Anthony James: basking in complete ignorance, mindlessly praying for deliverance to a more quiescent place – to silence the revilement for good – hoping to somehow, somewhere, find a way to escape notice. But that nagging voice, that inward monitor, won't let him forget that unless all hope has been surrendered, every bit of faith elapsed, and driving initiative decimated, he can't, nor will he ever enjoy true satisfying repose.

Can they hear it, ever? Anyone?

Who wants to be one foot in the dirt, feeling bitter and old, looking at a real short dollar and wondering what the fuck went wrong... and where? Therefore, he <u>must</u> be a doer, a self-serving steward. He must deal. Maintain. Looking right into the eyes of the world during these bouts, he offers everything he's got from deep within.

Help carry my being and spirit up and out from this hell.

Another challenge altogether is to resist the cynicism so quick to jump:

"Hey! Don't you get it? We live, and then… Fuck it! We die! And if you're real fuckin' lucky, and you believe in reincar-fucking-nation, you get to live it all over again. Maybe as a fucking dog or a cat or maybe even a lab rat!"

"...Aaahh! Anyone, at all?"

You know what, though? That's the same crapped out, cop-out disposition that he much younger felt himself, and saw in so many others, so many times before. The ever popular nineties mantra, "No Hope = No Fear!" makes Tony want to puke. It even passes now for human nature, a way of life, and the motto of a whole goddamn generation – and it makes Tony sick. With, however, his amendment to this way over-used coin, this is as recognizably optimistic as he can relay, and remains his own stock answer:

"Life is what you make it - (within the realm of what your life has to offer, that is)."

Tony entertains internally, every argument one can endure. He winds himself weary and wretchedly tight over everything from which shirt to wear to a party, or what side of his head the part should go in. It reaches all the way to his romantic inclination toward, or anxious dismissal of suicide - selfish and spiteful - at any given time during his life.

Am I the only one who feels this?

Those heady, gray, adolescent years brought with them an overwhelming amount of confusion. Reflections sometimes lasting hours at a time would circle and weave, usually putting Anthony, finally, to sleep, exhausted. Sometimes he'd wake-up with twice the weight behind his eyes. But the deliberations sometimes did indeed produce the resolution for which he had been striving, even if it did seem like a trip around an elbow just to get to a thumb.

He listens carefully.

"...I'm shunning life itself"

"What life?"

"...The life given me"

"No, the shit-fer-life that the former generation left you with!"

"...I can do something about it"

"It's too far gone. The wars, the corruption, population, politics, prejudice, the judicial system, prohibitions, poverty, suppression, oppression? We're dead, Dude"

"...I'm making it worse"

"You're not helping a goddamn thing."

"...What can I do to make a difference?"

"Even secondarily you may be contributing to the death of an innocent being, a child even, but everybody got to go sometime; it's part of The Plan."

"...It's an act of defiance, against every intelligent grown-up's better wishes."

"Realize that the act itself defeats the purpose of what the rebellion and revolution are all about in the first place."

"...But I LIKE IT...I really, really enjoy it."

"I bet Pression doesn't approve."

"...Her love for me is unconditional."

"For now."

"...I can *do without* a pleasure that charges twice sometimes thrice upon purchase with tax, health and maybe life itself."

"Back to LIFE again, TAKE CONTROL, if you

die tomorrow, you die knowing you lived life for yourself and nobody else, you're free. Live Free or Die, Mate!"

"...Yeah, to "Live Free and Die", the motto is "Live Free <u>OR</u> Die", asshole!"

"Not much room for alternative there, either."

"...How free can I possibly be when every day I let myself be controlled by the contents in a box?"

"One does indeed lose control."

"...My idea of freedom is having control over what I do without having to relinquish it to anyone or anything... especially those man-made."

"Product or ordinance?"

"...YES!"

"Then by God, if YOU don't cherish life,

don't draw it out any longer than it already is by making yourself, me and everybody else sick with it... just go get yourself a copy of "Final Exit," abuse it, and run. Run away from it. Jesus! GET OUT! GOD!"

"...I should try to quit ...again."

"You tried once before, you failed. You missed it."

"...I bet Pression thinks I stink and that my mouth tastes rancid, and I bet she hates those brown and yellow, reeking finger tips. Especially when I touch her... down there, on the inside."

"Cigarettes. I just want to quit smoking cigarettes." Tony is crying now, and tired. The ringing, pops, chirps, coughs and laughs continue. That's all.

*

By this time, Tony had already buried the Miami incident, assumed responsibility and decided there was no place for recourse or punishment. That is, except for the physical punishment <u>he</u> already received. He hadn't the need right away to address all three of the forenamed queries, but did indeed consider one under the moon tonight.

How was *it then that I came to be here?*

Right here.

Right now.

Feeling like I do, looking like I do, and with or without consequence, having so far done all that I have done, have not, and shouldn't have.

*

It took a cool October night in New Hampshire; with a witch-like girl he wanted for too long a time; that's where it was, moving Tony into thinking he belonged elsewhere. His place of birth, of becoming, was there in The Granite State, far above and away from the place where Pression and he were to land before month end. Sometime earlier that year, Pression's entire family, save older brother Bear, returned to Mississippi. Biloxi, Pression said it was, on the Gulf of Mexico. Tony had been entertaining the thought of packing it up and heading south, because many of his musical heroes hailed from the south. It was commonly known on the circuit that the young musicians down there were not only exceptionally versed in roots music, they are quality players. The music scene in its entirety thrived with young and old alike, delving into the fusion mixing rock and roll with country, blues and jazz. So, it was more than just a convenience for Tony, when on this night he took Pression up on her and her parents' proposition – a ride down for a place to stay. Taking up the invitation, he felt comfortable with the idea of staying with her and her family in Mississippi until he found a gig. He felt confident that all he really had to worry about was fitting her into the car with him and his drums. As they fell off to sleep that pivotal evening, after sealing an agreement with a drink, a toke and some fine autumnal love, they were already making up their personal itineraries, to follow up on tomorrow, the plans they together made tonight.

*

Having been a traveling musician for the past three years, trying his way with every jazz, blues, and rock band in the area, it was time for a formative move. Tony bent his step throughout the New England and Canadian circuits, and even though he was a Yankee boy through and through, he carried the attitude and disposition stereotypically reserved for a long-haired country boy. Influenced in might by some of the greatest musicians of the time, Tony even sometimes felt like a lonely, displaced and hybrid form of southern rocker.

I can't wait to get down there and show those boys what a sand spur in the ass really felt like. How high a snow bird can fly...?

Less than one week later, with everything that ever really mattered to him, everything needed; his drums, stereo, records, some books and a couple of bags of clothes – in that order – there he was, tooling down Route 95 South.

Oh, yes, and Pression, of course.

The trip down was fairly uneventful. They stopped in Washington, DC to visit friends of hers the first night. There's nothing like getting lost in DC in the middle of the night. It was dark, in every sense of the word, and it was scary. Without going-off on a defensive tangent so typical of a white guy who sure enough has black friends, Tony felt a little out of his element there. He remembers thinking that an ill fate may be closing in on him, as he reeled and rolled slowly through the inner city streets of DC, and his mind rewound to an occurrence that had passed several years before.

*

Mom and Tony were in her car driving slowly through the south end of Portsmouth, on their way to The Blue Fin Fish Market. The streets are winding with cars parked on both sides, so you have to drive slowly. Out from between two vans that were curbed on the right came this black, foolish kid that Tony knew from school, along with three others. They started to cross the street, rhythmically, slowly, shuffling the way they do, you know. Then, as the kid that Tony knew looked into the car - at first, through the glare of the sun, saw only mom. She was forced to yield to this small troop of dark pedestrians, then, he stopped. She slammed on the brakes for fear of hitting the boy. In the middle of the road, they stopped behind him.

They approached the car and pumped it up and down on the front shocks, bouncing on the hood, howling like chimps at feeding time. Mom instinctively started to yell at them. She didn't scream, it's just not in a farm girl from northern Maine to scream, but she hollered at them to "STOP IT" and yelled that they were being "PESTS". Bless her.

She once impressed Tony to no end when he witnessed her calling to the mat a biker from Salem, and arguing him right out of her face. He cut her off as he swung a too-close-left at the intersection she wanted to take a left out of. He cut it so close that it scared her, almost hitting the car, and she yelled at him out her open window to "LEARN HOW TO RIDE THAT THING, WILL YOU?!" He turned around quickly and came back to the intersection and went nose to nose with her before he got disgusted and just drove away embarrassed. Bless her again.

The boys were getting a kick out of the feared harassing, and the more mom yells, the closer they come to her window, and, the more they laugh and make ugly faces at her. By the time they reach her window, they are no longer facing the sun and are able to see Tony sitting there in the front seat with her. Not that he presented much of a threat; there were four of them and one of him.

"Ain't that always the way..."

Tony realizes that he recognizes one of them, the one who appears to be the author of this afternoon's twisted pleasure. He and the other boys had been pressing their faces against the driver's side window, shrieking lewd remarks and presenting mom with all the radical gestures of the times. It was just then, that Tony knew he was recognized. As soon as he looked in at Tony, he backed just far enough away from her window to see, and their eyes met. In that second, just before mother decided to simply gun it away with her right foot, Tony's eyes glaring into his, Tony grinned, winked and nodded ever slowly, and mouthed the words "One Day."

"One Day."

The South End boy stopped, expressionless, looking in at Tone, then backed-up just a step, but not before Mom - not caring that she had run over a white Converse All-Star, no doubt mutilating what were inside it, nothing more than five nigger-toes - gave it the fucking gas. With one poor boy hopping around on one foot and crying out in pain that his toes wuzza bleeedin', Mom and Anthony are once again on their way.

"Give any species too much rope… and they'll fuck it up."

Although Tony is empathetic, sympathetic, and even contributes to the cause, he chooses not to tolerate aggressive, dead-end actions, and he never entertains any asshole that chooses to make him or anyone he loves a part of their over-assertive or terrorist-like message.

Do you understand me? Does anyone? I'm actually a peaceful guy, but sometimes I just cannot wait for God.

Even though he had jammed with lots of black musicians, shared many a smoke with many a folk, and had even gone to jail for, and bailed out fellow humanitarians, black and white, for among other causes, racial equality and peace, Tony knows he will someday make that kid regret he ever fucked with him and his mother.

CHAPTER SEVEN

He could not have known. Tony was one of the freaks at school that hung out by the nurse's office doors. That is their corridor, their entrance, their dooryard. Them, the work-booted bunch that lived in denim field coats and jeans, all hair, jewelry and patchouli – Love, peace, bare feet and Granola. They weren't exactly an attractive bunch, but there was something mysterious, that turned curiosity into attraction. Most everyone simply ignored them, some for the fear of knowing too much.

Just as those glances exchanged on South

Street, there was an element of queasiness coursing through the over-confident black body, and an unsettling shudder into his young, tortured mind. He and his little South End posse done messed with someone they knew nothing about. That's a big mistake that many people make. It's Street 101: *Do not mess with anyone you do not know.*

Tony actually looked forward to going to school that coming Monday. He hung like he always did, at the end of the hall across from the nurse's office. He made no mention of the South End incident to anyone. Today is just another day at the beach. The only difference is that Tony discreetly, yet consistently keeps a keen eye on the black boy, like prey through a scope. That is exactly how Tony thinks of him these days: prey. The boy moshed through the halls and parking lot in the middle of what Tony saw as a black cloud, like Linus's, though he never lost sight of him. He alone.

Tony learned, carefully watching, who the boy hung with, what he did after school, arrival and departure, where he lived. Anthony followed him through The Pines, eventually out to Middle Street to South. The boy, none the wiser, habitually made his way down his shortcut toward home.

Bingo.

Tony positions himself just off the path Sambo took, and waits day after day. He is waiting for the one day Sam would make this trek alone, without the company and protection of peers. He waited-out every day, never to tire. He knew that someday the boy would pass this way by himself, and when he did, Tony'd take him. Contemplated and premeditatedly, Tony knows he doesn't want to have to chase the kid… Even though he will have, in his time, outrun exactly one slightly overweight police officer on a Friday night. He also in the past got away from one moderately deranged and decrepit neighborhood phobic on a Halloween night; he knew he would never, ever be able to outrun an intimidated, frightened black kid.

It's a Friday, and Tony is right there where he always was just off the path, alone, waiting.

Ah, yes...

There Black Sammy is, coming through The Pines, and he is all alone. Even though Tony had played this scenario many times through in mind, the real world anticipation (or blast of adrenalin) converts into a volcanic intoxication. It was an emotional appeal – not unlike delirium. All one can reason is that he is otherwise unarmed. The thought of the south-ender holding anything under his jacket or stuck in his pants did not so much as cross Tony's mind. Let alone thwart his plan of action.

Tony jumps down from the tree, crying out like a painted banshee and he hit the ground running. Sam screamed like a woman, arms shot up toward the sky in a violent, involuntary jerk, started, and tried to turn and run away. 'Plan A' was for Tony to run right into him full force, like a left tackle, then work on him from there. He hit him like so, and when he did they both went rolling through the pine needles. Sam got up before Tony could, but froze for a second. He wanted to see exactly who or what it was that had flown from the trees and into his path. Tony is up walking toward him, laughing, giggling.

Tony could tell by the look on the face opposite his the exact millisecond that recognition again took hold. Heat flooded into his Afro-rounded and circular looking head, like mercury in a hot thermometer, as he realized all at once what was unfolding before him and why. His eyes got comically large and bulged theatrically; Tony thought he could have passed as a vaudevillian star!

The boy turned and took off running, but Tony caught him before the fourth stride. They fell again and they both got up and ran again. As Sambo runs back toward the high school, Tony knows that he has to follow through before they get too close to it. And, do it before anyone else starts down the same path. Tony caught-up with him again and grabbed at his right sleeve, which made Sam spin around and lose his footing. On the pivot he swung forcefully centrifugal right, into the trunk of a big old pine tree. That alone might have been enough, but the sight of his already broken and bleeding nose and the scrapes on his cheek didn't even register in Tony. Tony hit him once splitting his bottom lip. The boy screamed as his head snapped back and bounced off of the tree trunk behind him. He sways on his feet and cries, but Tony didn't hear it and hit him again. Sam's knees buckled and down he went, curling himself up, cowering against the trunk of the same tree he met with his face fifteen seconds before, covering the eye just now smote.

Tony stood there watching – waiting for the boy to look up at him – to see him just once more. Tony suddenly noticed that Sam stopped moving altogether. After what was at least a full minute, one of those moments that seem more like seven, Sam sheepishly tilted his head upward and looked at Tony. He whimpers snorts and coughs. Blood was running from facial lesions, his nose, eye and lips. He spit several times.

"It's over dude," Tony speaks calmly to him, but he is out of breath. However, he spent several days memorizing what he would say should he ever catch this kid, and by Jesus he shall spill gut, now.

"In review," Tony begins, "Lesson number one is that you behave yourself, especially with due respect to elders… ladies… humans. Lesson two, you know who I am, I know who you are, and we both know why this had to happen." Tony says in a moot tone.

"It's an eye for an eye, a tooth for a tooth," the boy says. "Right? Just like Mama said."

"Yeah, consider us… once again… even. Got it?"

Man, that boy was listening to Tony like he would his Sunday school teacher, paddle in hand.

"Yeah, yeah, I didn't mean…" the boy started to babble.

"DON'T SPEAK TO ME! PLEASE!" Tony interjected sharply. "Do you believe that WE ARE NOW EVEN?!"

"I do. I do. We even, man."

"I just want one more thing from you," Tony tells him.

"What that be?" he asked, sniffling. "Anything."

"I want you to apologize, so I can tell my mom how sorry you are for treating her the way you and your friends did." Tony replied. His eyes never blinked, nor did they once leave Sammy's.

"I sorry, I'm sorry, man; you KNOW I sorry. Please."

"You mean it?" Tony meant it when he asked.

"Oh, man, oh man. Tell her I mean it."

"In the immortal words of Joe Walsh, just… walk away."

*

Pression wanted Tony to stop and ask directions. He is not a guy who minds asking for direction when he thinks he needs it, but, uh, Sorry… not this time. In the middle of the night in DC, one couldn't have <u>paid</u> him enough to unlock the doors, let alone stop and get out of the car.

Like going into New York with your camera and Bermudas for Christ's sake!

All that excitement was almost worth the wonderful night's sleep they spent on an old Castro Convertible pull-out couch. Banana boat that it was, Tony wallowed glad to be locked indoors with a couple of acquaintances that he believed, for no good reason, would not intentionally harm him. The trip to North Carolina, their next stop, is half the drive they took the day before. Tony had been driving about four-and-a-half hours it took to get there, and feels tired already.

I am so fucking glad Pression's sister Genevieve invited us to stay over.

They didn't get lost on their way, but Tony was a little uncomfortable nonetheless, because even though his dad had been a serviceman, Anthony never quite felt relaxed with GIs, ARMY men, Marines or any service guys, in general. It's not as discomforting as hanging out with cops, but Tone feels a dite tense around Genevieve's husband. Big Jay, being a Green Beret, exaggerated Tony's distress, although ironical that the straight guy's name is jay.

Genevieve and Jay live on base, which stirs a little more spice into the stew.

Surrounded by barbed wire and secured by armed gatekeepers surely made it the safest place to settle, as long as one could trust all those armed surrounding. Fort Bragg: where Dr. Jeffery McDonald recently slain his beautiful family. For Tony, it was the highlight of the trip to have gone by and visited the murder scene, at that time still behind the yellow and black tape. He does not sympathize or house empathy for McDonald. It's nothing like that. Tony thought Jeffery was mentally an idiot and quite critically ill, and obviously a narcissistic sociopath. He killed his own family. Besides that, Tony took his defense personal; that he dare try to imply hippies, a la The Manson Family debacle. To most, it's just morbid curiosity. To Anthony it becomes some kind of personal case study. He's always been interested to learn, immersing himself into the criminal law and forensic science aspects of solving the crime, rather than the crime itself. There is always so much to learn.

He doesn't know exactly why soldier-types unnerve him so. It's not a matter of trust, but it's something like that. Tony has over the years sold a lot of pot and acid to a lot of soldiers at Pease. Same with the Ship Yard… Yet, he couldn't help but think of them being right out there with the infamous disgruntled postal workers of the time. It has something to do with giving up personal choice for a living. Someone that allows another being to program them into an obedient machine, but deserve respect because they are the lean, mean machine securing freedom represents conflict to Anthony. The whole chain-of-command methodology falls apart for Anthony. He thinks top-down mentality is dangerous. It lacks characterization of emotional intelligence, but is great at learned combat, defense, militarism and artillery.

Who are you when your boss isn't around?

Who are you when your missus isn't around?

Anthony has learned to appreciate some sort of military organization, even though he was a border-line socialist a few short years ago. He spent a short time in jail for pamphleteering in support of Davis and Pulley in the early '70s. He joined the Berrigan Brothers in covering up the "Or Die" part of the New Hampshire state motto "Live Free or Die" on his license plates. Tony toyed with the ideals, and never saw himself a threat to society. Even though, he was all but convinced by Rubin and Hoffman that all capitalists were pigs, and by John Kay that the government was a monster on the loose... who had our heads into the noose.

Shit, I still kind of feel that way. See the NEWS lately?

Tony secretly held a personal vendetta with the US government. Although it started at age ten, when he was abused by a Coast Guard General Practitioner at the dispensary on the base at Governors Island, what put him over the edge was the cover-up involving a medical malpractice that killed his father less than two years later.

Anthony's Dad was a twenty-seven year service veteran, with three wars and several tours of duty worn on his chest. He went into the Chelsea Naval Hospital to have an ulcer treated, and should have been home inside of a few days. Instead, the team of Navel doctors assigned decided to do exploratory surgery on him, because of a found gall stone. Not one, but two exploratory surgery procedures within two weeks of each other. The forty-four year old survived those, incredibly. He was killed when a scalpel ruptured his spleen just before they closed him up that second time around. Tony's father bled to death overnight, and was found dead early the following morning. They contended that an x-ray showing an unusually large gall stone mandated the operations performed. That might have held up, but that same stone in that same x-ray later displayed for several civilian (and more highly qualified, apparently) physicians, proved to be nothing more than a shadow.

He bled to death, internally, just lying there in the Chelsea Naval hospital, where no one knew the difference. There in Dad was a man who gave every part of himself to his country through World War II, the Korean Conflict and the Vietnam War, killed by his own, just one year after retirement. That was all documented in autopsy records and criminal investigative affidavits and reports. Mrs. James, at one point, had a malpractice law suit against the Navy. The legal papers sat on Judge Garrity's desk in Boston for too long a time, collecting interest as well as dust. Just before the case was to finally go to trial, the one and only witness – one of the surgeons that agreed to testify for the James's, that indeed Tony's father was grossly mistreated and abused – mysteriously disappeared. He was later found dead in the woods not far from his home in Dover. The momentum was gone, the resources were gone and like Dad's blood, any money the family had, bled all over the streets of Boston.

Meanwhile, the pricks run free.

Judge Francis Garrity went on to fuck-up the Boston bussing issue, and he still presides on the bench there. Judge Flynn, The James's family lawyer, dragged his own feet and no doubt received his share of inducement, until the statute of limitations came up. Shortly after it did, he died in a truly bizarre and tragic way, when he, along with one of his many young boyfriend lover boys was found dead. It involved a ferret, a 16 ounce coke bottle and a home-spun bomb made out of eight strategically placed mayonnaise jars, each hooked to a spark plug screwed into the top, and filled with butane. They were extended with telephone wire and duct taped to various vulnerable places on the underside of the car they were in.

The bombs and cause of the blast and ensuing fire were never discovered. As usual, the more controversial aspects of the crime overshadowed the reports. They also interfered with the investigation. When Marilyn Monroe died, all that mattered was that she had been found in the nude; all that mattered was that Judge Flynn was found dead; unclothed with a boy, a bottle, and a ferret, outside of the infamously gay Sagamore Club. Conveniently, and not unfortunately for Anthony, Flynn was not a well-liked man in Portsmouth to begin with. Corrupt and gay to boot never did make it in an old salt town like Portsmouth, New Hampshire.

Tony and his mom hadn't yet lost the fifty acres of prime land on Banfield Road that constituted most of the estate left her by Anthony's father. Tony had a shooting range set-up where his dad's garden used to be, and he used it often. Anthony was a NRA Certified Pro Marksman by the time he was eleven years old. Since his father's untimely death, Tony took to sitting at the edge of the woods, at the target end of the range, and shoot at the Air Force planes flying directly above. The James residence was situated on the highest point in Portsmouth, and right underneath the flight pattern for Pease Air Force base. Tony was not only high, he was hot and he was angered. With never a thought of who may be in the cockpit, or nary a thought about what he might say in defense should he ever bring one down, Tony continued to fire.

"I was target shooting, musta been a ricochet."

In reality, he was once again posing as The Catholicized Martyr, and acting as The Fronted Schemer. Although he owned and earned his Pro Marksman pin using a .22 caliber rifle, Tony inherited from his dad a Winchester 30.30 and a vintage M1-Carbine, standard Korean War issue. That is the one he used out there on the USAF. Those moving target shooting days came to an abrupt finish on a hazy Saturday afternoon in the fall. A neighbor, who coincidentally served in Korea with Anthony's father, and had been friends and neighbors ever since, inadvertently did Tony and perhaps, potentially some poor, random, and unknowing pilot a big, big favor.

Until Mr. Paquette came barrel-assing

through the woods in his four wheel drive laying down on the horn, screaming insanely, Anthony hardly gave this form of recreation second thought. It seemed a round had somehow ricocheted, shooting right through the Paquette's living room window, and worse, came dangerously close to hitting his wife who was standing in the kitchen. She didn't hear the bullet go through the window, but felt the breeze and heard the buzz as the bullet went whizzing by her right ear the same second her living room bay window exploded.

Mr. Paquette never turned Tony in, and he never told Mrs. James. Tony's mom had no idea that the incident ever took place until twenty-five years later, when, as the family had Christmas dinner together with Jean. Tony told the whole story over coffee and chocolate cheese cake. He was such a great friend of Tony's dad and mom, especially with

the man he knew who had died too short a
time before, he felt too much compassion for
Mrs. James to serve up any more grief than
she already had on her plate.

CHAPTER EIGHT

The third night of their journey brought with it Anthony's birthday. They pulled off Interstate 85 to spend the night at a Motel-6 just past the Georgia-Alabama border. The most eventful happening on the trip would have been that third stop, where Pression wanted to give Tony something "really special" for the occasion. Tony, however, experienced a pre-premature ejaculation. That may well be able to put a damper over much of the plan she had for him that night. Fortunately, they are both mature in the relationship, so it's not as though they didn't know a premature ejaculation could ever be timely. Tony was hard again within moments. There's nothing like a dose of TLC.

It is such a shame that we were all once too young to know how to turn it all around. When, if ever a premature ejaculation occurs, Tony has heard some women take it as a compliment to her sexual appeal, like she is so fucking sexy that the man cannot help himself. She'll go the extra step or two in excitement to wind a man back up. Everybody is happy.

Other times, however, the woman is just totally insulted by the whole scene. She thinks that the man doesn't think enough of her to keep it up until she is able to, or decides it's time to climax. Everybody is a loser.

Tony doesn't let it bother him as once he did. He never suffered with chronic premature ejaculation, but if he does happen to climax before he thinks he is expected to, before his Pression has experienced her orgasm, he'll go for a dive. And there he'll remain until he gets that smashing, crashing clitoral orgasm; and he always does. The bonus is that cunnilingus, without fail, gets him hard as rock (again) - whenever a woman comes in his face. Then, all is well all over again.

*

Tony tried his first plate of grits the next morning, and found them pretty good with lots of butter, lots of pepper, and a little bit of salt. Pression repeatedly referred to their destination – Biloxi, Mississippi – all along the way. Tony looked at the map and saw that Biloxi was right on the Gulf Coast. He knew of all the legendary jazz musicians that live in, and frequent the area. If for no other reason, going there to jam with Pete

Fountain at the club he owned right there on the water front would be worth the trip.

The prospect of being right there between the Florida panhandle and the bayou country of Louisiana and the big easy city of New Orleans excites Tony. When they arrive and driving through town, the place shone of everything he had imagined. Welcome to Biloxi Mississippi! The beaches are sugar-white and the gulf a perfect aquamarine. He had to stop for a short walk on the beach. The sand actually squeak's with each step. He takes his shoes and socks off. The water is warm. So warm. Warmer than the August ocean water in New Hampshire! The structures along the ocean front road were large and sturdy, mostly stucco, and the streets were clean.

We have arrived!

"Where to from here, Presh?"

"Take the next right," she said. "Then go over the bridge."

Tony was a little uneasy when he saw the sign reading <u>Welcome to D'Iberville, Mississippi</u>.

"I thought we were coming to Biloxi," Tony more asks then says.

"Well, I wanted to give you a city you'd easily recognize on a map. Besides, it's just the next town over."

All right… How much of a difference could there really be?

Just over the bridge turned out to be the epitome of The Other Side of the Tracks, or as Johnny Rivers so aptly put it: "The po' side of town." The homes were small and ramshackle. Most had piles of refuse in the yard. Pression's house was no different. Driving through Biloxi had been beautiful.

It was clean and busy, and inspiring to the look. Then, just over the bridge, delivered them into an urban looking slum town. The difference between Biloxi and D'Iberville was like the difference between what your imagination, no matter what your beliefs, might place between heaven and hell. This represents no surprise to Pression, having spent part of her childhood there, but it is culture shock to Tony.

Although her mother and father are some of the most interesting people he will have ever met, Tony is uncomfortable. The little shack of a house was infested with bugs, and was hotter than a sauna. Bugs: Talking roaches blues; La Cook-a-fucking-Rocha; baby ones; toddlers; medium sized ones; big ones; FUCKING big ones. Some crawled for a living; some flew around in search. Those are called Palmetto bugs, which is much too nice a name for those savages. Not only can you hear their presence in the night, you can literally feel it. Those airborne germ carriers, with the racket they made, keep Tony awake most every night. The buzz and the flutter of the wings, and the unbalanced breeze generated by them are extremely grotesque.

Her parents didn't want the young couple sleeping together, so whenever the house was empty during the day, Presh and Tony would have to rush through what little love making that time afforded. They had to fuck through their clothes, mostly, pulling his shorts to the side to free his erected penis and blue balls, yanking at and then having to hold Pression's shorts aside to gain entrance into her waiting vagina. It was better than nothing, but that was all. Quick fucks get tired fast, because after several forced and none spontaneous, you cannot refer to the act as making love. Under the covers, it was just desperate, hungry fucking.

Pression's mom worked a few days a week at the local hospital, where she held some kind of clerical position. Her poor old dad hadn't worked a day in over twenty years, so he was usually always at home, on the couch, reading. One thing about him was that he never, ever watched the TV. He read. He read multiple books at once and went through a stack of readings in the course of a week. He also walked. A very peculiar man is he. He once suggested Tony become a square dance caller, or an auctioneer or something like that. He thought Tony had a striking voice.

"Presh, why doesn't your Dad work? He doesn't act or look disabled."

"He's not disabled. He just didn't like working for people, and he is otherwise unskilled, I guess."

"So, he decided to just, like, not work?"

"Right. He reads and learns so much that I think he may believe he is over-qualified."

"For everything?"

"Everything."

Tony could barely sleep for the three weeks he spent in that hell hole, but he never forgot their southern hospitality. Anthony immediately found a gig with a local Dixieland jazz/blues/top 40 band. They definitely were *not* what he was looking for, but it was bucks in the wallet and it helped keep his chops up for the meanwhile. He spent his days placing ads up all over Biloxi. He hung ads in every music store, laundry mat and 7-11 to be found. Any band coming through *that* town was going to see *his* ads, by God!

Sure enough, Anthony received a call on an early Monday evening from a fellow who said he saw Tony's ad in the Biloxi Bubble

Wash & Dry launderette. After establishing through conversation, questions and answers, they were indeed on the same page, Dolphin invited Tony down to the hall that night to check out his band – he'd be on the guest list. They were playing at Captain Jack's on Biloxi Beach, right down the street from the world famous Fountaine Bleau.

Tony went, and he was impressed. They had a sound, they were tight and best of all, and they played no disco! Anthony was chilled. He was thrilled. It was AOR. As opposed to AM Top 40, it was FM Top 100, classics, and blues! The blues! The original tunes they played Tony thinks sound decent, as well. Caught up in the initial excitement, Tony really didn't have the wherewithal to be constructively critical in any way. Just *hearing* original tunes in a club in those days was refreshing, rare, and bold.

Dolphin and Tony spent band break times talking. They got along surprisingly well, right from the start. Tony is used to considering the temperament of most guitarists he'd met, as was Dolphin the boisterousness of most drummers. But, Tony is different. He has a professional air – a bright aura. They were both serious musicians and playful humans. They clicked. Dolphin had, as Tony, been a professional, traveling musician from a very early age. He had been traveling throughout the South since his early teenage years, and he was considered by many in the business to be somewhat of a prodigy.

Dolphin was heavily influenced by The Beatles, as well as other British rock acts, and by traditional blues. The complimentary outpouring was a unique songwriting skill and presence that smacked not only of fresh rock hooks and productive sound, but also of traditional progressions and thoughtful, meaningful and very clever lyrics. Not all yeah, baby and love.

His extraordinary guitar playing was easily apparent within moments of the first set, and Dolphin, also being the lead vocalist, impressed Tony to no end with his ability to maintain an extremely noteworthy style amidst what was extremely complicated guitar playing. He has a fluent voice with a dynamic range. He had even mastered his vibrato technique, which most rock vocalists never bother with. Dolphin was also clearly the leader of the band. An audition was scheduled for the following afternoon. It would be held there at the club. Tony promises he'll be there by two.

When Tony showed up at the hall the next day, the band's truck and trailer were backed up to the loading dock. When Tony walked in he saw that all but the essential stage gear needed for the audition had been loaded out.

"What the fuck?" He had to ask.

"Fired," replied Dolphin.

"You are shitting me," Tony was shocked, because frankly, they were one of the best acts he'd seen outside of hall or stadium.

"For what?"

"Didn't play enough Top 40," Dolphin said matter-of-factly.

So, Tony thinks, they had been fired. Could this be true? This, thereby being an answer to his prayers – that is, a band of musicians that refused to sell-out? Tony could not *wait* to show them the banner across the top of the tattoo on his right arm. It's a picture of the American Flag and a Confederate Jack, both hanging on Civil War swords, crossed in union, with the words "Rock and Roll Forever" written in a banner across the bottom, and the words "Disco Sure As Hell Sucks" written in a banner across the top.

Any group can play any one of the popular songs of the day, and get plenty of work, but not every band would justify the affordability of just flat out refusing to do so, despite the money. Tony loves it, and says so. Neither Dolphin nor Anthony was in it for the weekends; they wanted to do their own stuff and would do only covers selectively chosen by the group, not entirely by the resident radio-heads. His band of mates apparently felt as strongly about that as did he and Tone.

The technical interview/live audition went well. The band and Tony rallied through a good number of tunes, some Tony knew fairly well, some he had never played before, and probably at least one or two that he never even heard. The coolest realization came at the start because right away their bass player and drummer Tony locked together and kept a good groove going. That groove never let up. Dee is very good at listening and following leads, as is Tony. The band pushed each other pretty hard and well, playing off each other, considering they had never played with Tony. Moreover, they didn't know each other whatsoever. Tony has a great ear and he's keen on playing off others. They liked that. Tony garnered his fun in feedback from *not* knowing someone in order to get along so well.

Oh yes, Tony did have to do the token drum solo. Everyone wants a drum solo. Tony, of course, had one handy and he laid it on them smartly and properly, without word, question or hesitation. They liked that, too. He was never a whiner. After the audition they left Tony sitting up there on the riser while they all, as a unit, went off to a table in the corner of the adjacent dining room to huddle up. fifteen minutes go by before they return, at which time Dolphin offers Tony the drum seat.

It sure is nice to be loved.

CHAPTER NINE

Tony officially joins the outfit on Tuesday, Election Day, 1976, one day after their being fired and the same day he auditioned. Pression and he are on their way to Panama City, Florida, traveling with the band in a small caravan of vehicles. Pression invited the other girls to ride with her in the VW, and sent Tony up to ride in the large van with the boys in the band.

Dovid asks if he can see one of Tony's drums. So, Tony pulls out a rack tom. Dovid noticed right away the different looking finish and asked what it was.

"It is a 3D Satin finish. Take your finger and poke the shell. Push a little as though you are trying to put your finger through it."

"Holy shit!" Dovid hollers. "It looked like my finger was going right through it!"

"Yeah Dovid, they're cool. Wait till you see them under the lights! They are original Camco Drums made in Oaklawn Illinois and are rare to find anymore, and they sound great playing any genre."

They both learned from the very first day – one of the rules of the road: never go anywhere without a couple coolers full of beer. Alcohol is not available in Mississippi on Election Day, which threw a wrench into the traveling machine; they righted the situation as soon as they crossed the border into Alabama. Tony is never without weed, so between the spirits and smoke, the inquisitiveness pours from the group. Plans made over a warm buzz; the trip was fun, felt short, and was conversationally conducive and productive.

Pression and Tony would stay with Dee, until they found a more opportune place to live. The lusty trip over Route 98 sends everyone to bed rather early, which was just as well, because the band planned to start rehearsals tomorrow. They pulled into Lynne Haven in the middle of the evening, and Dee's parents are not around.

"Well, Presh," Tony whispers. "Sleep well this first night into our new existence."

"Mmm," she responds in his ear. They are on the couch together, snuggled and ready to go to sleep.

Tony wakes up the next morning - *feels early* - with Dee's mother and father crouched down, staring into his face. He opened his eyes, to see their noses just inches from his! They were studying him as though he were a being from another dimension. Presh was up at the table sipping tea. It took a moment for Anthony's eyes to open, and brain to kick-in, but he is able to focus enough after a moment to say to them a simple, "Hi?"

"Do you know the difference between a Yankee and a Damn Yankee?" Nell asks loud and clear.

"Uh… no."

"The Damn Yankee never goes back!" She cackles with laughter, as Benny, her husband smiles wryly. It's as though they heard the joke told by someone else, on The Tonight Show, or something. Just the sound of her voice as she answered, in her deep southern accent, was enough to cause Tony to laugh. She is a parody of herself! The funny scene has Tony laughing now, too.

Three days of rehearsal supported Tony's first gig with the band. They practiced in Dee's house from around ten until six. Dee's daddy is remodeling the large living area, which makes a great practice place - there are no walls, yet, which offered more space. There were only a few studs on the outside perimeter. Both Dee's parents worked during the day, so the band had several hours to work with on Wednesday, Thursday and Friday. Their first gig with Tony is Saturday at The Beach Shack, and they have to get ready.

The Beach Shack is on Panama City Beach. With a full bar and game room, it's atypical with a lofty, open barn-like atmosphere. It attracts the locals, so crowds are a given whether Snake and Mitch offer entertainment, or not. The huge open room, with a bar and seating on one side and a poolroom on the other, offered no space for a stage, but the gear fit at the end of the long wall, seating side, facing diagonally outward. They all worked as hard as Tony did over the past three days, rehearsing song after song, and they professionally and easily survived that first night.

Starting there, the Fool Star and his band hit the road, and hit it hard. They were due in Albany, Georgia the following week, and never looked back from there. Over the next ten years plus, they would log more than two hundred seventy five thousand miles, covering a two hundred sixty-city circuit, in fourteen southeastern states. They agree that rich, or not, they shall afford a look back on life someday they'll not regret. For it was verily becoming a whole different life for Tony and Pression. Right away, they feel the group has what it takes to make it in the business, not to mention a habit of self-sustenance.

"As a working unit, this group is tighter

than a grasshopper's asshole," Tony shares with Presh. "You know that, don't you?"

"I heard it the first night. They're good."

"Dolphin is awesome."

"You all do well as a group," Presh says. "Gene is kind of clunky."

"Yeah, I noticed - but he can hold a fair rhythm, and has a wide vocal range. Allen is a little sloppy."

"I agree, but they're still young," says Pression. "They can only get better, right? Think projection."

No matter what lay ahead, Tony finally found the all-devoted unit dedicated to making history with music. Their goal as individual musicians and as a band was a single, simple vision: Success by music. Success meant publishing their compositions. Success meant recordings. An album represented a milestone to success.

>>They play the bar scene for a while, to pay the bills. For every artist to whom they played tribute, however, they had two originals in store. Therefore, never a set went by they didn't turn their audience on to a blast of their own music. The best part, aside from the fact that it felt great jamming their own music into the heads of those before them, is that everyone out there enjoys it. Unheard of in a non-showcase situation back then, they consistently received more requests for their own music than they did for the covers.

Tony felt it became a priority to become and remain totally self-sufficient. He shared with them he wanted the group to be a completely self-contained unit, work nor livelihood dependent on no one – nothing extraneous. They traded in their trailer for a larger moving van. They hired a full-time road crew to help get them there, keep them up, and tear them down. The band remains devoted to the music (only). The crew is dedicated to the band (first).

"Our crew is a phenomenal team of humans," Tony tells Pression.

"I get along good with their girlfriends, too," Presh replies.

They serve each as a personal for each member of the band, and they share all the responsibilities of managing the transportation and production assets. The band members own their own stage gear, and band carries their own production: sound and lights. Tony quickly became the manager of the group, so he made them an S-Corp Partnership-LLC. It names him Owner of the Enterprise. It also implicitly put the burden of managing, booking and promotion into his lap.

The Fool Star's group picked up a used Mayflower to carry the equipment in. Economically, they spray-painted by hand, the old beast flat black. Stump, the resident stage manager, and artist of the group used silver paint to finish it off by adding images of corner guards and handles. It looked just like a gigantic rolling hard shell road case, or an old steam trunk rolling down the road.

The band and crew didn't do all that work themselves. When faced with a task, like painting a truck, what they saw was a perfect opportunity for a party. Therefore, as always, party they did. Being in a rock and roll band is a lot like going to college – bon fires, frat parties, panty raids and all. Topless!

Higher edge-ucation.

Some contend to this day that all remain open to time spent on the road, the nursery of life; one could never have picked-up those lessons in school. The whole analogy is a bi-way avenue. It opens up a completely new level of matter for discussion and debate. The off-the-top argument from the right is that one must have a degree to get a job, thus opening the door toward gaining experience. One cannot argue against such a stance. However, from the left, experience – not necessarily in a field – but world renowned human experience, in general, offers opportunities one would be lucky, if not unlikely, to encounter within the confines of the typical campus, college theater or classroom.

Whether or not an individual derives a career out of her college major, or works in a position based on the degree in hand, is dependent on many factors. The future is extremely volatile and never offers a guarantee. One must look beyond the education that simply gains entrance into a world based on material and money, and look toward education based on experiential recognition, analysis, reflection and realization – human condition. Every instance, word and glance may represent a different emotion, meaning or result. It is up to the individual to make or turn every event into experience by drawing upon it honestly and spiritually, but not dwelling upon it literally or within the confines of shallow selfishness, naivety or programmed stubbornness.

Learning to ride logical progression makes a big difference. Continuing education is a huge factor in the human experience equation. It may include a classroom setting, or it may not. One may fall in with an instructor who has done little more than base his own theories, evidence and presentation on someone else's experience and documented case studies. That's history. That instructor has merely memorized the textbooks. One should hope that the instructor will have had real world and modern day experience, or better yet be an active practitioner in the field when not in the classroom.

Continuing education can take on many meaningful façades. Regardless of the setting – sitting on a rock or sitting at a desk - it is a matter of one being a listener and watcher, being conscientiously communicative, well-read, well-travelled, well-versed, open, and most of all, honest and sensitive to humility and the human condition. People learn from people. People learn from events. People learn from themselves.

This, Tony believes – and can explain it free form – on or off a soapbox. It's as simple as that. The rest of the guys half get it. The girls do, all the way. The only point he intends to make is that education doesn't have to end when school does. To put a welcome end to this narrative, he offers this bottom line: "While I could never discount a college education, I will also never discount an individual who happens not to have one."

The Fool Star's group took full advantage of being a rock and roll band, of not having to follow the rules, answer to anyone at any time, and answered every excuse for doing what they wanted. Tony taught them that. In this case, that meant doing what they needed, which was having that party to get the truck painted. With the wine, women, song and all, it was a regular barn-raising, again, not unlike a weekend at the old frat house. Every band does this. Ask any musician who's been on the road. Every occasion is a party and event of continuity.

The band sponsored the truck painting

party in their hometown, in the parking lot of JJ's. JJ's is a small venue, but a room the band loves to play. Being such a small room, JJ's offers an intimate setting within which to play for their hometown crowd. In addition, the owner let them rehearse there in the daytime – much to the chagrin of the noontime drunks at the bar. Eventually, they played every venue in Panama City, but JJ's was no doubt the most qualified to call home.

There were two full kegs of beer at the painting ceremony, and enough people to finish them off in one long, sunny afternoon. As if an even coat of flat black required the extra space, there was also, as always, plenty of stinky-sweet, green, seedless orbile. It took almost all of a gross of cases of spray paint to cover the monster Mayflower. That's one hundred forty-four cases of twenty-four cans of paint. Layered underneath, that yellow, orange, red and green colored Mayflower logo seemed to absorb the black. The crew used the paint left over to cover their old Chevy Suburban. You know… So it would match.

The caravan included numerous automobiles at any given time, depending on who happened to be traveling with the band. Although the group once traveled using just one decrepit, old van and a home spun trailer, as they grew professionally, and with guidance from Tony, so did their fleet. Within eighteen months, they had the big truck for the equipment, the Suburban for the luggage and wardrobe, and a new band RV and a couple vans for musicians, crew and guests. Those are what got them there and back.

…At least there.

…Usually.

Among the menial tasks, such as driving the trucks and babysitting the band members when they got too high, the band relied heavily on their road crew to make sure the sound and look was as professional and polished as possible when the band took the stage. As any musician who has played to live audiences knows, no matter who you are, the hired help will make you what you are, or break you in the end.

As hypocritical as it seems, while they strive to be as self-sufficient as possible, they also feel a void. Tony has been the acting promoter, manager and booking agent of the group for the first few years. It wasn't difficult keeping the group busy with roadwork, but it was difficult trying to manage the business of rock and roll in the midst of creating the product itself, on top of the brokering. Something was missing. What did all the great bands have that they didn't have?

It was nothing material.

Nothing emotional.

It was more a connection.

"We need a manager. A real manager," Tony says, and continued with a vow to find one to take over some tasks with or for him.

"Someone to go to bat for us."

"Somebody to strike that deal."

"Stroke the lion's belly."

"Kiss some ass."

"Lick some boot."

"Stick the neck out."

"Put his dick out there on the block over us."

"Shop our tunes."

"Turn a trick."

"Yeah. That's it."

"An innovator."

"An idea man."

"A genius."

"A sneak."

"A crook."

"Most of all," Tony finishes. "Someone who believes."

They had to face it. The Beatles had Epstein; Bruce had Landau; the Allmans had Walden; the Eagles had Sczymczk; Santana had Graham, etc.

Yes, we should be concentrating more on the product and the music, not where the next gig was going to come from, what the newest public relations game was, or who the hottest producer on the charts happened to be.

Tony was ready to shed the load, but was more anxious to hire a real manager to take up the slack that he had inadvertently let out. The local record store manager was a big fan. Dambert had, in the past, approached them on a number of occasions with desires to manage the band, but often burdened the group by expressing pipe dreams of his own. He was a radio personality, a frustrated musician, as most of those jocks are, you know, but he moonlighted at the store during his off-air time. He was also a songwriter.

Regardless of his background, he seemed to have a sense of what the business was supposed to be all about, so Tony decided to talk to him. The Fool Star got the feeling very early on that Dambert didn't have what it would take to slip the group successfully into the majors. The first day Tony met him, he reminded him of a cross between Paul

Williams and the Oscar Meyer wiener kid. But hey, he needn't rely on impression, right?

He was supposed to make us look good!

Unlike the hair bands of the day, they aren't pretty. The music, they believe, will do the talking. It was Dambert's little, tiny, beady eyes that were too close together, along with that canned, butt-head laugh of his that made him a hard person for Tony to trust right away. His eyes never really met Tony's when he spoke to him, but glared back into them as Tony spoke to him. Additionally, he laughed far too often, at far too much.

Classic symptoms of the nervous and the unwritten confession of the guilty.

He being the unknown record store manager falling in with the local rock and roll heroes sounds all too familiar doesn't it? Well, don't think the band didn't think about that either. We did, but rather than introducing rhetorical cynicism, it injected excitement into them. The "what goes around - comes around" mentality had Tony and Dolphin talking themselves into the relationship before they ever talked deal with Dambert, or the rest of the band.

The group represents, they think, that what the country needs is, a new alternative to commercial radio and disco. Manufactured music had saturated and numbed the public and setback the young and impressionable. It began to make weary the boomers that had pioneered rock and roll thus far, with a rock and roll listener's brand of disillusionment and discontent.

With all their initiative, drive and intangible incentive behind them and the dreamy phraseology of "Hey, you never know", dangling in front of them, not unlike the proverbial carrot leading the horse - along with their outstretched hands, too eager to shake on a deal – they unanimously decide that 20% of their gross would be worth it. If Dambert could score a record deal and help secure a producer for a world-class record, it would be worth it. Hell, Tony thinks if a record deal clause were written in as part of that initial contract, he would have paid him a bit more than the better than standard twenty! Regardless, Tony has a rider of his own prepared for Dambert, and it's an offer he shan't refuse.

Working with Dambert started out all right, lucrative. He managed to keep the band working live all over the south, but in a haphazard circuit. The money was fair, but the miles rolled out before them week by week. To the very end, however, they noticed that's about all Dambert ever did, besides get on their nerves.

A typical road trip, mapped-out by Dambert, may have been Panama City down to Orlando; all the way up to Wise, Virginia; back down to Daytona Beach, Florida; then way to hell back up to Johnson City, Tennessee; and then down to Thibodaux, Louisiana… and so on. Many times those dates came without a day between, so the group will have driven all night to get to the next venue; hardly the time to set up and play on schedule. Refer to your favorite atlas for details. It was nonsense: a burnout circuit to be certain.

Dam's formula to make it in the music business was very different from the Fool Star's. When the group found out all he was doing – which cost the band even more money in brokerage fees – was subcontracting other booking agents to keep them working, they flipped. They could have done that much on their own (and later would go back to booking themselves). On top of that, Dambert had laid claim that there was little time for him to do much else. They knew in his heart he meant well, but he and they truly were in two different leagues before long, and meaning well and doing well are two very different things.

*

In the music business, one has to have an ear. One has to have some insight and have a sense of timing, cannot be afraid to take a few chances nor be intimidated by difference. Simply stated, one must learn of history, of course, but also have the stamina to withstand change, most importantly to take risks that create change and something new.

Dambert tried to make them as he saw others. Even worse, he tried to make them as he once saw himself. The one he let go of when he married his bride and began having kids. Every time they met with him to discuss their music, he would invariably introduce them to one or more of his own songs, or one of which he had co-written with some friend of his or another. He would try to convince them that it could be their one chance. He suggested that he held the vehicle upon which they had been waiting to take them to the big stage.

He probably still doesn't know how much that hurt. The worse part of it all was that he sincerely thought that what he brought to the table was superior to their stuff. The saddest note was that it wasn't. Anyone with half an ear would have agreed, all egos aside, this was enough for Tony to want to get away. He didn't want his band blatantly used by a fledgling songwriter as a wing to the summit.

Understand that Tony understood

marketability, as well as timing and delivery. He tried to accept the idea that industry bigs sometimes wouldn't see or hear things the way he did. He and the group resigned that, unfortunately, it would aesthetically be their loss, but in reality, it's always the loss of the hungry musician. They just wanted a chance to show off what they had, and what they were capable of doing, that's all.

They were also quite up for production. Lyrics here and sweeteners there, and any collaboration that may enrich the effort were always welcome and gear. What makes something special, however, is its natural charisma and freshness. Losing that is like squandering the gift itself.

"This band is a devoted and dedicated group in need of a serious partner," Tony says, "And a serious break."

"You're a damn strong band," declares Pression back.

They resented hiring a manager who dwelled more on image and standards set by someone else, and less on the art of building something original from the foundation lay by the Fool Star's band. Under Dambert, they had produced an independent single, just to see where it would go in the regional Billboard. It was Dambert's practice to make some kind of deal with the studio he would book that invariably included the band having to back up some other artist. He made the group agree to that before he would agree to provide them the time and resources to record their own project. The other artist would inevitably perform one of Dambert's compositions.

Side one of that first single went to number one and stayed there for over three weeks. The song remained in the top ten for months. The group felt like they had scored a springboard to a break with a major label deal. This also introduces the saddest part of their time with Dambert. He failed to capitalize on the success.

The music business is hard enough when you are single with no responsibilities, let alone when you have a wife and family to support, as Dambert had. So, when his crying for more no longer helped, and they had resigned to the thought that their manager blew a significant opportunity, the band had to let him go. Tony continued his search for truth, in the meantime booking the group while he rode out his contract. He hoped to find eventually that special party who might see the real potential in his band, crew, songwriting and self-sufficiency.

They eventually found themselves talking with one of the fellows Dambert had been using to book them around Orlando. Tony booked a gig down in Orlando, where the band used the opportunity to set up an informal meeting with the subcontractor. It was a petting session, just to feel each other out a bit. The intention was to stress the importance behind getting along, attitude and disposition. Plans and dreams, and love and money were not supposed to enter the conversation, but somehow, they did.

That first meeting with Scar was surely impressive. He lived in a gorgeous home; all pastels, palm trees and wicker furniture. He drove a nice, new Beamer, and wore island clothes. Dare Tony forget the cross-thought that Scar also had a young goddess living there with him? She was a working, struggling model who nonetheless managed to stay busy in a business that was as crazy as the one within which the group had a foot.

There was little to no remorse or guilt felt by anyone as discussion ensued at Scar's house with talk of him replacing Dambert. Had it not been for Dambert, they probably would not have been there in the first place. So acknowledgement that Dambert had indeed been a stepping-stone closed the conversation. The combination of the surroundings, excitement, summer drinks, and, the prospect of forming what they were all hoping would be a fresh, lucrative and strategic alliance, obliterated any other feelings of guilt any one of them may have had to begin with. Scar, they discovered by his own admission, had always loved them. Scar had always wanted them. Now, he would have them.

They were a band well known for being the best-sounding in the south. They were also one of the few unsigned bands from the south who had had a hit record on the air. Their first single, which they wrote and produced, knocked Andy Gibb's latest hit out of the Number One position on the regional Billboard Charts, and it stayed there for over three weeks. Andy was the younger Gibb brother of the world-renowned Bee Gees trio. He would one year later die suddenly and sadly due to a heart problem, supposedly agitated by recreational overindulgence. Regional popularity had many of the up and coming local bands including the hit in their live sets. Therein lay the main complaint with Dambert, after all. He was unable to capitalize on that unprecedented milestone. What other band could knock-off a Gibb and stave off a Michael fucking Jackson for multiple weeks at # 1, and still go unsigned?!

*

Along with the club and theater dates that they, coincidentally, no longer had any trouble booking themselves, they also started doing a lot more concerts, often opening for the momentary top of the main. But, with the song on the radio, they also headlined many shows.

One power that Dolphin has is what every songwriter in the world wishes he or she had; the uncanny ability to produce smart, intelligent pieces that are almost invariably, naturally hooked. Dolphin wrote from his heart, always, but you'd swear he was writing from his wallet. That, he did to the point where at times you would be justified in calling him a blues man. It really is a phenomenon, a real balancing act, and a true blessing and calling. Musically strong and lyrically fair, his are some of the most comfortable and exciting songs ever heard. They are some of the most pleasurable Tony ever co-wrote and played.

Scar was well aware of their talents as a

group, and of Dolphin's advanced abilities as a songwriter. He made it clear that he was eager to join. Through long deliberations, the band and Scar decided that they needed to follow through with a plan to settle for a while in a town where they could procure plenty of live work. That need would become necessary, but more, Tony was anxious to secure a studio in which to record.

"Play all day and rock all night..."

They had already spent a significant amount of time and money trying different markets and studios in Orlando, Tampa, and Atlanta, Georgia, but they were not satisfied with the facilities or the output of any of those. The takes sounded experimental. They had yet to try Miami.

Miami is one of the busiest areas around for modeling as well as for music, yet Scar's fiancé wanted nothing to do with moving with us. She was very happy living up in Orlando, and wanted to remain close to her parents. Tony already decided to set up shop down there, with or without Scar. The band agreed. Scar, with dollar signs flashing before him, his eyes on the prize, disagreed. Then, in a move that surprised and impressed both band and crew, he up and left her in Orlando and came with the group. He cashed in, bought himself a thirty-six foot motor home and traveled with the group until they finalized arrangements and secured work and space for themselves and Scar down Miami.

With that move alone, he proved to be someone willing to take a giant step on chance, a leap of faith, solely on the promise of, and talent behind the group. Moreover, for the sake of the music itself. Scar, in the end, took quite a loss on chance. The goddess and he, as a couple, lasted for a short while longer, but as everyone knows who has ever been through it, absence does not make the heart grow fonder.

Absence makes the mind go wander (and wonder).

Absence makes the eyes look yonder.

Absence makes the woman lonely.

Ah, the man, well… a hard dick, as it has been stated by many a wise man before, has no conscience.

Faced with an ultimatum, Scar chose to continue to pursue what he would declare his new career, his dream, without her. She would in turn continue with her own established career, without him. The group was surprised to learn, when Scar lost his love, that essentially everything; the car, the property, the house and everything in it was really the old lady's. Everything was in her name. (That woman was so substantially beautiful that one may feel slightly perverted and a little queer referring to her as merely "the old lady.") She had been carrying Scar from day to day, week to week, and eventually month to month. Who knows what might have been had he not gone on that rock and roll binge with the Fool Star and his band? Tony and Pression felt the break-up was understandable, yet a terribly sad thing. Now, well, they know she got what she deserved, for she sure deserved better than Scar.

That one monumental meeting and a band head-scratching session later is about all it took. Their offer to Scar was numerically the same as they had been paying Dambert.

"When you ain't got nothin'…"

"The difference between the boys
in Zimeron and Fool Star's band,
besides the musical, was that Zimeron
actually *did* go out and get spandex,
perms in their hair and stuff their
crotches with old cotton socks."

PART III

CHAPTER TEN

Scar accepted the position, and the band elected Tony to call Dambert to break the news to him that the group would no longer be needing his services, thanks very much. Tony didn't really mind doing it, for he had always been the unofficial manager, spokesperson, mediator and leading decision maker for the group anyway. Pression loved seeing that in him. They hadn't renewed their contract with Dambert, because he never offered them one - beyond the original, that ever guaranteed any revenue from the road shows. They were free agents. Of course, Tony continued to collect his top secret dollar-per-mile.

From the business point of view, Dambert had done next to nothing to further their collective career, and for Tony, it was simply time to move on. Everybody was getting kind of tired of waiting and felt like they out-grew the odd, older fellow. Personally, all Tony had to do was think of just one of the many times Dambert had pissed him off… one of the many times he pissed them all off…

…like the time we all went over to his place for a band meeting. It was a Halloween day the Fool Star never forgot. We had stopped at a costume shop in Tampa and bought a bunch of goofy looking Halloween masks. Very much like the half-masks you see The Dead wearing in the liner notes of the Europe '72 album. Every one of us had one on and we were all there, band and crew, as usual. We always considered the crew more as an extension of the band, even to the point where, sans Tony, never did any member of the

band take home any more money than did the crewmembers. Therefore, the crew was with us as they most times were. We relied on their input at these get-it-together meetings as well as each other's, you understand.

So, we were all at Dambert's apartment doorstep, in our masks, brewing and giggling, like children bubbling with the excitement that only Halloween can proliferate, and we give a knock. We are expected, so it's no big deal, right? Well, when he opened the door, there we were; heads bobbing and twitching, our hands in the air, arms waving and us hollering a long, loud, vaudevillian, black faced and anguishing "AAAAAGGGGGHHHHH". And that did it. Immediately, Dambert's own arms shot up into the air, and his jaw bounced off his chest. Then, just after that one second, like a skip on a vinyl record album, or a hiccup, he gave quite a start, his eyes went wide, then they went squinty on us. He then twisted this really pissed off look into his face. He yelled at us that the meeting was off and to get the hell out. We all figured that it must have been a lot of embarrassment after the initial scare, although I swear he liked to have shit right in his jockeys when he first opened that door! We waited there anyway. He was more than just a little pissed-off. He refused to answer the door, let alone let us in. We waited for - it must have been - fifteen or twenty minutes. Then, when he'd decided he was cooled down, he opened the door. Oh, we still had our masks on. This is what did it for me: Just to be an asshole, he refused to let the crew in to the meeting. Seems petty enough, but Tony didn't go for that kind of bullshit. The rest of the band went in, and guessing, went on with some kind of discussion about whatever to do with the band. Meanwhile, I stayed outside with the crew.

Fugg that. Fugg him.

…and the task of firing him took on an easier, almost appealing tone. The last Tony heard, Dambert was doing commercial radio jingles and advertisements in Tennessee. In fact, it was that asshole responsible for the Wuv's fast food chain using The Beatles' "All You Need is Love" as their pseudo-anthem; sang, "All You Need is WUVS"! Can you believe he would do such a thing?

I can.

After the storm settled, and Dambert found himself another means by which to pay the bills, he began phoning the group. He continued to call, from time to time, from different locations around the country, with always a different, often whimsical proposition. His ideas were each one cumulatively crazier than the one before. The most amusing of which was the one he laid on them after tracking them down in Ormond Beach, Florida on New Year's Eve. He was calling from Nashville that particular time, in essence promising instant success in the Country market if we would only change the name of the band to "Jack Rowbison".

And record a catalog of songs that he had written, of course.

Actually, aside from the song list and name change, that was probably the smartest idea he had ever contributed. The country market within the year boomed into an Eagles-Rock-like manifestation that would last a decade, seemingly forever in the music business. For a while there, country music was sounding much like the country rock genre of the seventies. They turned him down, but that would have been an easy market for them to fit into, even thrive. Their motley look even became hot in country. It sure would have been an easy market for Dolphin to write.

Who knew?

*

Even after dumping Dambert, the circuit didn't change right away. It continued to bring the outfit up, down and across every highway, blue, green and red in the southeast. The road also brought them face to face with many other bands and artists traveling through that same breadth. They were in a land that was a virtual Mecca of hungry rebels looking for the party, as well as vacationers, who had left their scruples up north, along with their troubles.

The Fool Star had to come up with a plan that was going to solve a few of his band's financial problems. In truth, they were alluded to one by *Molly Hatchet.* Molly was one of the road bands the Fool Star's band had come to know and love, and had been running with and running into fairly often. They were just on the verge of striking the deal they eventually signed that would yield that first monumental Hatchet album: *"Flirtin' with Disaster"*.

Molly had their own problems, though they did enjoy some success, and still to this day tour every year. Those poor guys, back in the day, the critics all said, were doing nothing but capitalizing on the tragedy suffered by *Lynyrd Skynyrd.* It wasn't Molly's fault that the release of their album was untimely, released much too soon after the plane crash that killed members of the *Skynyrd* band and crew. The record company no doubt had a say in the matter. It's tough bearing a label of rip-off. Of all that the Fool Star's group had ever been accused, never had they been labeled a rip. It's a mean, cruel business.

Besides coming from Florida and being ugly, Tony's band already had quite a bit in common with Molly. The way they traveled and the way they handled band business were similar. They even had a used moving van that they had spray painted - brown! It was *Molly Hatchett* however, whom the Fool Star would credit for having turned them on to something that would change the way they lived. Something later christened "The PBC Budget".

Molly described to them something they had been doing over the course of the past eighteen months that had saved the band, or made the band – depending on how one wanted to look at it – close to sixty-five percent their gross earnings. Simply stated, it was a budget based on everyone in the road show taking home no more than thirty-five dollars a week in salary. The business paid all expenses, but all other dollars went straight back into the business, or the show – every red cent.

The Peanut Butter Cracker Budget. Hence, "PBC".

In the hotel they were sharing with Molly, in Ludowici, Georgia, desperate to get themselves into a studio even if they had to buy their way in themselves, they agreed to give it a go. The entire entourage agreed that the struggle might be worth it, personally each, if for the good of "THE BAND". That may have actually represented the beginning of the end for them as a group, for appreciative, mutual starvation does not nurture relationships, that is, unless you're a frustrated prisoner.

The PBC Budget did enable the Fool Star's group to put away a lot more money than before. It wasn't hard to figure out. At first, it looked very promising, as they thought to their selves "Shit, we'll just pay our own way into success." As facetious as the intent, that would not have been unlike what a few other musicians have done in the past - and continue to do. They must, for it's so often, so obviously, not the talent! It just can't be.

Little by little, Tony continued to put away their money, as they all continued to keep their weight down. Weight had never been an issue for Tony. Being a drummer, he would easily sweat-off anywhere from six to eight pounds a night, usually averaging around seven. There were at first many peanut butter cracker dinners, but the entourage eventually worked the whole idea down to a science. Each of them carried from place to place what was in essence a small kitchenette in a steam trunk, and they always stayed in the least expensive hotels they could find.

There were many a night when Dee would plug in that second-hand hot plate and portable deep fryer, while his roommate, Allen, was busy blow-drying his hair... and... PsssPHeweeOOOOMPah! Every light in the hotel would go out, the fuses blown, no doubt smoldering, or the breakers tripped. The rest of the group, along with any other guests that hadn't already been scared away, would wander around outside, murmuring, mumbling, grumbling and suggesting, until the power came back up.

They carried with them from town to town, hot plates, skillets, pots, pans, utensils, plates, crock-pots, bowls, mugs, coffee makers, cups, coolers and trunks that served as portable pantries full of non-perishables. It was quite the operation, really. Tony and Pression ate a lot of spinach linguini with olive oil and Italian Three Cheese, rice and beans, American chop-suey, cucumber sandwiches, grilled cheeses, salads, and of course peanut butter and jelly, peanut butter and banana, and banana and mayonnaise sandwiches. The band paid for all the fast food joints patronized while traveling over the road. Fortunately, in the evenings at the venue, as part of the rider, they got food and drinks free. The rider is always the best part of the contract, besides the money.

The discipline behind the PBC was almost like that of the famous Rice Diet. During the first phase of the Rice Diet, the dieter must eat only rice and fruit. One restricts oneself to one fruit for breakfast, two fruits and three quarters of a cup of rice for lunch, and the same for supper. It breaks you into living a completely new lifestyle. Within a year they were able to afford the very best equipment.

The Fool Star's band had the finest PA and lights in the land! Some disadvantages to scrimping cannot be justified by the business of the band mysteriously looking and sounding so damn good on the follow up visits on the circuit. They stayed in the least expensive places in town, as opposed to the cheapest. The line is so thin between the two that it often goes undetected, until it's too late. Like when someone in the crew discovers two thighs swollen with red, itching, scabies, as the Audio Tech did in Hollywood. Or when one or more of the band members comes up with a crawling crotch full of the crabs, as they all did in Fort Walton Beach.

Tony was so paranoid upon discovering he had them that after having self-administered two RID shampoos and combings, he shaved his entire genital area, from his fucking knees to his chest. After he shaved he stayed in that shower with a third bottle of RID and a fucking pot scrubber, and he scrubbed until he fuckin' bled, he did. Pression, for a time, tried her best to stay away from the area best she could.

Luckily, times like those were rare and temporary, but they did at one time occur. Eventually, all of them, band and crew, had come up against most of the other not-so-nice hazards of the road, as well. Those challenges had little to do with the place within which they were staying, and everything to do with whose company they kept when they were a long, long way from home.

They had been so hardened and tempered by it all, for instance, that when poor old Dee contracted venereal warts in Atlanta, he came home from the doctor insouciantly telling the group that he had "Penis-sore-ises" (like Dinosaur-ises), and all were able and willing to laugh along with his own sense of humor over it. There was nothing funny about any STD, especially the wart and syph, but over the years they had each seen, at least second hand – worse case, first hand – every specimen of funk then known to man. Repeatedly, the humor just helped them get through it all, much the same as a team of homicide detectives is able to laugh together, notebook in one hand, a ham sandwich or jelly donut in the other, while almost blindly looking down at the bloody corpse before them, which has just become the latest statistic. No one knew what AIDS was back then. Oh, it was out there all right, but no one yet knew it. Our government had everyone convinced that it was contained to African homosexual men. They damn sure know it now, and they all know they are damned lucky not to have picked it up somewhere along the way.

"I thank God every day for that small, yet significant favor," Tony says.

"So do I," agrees Presh. "So…do… I!"

Other misfortunes also come-up every now and then, besides those visits to the local health clinic for the free penicillin. For instance, they had rented a house in Destin Beach on one occasion. It was not far from the hall where they had secured a two-week long engagement. Many good things happened that first week. A friend of the band landed a spot on General Hospital, and they got to watch her everyday as she waited on the customers in "Kelly's Diner". She hardly had speaking parts, but like all those must when in the background shots for any restaurant scene, she and the guests mouthed the silence beautifully.

Bob Seger released a new album and did a great interview on Westward One Radio Network. Bob is one of those righteous mid-western people - he is genuinely cool. He let the band and crew sit-in on his practice and sound check at a stop in South Carolina, and would have had them as guests at the show, accept that the band had to play across town that same night at Columbia University. Heavy competition. Lennono released Double Fantasy, and they sat around and listened to that one a couple hundred times. At least the John songs.

The one bad thing that happened obliterated all the good. On the first Friday night, a group of kids, who knew exactly who we were and where the group was playing, broke into the rented house. They had noted that we were playing every night that week from 9:30 P.M., until about 2:00 or 2:30 A.M. A break-in can be emotionally shattering, to say the least, but when the band and crew walked into a ransacked house, every cabinet, drawer, bureau, suitcase and dresser emptied, and the contents strewn everywhere, it was an assault on their very privacy.

The kids had also taken the trash bags from the back yard and had spread the waste and spoilage about every room in the house. It was as if they took each bag by the bottom and stood in the middle of each room and just started spinning around, centrifugally freeing the bag-tie, letting the trash fly, and fly about.

In return, they clearly outdid themselves when they decided to defecate. There had to have been five or six of those ass-holes in on it, because a lesser number could never have produced the amount of shit that they did, unless they had been saving it up for days. Sick indeed, they shit in our suitcases, in our shoes, in our headphones, in the closets and even left some in the refrigerator.

The band and crew stayed up all of that

Friday night and spent most of Saturday cleaning up the place and their belongings. That was ample time for Tony to put through the grinder his idea of the education due those little vandals; those little shitters. He shared the scheme with only his ever-faithful comrade Hogweed, who, in full concurrence transformed it into intention. Tony wanted nothing more than to teach those little beat-offs a lesson in life.

You know…

The Fool Star's own kind of lesson.

On the following night, Saturday, Hog and Tony planned to sneak back to the house during the intermission they will have been afforded. Little did those neighborhood creeps know that on Saturday, Tony's band would open for Vassar Clemmons. After the warm-up set, they were essentially off and free until about half past midnight. That's when the Fool Star's band went back onstage for the big encore jam. The hope was that the kids had planned a second attack.

The fact that the band could on one night share a bill with Vassar, and on the next with Rick Derringer, or one night with Fog Hat and the next with Doc Holliday, for example, always seemed like an asset. In reality, it may have confused the executives, for they could not visualize us fitting into any particular or trendy mold. They were, in Tony's eyes, either too blind to see, or they lacked imagination. The Fool Star's group could have *been* the mold. Moreover, they could have been anything. They were fresh. The expectation in those days was that a band from the south played southern rock. None of the labels wanted southern rock: Catch-22. It was a very ignorant, closed-minded and bigoted marketing business.

On the intermission, Hog and Tony jumped into the black Suburban. They drove along slowly, deliberately, talking little, but only of the plan. They parked two blocks away from the house and walked behind a row of homes to get to theirs. Tony knew that those children had no reason to despise the band personally – that they were probably just being kids – but that did nothing to thwart the determination.

Who was it that said, "Teach your children…? You, who are on the road…?"

Tony had an uncanny ability to twist the most forthright and positive message, turning it into his own caliginous, convoluted and intorted anthem. His answer to you, naturally, may be "…because you know sometimes words have two meanings…"

Tony and Hog were reeling with excitement at the thought of confronting the little barstids. As the two approached, lowly and veiled, noctivagant behind the hedgerow, their hearts pounded steady. Then, sure enough, just as they had suspected, they saw that the vandals had indeed planned a repeat performance. They were smart enough to keep the lights down, but Tony could see at the borders of the window shades the intermittent flickering of the flashlights they carried. The scene could have easily passed as a couple innocently slouched on their couch, eating popcorn and watching a TV movie or something behind the protection of their blinds, or maybe enjoying each other, there in the darkness of their own family room. But hell, Tony and Hog knew better.

They appeared centralized in that one area - the living room. Hog and Tony figured that they probably just got there, and were at this time planning their activities for the night, possibly waiting for others to join them. Knowing that they had gotten in through the sliding glass doors at the rear of the house, and knowing that they would have left those doors open, or at least unlocked to insure an easy getaway upon an unforeseen surprise through the front, Tony and Hog headed toward that back door themselves. Hog was carrying the sawed-off 12 gauge, and Tony was carrying a .380. They both had their Buck knives on their belts. It was not a snub revolver, but a longer barrel Walther that actually made the small gauge look a lot bigger than it actually was – kind of like a nine millimeter. Once the duo got to the back of the house they were able to see and pretty much verify that there were only two of them there by that point in the night.

Upon closer investigation, Tony saw, surprisingly, that although one of the boys was white, his accomplice was black. There are but two real phobias that almost every southern boy grows up with, unless he is, in every sense of the word, a hillbilly. One is, of course, afro-phobia. The other is homophobia. The first is obviously irrelevant here, but ah, the second is not. Tony had prompted Hog on the detailed POA on their way to the house, and, always the fun-loving companion, Hog agreed it was a capital idea, and should serve its purpose well.

Tony had his eye on the goings-on inside the house, and Hog was watching the perimeter of the yard behind us. They waited for eight or ten minutes, then decided that it would be safe to assume that the two inside would be the lone players in the game on this fair and classic Panhandle kind of night. They also assumed that the boys who passed on the festivities for night number two (no pun intended), were instinctively the smarter subset of the gang.

They saw the boys wander down the hallway toward the bedrooms. Hog and Tony then, ever so gingerly, slid open the glass panels that served as the outside entryway from the back that led into the kitchen. They would crawl behind a kitchen island. They pulled their ski masks down, slithered into the kitchen and stopped. They sat there for a few seconds, leaning on and hiding behind the island in the middle of the galley floor space.

One of the boys is coming back up the hallway, toward the living room. Hog and Tony tense, but then the boy seemed to have just stopped. Hog and Tony look at each other, just barely able to make out the inquisitiveness in each other's eyes, and then it hit them. The kid came back up the hallway to use the bathroom. The other one ducked into one of the two bedrooms nearest this end of the house. The boy in the john had shut the door behind himself, apparently having an evening B.M. Why he didn't just shit in the shoes the way he did the night before was beyond reason.

This opened up an excellent opportunity. While the first kid was still in the bathroom, Hog crept down the hall, listening, and finally zeroing-in on the other boy, who, ironically, was in Hog's own bedroom. The young teen was digging busily through the open suitcase at the bottom of the closet. He heard Hog come up behind him, and thinking that it was his partner instead, says without looking up:

"I show am glad we came back to see what we missed, ain't chew? Ah cain't b'leeve them ass-holes went off and left everthang here agin after what we done to 'em laist naght."

In the voice that was so unmistakably and intrinsically Hog, so low, resonant, gravelly and downright classically frightening, the weed groaned a long and pain inflicting:

"Uuuggghhharrrrg…," and then replied, "B'leeve it, sawn."

The boy in the latrine faintly heard the other boy talking, and half-hollered:

"Don't y'all know it be impolaht to convoise wid a main when he be on da throne, you whaht trim-licker?!… Shut-the-fuck-up, I be out n'a minute."

By the time that sentence was finished, Hog had blanketed his boy with an oversized beach towel, pulled him down, pinned him, and then duct-taped his mouth. That done, he swiftly flipped the kid over so that he was lying prostrate on the floor. Hogweed then taped the boy's wrists together. Don't think the kid didn't want to put up a fight, but even in his youth he was no match for the six foot, three inch, three-hundred pound Hog. Next came the ankles, and once that was done, Hog dragged him by the feet into the middle of the room and left him there.

Tony stations himself just outside the bathroom door, at the living room end, and waits. Hearing the paper dispenser rolling, and the toilet flush, he readied himself for the bound. He squats with his own towel, ready. When that little brown boy came out of the bathroom and turned toward the bedrooms, instinctively glancing down at, and touching his zipper to make sure he had remembered to pull it up all the way, Tony pounced. That young black one was really wiry and strong for his age, but adrenaline was like fire in Tony's heart, and he took him down right there in the hall, screams fading into the towel, sounding more like muffled chants of hope instead. On the way down to the floor Tony could feel the little fucker trying to bite him through the towel, and he was kicking like a castrated jackass. Hog was right there by the time Tony got him down, and he did the honors of taping the young prick up.

Hog and Tony drag him head last into the room where the other kid lay, and just kind of drop his feet up side of the white boy's head. They flipped them both over forcing them to look at their captors. They both look up, wide eyed, trembling, obviously frightened, if not downright terrified.

Tony had the .380 sticking out of the back of his pants, and when he produced the long nosed pistol, an audible click comes from the throats of both boys. They both began to kick, but to no avail. Tony told Hog to go get his friend, and when he came back in, carrying the sawed-off, looking a little like a futuristic Chuck Connors in colors, the poor white kid farted tremendously loud, and then involuntarily shit his pants.

"Now, *that* was impressive." Tony said.

"And you there, my fine milk chocolate colored friend, why did you bother using the commode tonight?"

Hog chuckled a little, and commented to the white boy:

"Jeeziz' kid, you stink."

Surely the black boy would have shit himself as well, had he not spent what he had in the bathroom a few minutes before. Now it was time for the lesson of the day.

"Well now," Tony said, speaking very deliberately and very slowly, "Look at me, I'm laughing… right here," pointing to his throat, just below the Adam's apple.

Hog, without having to try, sounds like Lurch from the Addams Family with strep throat. He gave 'em another slow, low "uugghharrg…"

Their eyes were darting back and forth speedily between each other and at Tony and Hog most insanely.

"We could kill you, right here, right now, and take y'all out to Pinnacle Point, where no one would ever find you," said Tony. "But that just ain't my style."

"I would really like to hurt you, let you get all better, and come back and hurt you again. That is not an option, because I don't think I ever want to come back to this fucking hellhole, even for that kind of fun. We have come up with alternative measures for you both... unless of course, you'd rather die, right Pard'?" Tony nodded toward the Weed.

"That's it." Hog confirmed.

"So, who wants to be the spokesperson for the two of you numb little dubbers?" Tony asked.

They both looked quickly at each other, both shrugging their shoulders and one nodding at the other.

"That's real team work, there fellas," Tony said. "Hog spot for me."

Hog rested the barrel end of the shotgun against the white boys head, and after cautioning him not to do anything that may be detrimental to his health; Tony ripped the duct tape from his mouth. He made a yelp like a puppy, then a course, yet quiet "SCHSCHSCH" from the Hog was all it took to shut him up again.

"I read a little something, as I, myself, was sitting in the john not long ago, having a well-deserved shit of my own," Tony began, addressing the young brown one. "It was merely some nasty graffiti from the shit house wall at a bar, but oh, it really got my attention. It went something like this:

'The fat blonde behind the bar with the big tits let me fuck in her ass…

…then she licked my dick clean'

Now *that* was some good readin'." Tony deadpanned.

Hog and Tony were giggling like displaced transvestite fairies, because Tony was improvising most of that stuff, but it was coming off just so good. Hogweed was a sight and a sound. Though his voice was extremely deep and rough, he had a slight lisp, which sometimes sounded comical, but only if you knew him well. Like Mike Tyson. He donned usually a red or black bandanna around and over his head - gypsy style - and wore an eye patch. Even when he didn't wear the patch, the sight of that one tired, droopy deadeye was enough to turn most people away. …Not unlike the Medusa.

"...but I'd much rather see a live show," Tony added. "So here are your choices. You may either play it out for us right here, right now, as I direct, without flaw, or, you can die. Now, who wants to die? Show of hands? Aw, shit, just nod your head yes if you'd rather die. No? OKAY, then.

Who wants to be the fat blonde with the big tits?"

Tony went out the back door, circled around the way Hog and he had come earlier, and retrieved the Suburban. Tony backed into the carport; Hog loaded the two of them into the rear, jumped in next to Tony, and then they drove out to Pinnacle Point. Both boys sobbed through their noses the entire way there. Tony had to give them the lecture on how they shouldn't be fucking with anyone unless they by-God know whom they're fucking *with*. Tony asked them to be thankful for the gift of life and a second chance. He told them they should consider this a warning, because if they ever again crossed us, or anyone else as crazy as us, things could be a lot worse. Just to confuse them, Hog added that we didn't appreciate young punks casing houses in our territory.

Hog and Tony were back at the club with fifteen minutes to spare.

*

After drinking too much it's a common occurrence for the adult drunkard to wet the bed. Sometimes he'll get up in the morning discovering that dampness down there, the dark spot on the couch, the carpet, or in the bed before realizing that the horrendous dream of the night before contained a bit of a twist. That is, he wasn't fucking that dream-girl, he was pissing on her, and the worst part is, of course, he had actually peed all over himself.

During any given binge, a drunkard is bound to get up, sleepwalking. His inebriated mind tells him he is heading to the bathroom, but he ends-up in another room of the house altogether. Once there, he starts peeing anyway, dreamily imagining that he is standing over the latrine. After a night of indulgence, Dee had drunkenly peed into poor Dovid's open suitcase. The bag had been lying open on the closet floor of an otherwise, clean, Motel 6. Hogweed certainly outdid himself, and Dee, when he stumbled right up to the refrigerator in a house they had on Daytona Beach, opened the door, stepped forward, and pissed right there. He did this just as though he had marched up to the bathroom door, opened it, took a step forward and bled his big, fat lizard in the friggin' toilet that otherwise should have been there. It is all very, very disgusting and grotesque, but somehow, what those kids in Destin did to the group, seemed so much worse. After all, they did number two.

Tony's band were often times the victims of circumstance. That is not to say that they didn't walk right into any given situation on the feet that carried them, but the occasional case of the crabs, or the clap, or the piss-in-the-bed, they all presumed were part of paying their dues. They accepted them as part of growing-up and cutting teeth. Life on the road with a rock and roll band. No apologies.

So, if nothing else, the years spent traveling and playing all over the south, conquering crowd upon crowd, in search of the almighty record deal, led at some points by their dick-strings and other times by heart-strings - getting shat upon, or shitting themselves and falling right back into it – were some of the group's most formative years. They learned a lot about each other, and their selves getting tougher and tougher with every town visited, experiences shared and every hardship endured. They learned a lot about people in general, the attitudinal, and the human condition.

Tony has seen many a big, burly biker doing the old farmer brown, blowing the mucous from his face to the ground no matter who happened to be around, or what street he happened to be on. He has also since been inside of at least two dozen Fortune 500 corporations throughout the New York metropolitan area, and can testify that there are bugars and snots hanging off the executive lavatory walls of every single one of them, as well as droplets of pee and smears of feces left on the toilet seat edges, as well. And those places are cleaned on a nightly basis!

So what's the difference?

Whether it's Wall Street or Swap Meet, most men in suits fake manners when others are looking. Essentially, men are all pretty much the same. Cosmetically we may appear different, but we are all driven by sex, power, procreation, greed and fear of God. Some believe that everything happens for a reason. Case in point: Any time on the road that was any less severe than the time spent thus far, could never have readied the Fool Star's band for Homestead, Florida!

CHAPTER ELEVEN

The Big Daddy's organization is an institution all around the south, headquartered in Florida, a home for itself in Miami. As popular as they are with the dance crowd, especially those who preferred a DJ to a band, the Big Daddies were known infamously to all rockers as nothing more than a collection of disco-licking joints one and all. The unnatural irony, unreal as it seems, is that the Fool Star's group is doing a lot of work for them! They were always selective about the places played, or more correctly, the music they were expected to play once there. The Big Daddies were justifiably very selective when faced with where to put them once they had them.

Tony's band is the black sheep of the club scene because of their repertoire, demeanor and following. They play rock and roll, they look like they play rock and roll, and, they act like they play rock and roll. And they have a rock and roll show. The Bohemian Brethren, listeners habitually and ecstatically blow their minds when they come to see the Fool Star's band play.

As a follow-up to the band's Number-One, they had been granted lots of air play on the couple Top Ten singles they released subsequently. Radio play helps tremendously in booking bargaining power. The "Dead Celeb" Circuit of the south - Big Daddy's, Level III, and Crown Lounge - is very much unlike the other club situations the band usually welcomed. They were more used to roadhouses, showcase, after hours clubs and theaters, such as The Whipping Post in Augusta, C.W. Shaw's in Atlanta, The Attic in Greensboro, and The Dancing Bear in Raleigh. All were excellent venues into which to deliver their original music.

Unfortunately, the musical temperament of the string clubs remains very unpredictable. The hired band is expected to *make people dance*. …Like the fucking Indians make it rain. The band is expected to *make the people drink*. …Like the fucking Indians share the pipe. But mostly to drink. And drink. And drink some more. Good times and American Bandstand are great and all, but attendance, sales and high number receipts rise above in every instance, in every way, when playing a club date.

Keeping busy often had nothing to do with how well-rehearsed, creative or professional

Tony's band is. Sometimes it seems like it's more about the brand of music his band played compared to the popular, and, what his band looked like. Again, he was proud to retort, "We play rock and roll and we look like we play rock and roll" to anyone who had to ask. So, not at all does the Fool Star's band appeal to the typical suburbanite, tippy-toeing, polyester vacationers, say, on Marco Island. They want disco.

Big Daddies and Level III's are multi-level, with a rock room and disco, both, separated by floors: Disco downstairs and rock upstairs. The group met some of their biggest, most devoted fans at clubs where Tony's band kinetically drew them out of the disco room and up into the rock hall. Once watching, and hearing the group play most people stayed in the rock hall to finish the night. And they returned time after time.

Daytona is a favorite stop every time around. They play there at least three or four times a year. They always have a date over Bike Week, and also culted with the collegiate swarm during the annual school Spring Breaks. They also played on DST fall back, having to perform the extra set at two. Their audience is wide. Even the older people like them. That's because many of the covers are songs that they no doubt remember from their younger years. Traditional music, and roots rock are a big influence on Tony's band. Much of the appeal was that they tried to have a lot of fun on stage – sometimes it showed – and when it did, it was contagious.

Be it Sarasota – Bradenton, Clearwater, Tampa - St. Pete, Naples - Miami, Orlando, Panama City, Tallahassee - Jacksonville, and any other good for something Florida town one can mention, virtually everyone the band ever played for, in Florida or away, who knew there was more to music than it being just something nice to dance to, became instant fans. The group is finally on their way, just what Tony and Pression planned, needed and wanted. It's working.

You would never have found the group, say, at the Big Daddy's out on Maribelle Island, asking the middle aged couples in their Polo outfits and Gucci sneakers "How They Were Doing Tonight?" and "Were They Ready to Party?!"

...breaking into a polished rendition of *Super Freak* or *Get the Funk Outa My Face* or friggin' *Celebrate!*

Though one'd be hard pressed to get a thumb on them any given moment within the years of 1975 and 1986, for they are, for the most part, all over the territorial musical map, for a few of those years in between, however, one could sure as betting find them at a Big Daddy's in Miami, and even more likely at the Big Daddy's Homestead.

Homestead. Homestead dear Homestead; besides Florida City, the farthest south you can travel by land before hitting the Keys. South Miami. Little Havana.

Upper Columbia.

Outer Alcatraz.

L.A. - Lower Alabama.

Biker City.

Drug Haven.

And for a while there… Home.

All it took was one week long engagement at the Big D's Homestead to consummate the deal. It was sort of a live audition; or rather, a five day "try before you buy" kind of thing. The Fool Star's band isn't sure whether that was where they wanted to be, but much more critical was that the organization wasn't sure they'd be accepted there. Few bands are. Indicative rejection might have come to a group by any sort or means, from heckling, booing and verbal slaughter, to hurling trajectories, plug-pulling and riot. Just like those bar scenes in the movies where there is a chain link fence protecting the band from the riotous crowd, is Homestead. ...Without the fence...

Homestead Big Daddy's is the one and only place Tony and Pression ever encountered the absolute premise that the customer is <u>always</u> right. The customers alone in Homestead call the shots. Homestead is the only Big Daddy's that did not, and could not, enforce a dress code. The club and the clientele both were Big Daddy exceptions. The reputation had been worn rough by the mistreatment of many, tarnished, and under the constant scrutiny of others that were leery and weary of the power that Big D commanded. It has to do with balance. Homestead Big Daddy's is one club that honestly is, almost always, too crowded to clean; yet the sore thumb. The libertine, loose women, prodigals, and ruffian and wealthy: Daddy's black sheep remains in the end, all of his. Bottom line: Homestead is also Big D's biggest money maker.

There, the band plays to the leathers, colors, silk suits, jeans and tee-shirts, as well as the naked high. Homestead is all hair, tits and tattoos. When their first week in Homestead came finally to a close – the band and crew finishing-up an encore of *Skynyrd* tunes that include a twenty minute tribute finale to "Freebird" – with everyone in the place tripping on mescaline, some kind of a pseudo-psycho-cosmic bond had been forged, metaphysically joining band to audience.

Yes, damn it, we are trippin' too…!

Forty-five minutes later, the crew went out to back the truck up for the load-out. They were stopped in their tracks about twenty feet or so from the back door, by Whale, who stood there with a handful of ignition wires, wearing a sheepishly funny looking, shit eating grin on his face. His eyes were on fire and jumping all over his universe. He was apparently acting spokesman and assumed leader of the legion of some fifty or sixty other bikers and friends whom behind him had gathered.

The crew; T.L., Hogweed, Droid and Stump bee-bopped elatedly out of the back door, the successful, wild, fun and tiring five-nighter behind them. Strolling along, they came soon to a classic domino-stooge-stop, however, when confronted with the sizable crowd that assembled magically and appeared before them. Whale said, without affectation, "We're not gonna let you go." As simple as it sounded, it was clear he was not kidding. They all were not kidding.

Meanwhile, another smaller task force had the manager of the bar, a super bowl ring bearing ex-Pittsburgh Steeler, cornered in his office. The assistant manager was frantically calling all over Florida trying to reach their booking agent, the band's agent, and their regional manager with the demands that had been placed before them this bizarre night. Management didn't mind. Why should they? Good business is good business, and they had had one hell of a week. That bar was packed Tuesday through Saturday, 8:30 PM till 2:30 AM every night.

To the band, once fired for not playing the right kind of music, it almost felt too good to be true. It is almost too peculiar to be true. The Homesteaders, after just one week, seemed like family that the group knew they had, but had yet to meet until now. The crowd, the bikers, the dealers and the consumers were so happy that they finally had a no-nonsense rock band in there that they, by God, were going to claim and protect their find by all means.

The group is equally pleased to play for a no-nonsense crowd. They rocked that week in Homestead, and would every week thereafter, playing every night like there would be no rock tomorrow. And the crowds kept coming. What could have been a typical week long engagement at just another club in the south, turned into a much longer and enduring relationship. Big Daddy gave the okay for an extension with only a verbal confirmation on the register tape totals, and the booking agent really didn't have a chance to decline so long as Big D had already spoken. The group went in there direct with Scar, who had previously established a working relationship of his own with Big D. The booking agent is Big Daddy's exclusive, so he isn't overly thrilled with the idea of the Fool Star's band moving in, because he wouldn't collect any commission. He has plenty of other bands and plenty of other Big Daddy's to work with, so no one involved is too awfully worried about him. I was the official manager of the group, so I was in the office all thumbs up!

The band that had been scheduled to start the following week, who had essentially worked their way into what was a house band position there in Big Daddy's Homestead, aren't too thrilled either. For them, it means knowing that they would have to find work elsewhere. It also meant replacement and rejection. Tony's band, however, is damned happy! After years of being on the road, having traveled more than a quarter million miles, playing fifty weeks a year, they couldn't even comprehend the concept of *not* traveling. Right away, the idea sounds seductive and inviting. What it means, as a band, is that they can concentrate more on recording than on chasing the next gig, which falls nicely in with their ulterior plans.

The band signed the six month, with six month option with Big D's. They first settled in to the house in Homestead that Big Daddy furnished, and then they concentrated on setting Scar up with an office. After scouring the Miami area for office space and studios, they found the needed vacant space at Studio Center in North Miami. It was available immediately and was the most reasonably priced. Without much research or deliberation, as manager, the Fool Star frugally took it.

*

Studio Center is owned and run by a big Italian fellow named Montalvo. He is rich and he is as nice a man as he could be. He is also the Governor's brother-in-law. That sure did not make Tony trust him any less, but all got along, and Montalvo loved the band.

"That kind of relationship couldn't hurt," Pression reminds Tony.

The Center itself, and the key players within, are known more for accomplishments in television and advertising than for any significant contributions to rock music. The neighboring Criteria Studios supported many great and classic rock acts, including Crosby, Stills, Nash and Young, Eric Clapton, The Allman Brothers, The Eagles and The Bee Gees. Wow! So many more! But Studio Center's fifteen minutes of musical fame came and went with the disco craze. They produced many of the various Miami-based pop stars of that thankfully short-lived era. Tony is hoping to change all that.

As is the case with most independent studios, day-by-day business at Studio Center survived contract to contract. A large part of the revenue comes from various production deals, such as the one they currently have with *Fayva Shoes.* The Center handles virtually everything for Fayva: the ad campaigns, the commercial shoots, film and video footage, the models, talent casting, the sound tracks, the arts and graphics, and even play a part in associated promotional distribution.

The truly impressive asset, as far as the band is concerned, is the ever-present swarm of female models that hang-out there. Every visit to the studio was for the band like going to the Playboy Mansion! Although the group lived and played down in South Miami, and they commute to Studio Center in North Miami, the recognized potential outweighs the distance. The group would soon be booking studio time, as they almost have what they need to fund the first engagement. They hope that, by virtue of his settling-in there, Scar would inevitably form an alliance of sorts with Mr. Montalvo.

Scar settled into his office and went about his business dealings for the band. He involves himself with, and recruits various local talents, and he called down a couple of old groups he had booked from Orlando. This helps put a few extra bucks in his pocket, not to mention a few more girls in his bunk. He continues to live in the studio parking lot, plugging his RV right into the center for his power and water supplies. Whether this is for simple convenience sake or shear shrewdness, Tony and Pression do not know.

"Certainly, he could have sold the motor home," Pression says.

"It is like he is still on the road, but his wheels aren't turning," Tony answered.

"Might have seen it then, if I had my eyes open," he laughs.

*

"Hey, I'm Kenny Benito," said one of those tee-shirts-and-jeans from the Homestead audience.

"Hey Kenny," says Pression.

"Hey man," Tony says. "Tony. This is my girl Pression."

Kenny Benito is a nineteen year old from New Jersey.

"So, what's up, Kenny?" Pression asks.

"I think you guys are fucking great!" Kenny went on to compliment. "Thanks," is all Tony can say. "I appreciate it. I'll tell the rest of the guys."

Throughout the south, there are many, many people who believe in the band. They believe in the band, and they cheer for them. The most loyal of the fan base supported literally the band and the crew. They down right spoiled them rotten! Kenny is one of those people. He does both. He loves to watch band play, and he listens well to the songs. He went out of his way to get to know the entire band and crew individually. He understands the band's goals and measures. He knows they want to make money without selling their souls.

He makes it a point to try to understand all of their strengths, and either accepts, make-well or medicate their weaknesses. Smart like that for his age. He asks for, and would accept nothing in return, except that the band just keep on rocking.

"Presh," Tony calls to Pression. "Kenny does more for the group than anyone, including Scar."

"It seems that way."

Kenny has an unconditional commitment to teaching the group to stop once in a while and to simply enjoy life. He appreciates the amount of time, effort and money the group has invested in itself, but sees clearly the sacrifices they made in order to do so. Kenny reintroduced them to the concept of a happy life – a happy life outside the band. Recreational cocaine.

Kenny, at nineteen, is netting easily over nine-hundred grand a year on the average, mostly tax free. All it takes is three big deals a year. He was looking for an interesting investment – something fun, with potential. He was looking for some guarantee, with little effort and risk. Realize that the boy started out at the bottom. He ran, as a young teen, for some of the largest men in Miami, taking real chances. Kenny treacherously climbed the dope rope – the Amazon bandit's corporate family ladder – when finally the day came Kenny B established the sizable numbers all his own.

They were all good, but the most lucrative was an exclusive and huge connection in Seattle. Three times a year, without fail, Seattle would fly into Miami, take a ten pack of kilos of white off Kenny and leave him with a bag full of cash. That quick and that simple was the plan. It was simply pro, a substantial, yet calculated risk at worse and a fairly safe proposition for a crazy person at best. Along with every deal came enough extra sniff to stash a bundle, or generate a little extra pocket change, if need be.

"Right-handers know more than anyone else

How intimate a handshake be –

That same hand firmly seal acquaintance

Do service them animatedly..."

PART IV

CHAPTER TWELVE

Tony dealt a little dope in his hometown, but coke hadn't yet really caught-on. Oh, he was, on occasion, doing it, but not selling it. His generation of consumers were into Speed, Weed and LSD. He and Pression had a good thing going, selling pot and acid part-time, dealing all through high school, right up until they left New Hampshire for Mississippi. Outside of the time they spent touring, dealing was their only source of income. They were moving twelve pounds of pot a week, along with eight hundred sheets of acid – sometimes more. It was enough to keep cash in the pocket and stash for the head. Beside music, that's all Tony had going to pay the rent and spread the high.

The nation's Great War on Drugs had not yet officially been declared, but there were several occasions when Tony and Pression – living together - did feel the heat, and those were some very close calls. The first time, Drew and Tony planned on meeting one of their local competitors, named Cap, who had called them to say he had been stood-up by his supplier. He just had to have his end for the buyer, as planned, on that very night, or he may well lose him for good. Tony and Drew could dig that. They could filter their shit through Cap and still come out ahead. So, they met him as planned, out behind the high school to deliver the goods.

There was a basketball game scheduled that brought with it lots of people, and generated plenty of commotion. The law and everyone else were as busy as they could be inside the auditorium and around the atrium in the school as usual at game time. Drew and Tony had come by the school earlier that night and had stashed the five pounds and the one hundred sheets just off the path that lead into the pines behind the school.

Tony left his car out on Middle Street and Drew and he walked onto the back grounds of the school to meet Cap. Things looked okay. He was right where he said he would be, standing to the side of the new training facility across the access road from the back of the school gymnasium. Everything fit nicely into one doubled, brown Pic N Pay grocery bag, and it took just a minute or so for Tony to retrieve it and bring it back to where Drew and Cap waited. Drew held the bag while Tony counted the money.

The two man police cruiser made its way

ever so slowly through the front parking lot. They were getting ready to turn left, down the side access drive that would bring them right to where the three were standing. Just as the cop car rounded the corner, its lights turned out, creeping, Tony saw a twitching look in Cap's eye. He looked over Cap's shoulder and saw it. He couldn't make it out clearly; he couldn't even see the roof lights, but his gut wrenched the reality up to his head in one sickening pulse.

"He set us up!"

The cop driving had stopped the car and both the officers were easing out of their respective doors. They began double stepping, one on each side of the drive, crouched at the waist, knees bent, with each step hustling a little faster toward the trio. They had their right hands on their guns. Tony could hear the thudding slap-click the heels and soles of their police issue patent leather brogans as they hurried up the walk.

The whole story about Cap's supplier had been a lie. John Cap got busted two days before and struck a deal with the law to rat on his connection. John was much too smart to genuinely do such a thing, so he concocted this arrangement to make it look as if Tony, Pression and Drew were his suppliers. That way, he's off the hook, and, he doesn't have to look over his own shoulder for the man from South Boston coming for him. All he did, as far as he was concerned, was to overtake a couple of competitive schmucks, much like himself.

All Tony could do was turn to Drew and yell:

"RUN!" as loud as he could.

And run they did.

Tony – surprising all of them – ran right at the officers, who were drawing and yelling at all of them to freeze. Drew ran in the opposite direction, but was, unfortunately, tackled right away. Drew had no idea that he had been burned. He thought the cops were after John. John did in fact feign a run to make it look good, and one of the cops did in fact feint after him. It was a ridiculous bit of improvised choreography. But that's all it took for Tony to get by that fat, blue-uniformed son-of-a-bitch.

Tony ran as fast as he had ever run in his life, past the police car, right around the corner, past the west wing of the school, right by another cop, who was probably just there working security on an off-night, picking up some extra loot, moonlighting. Tony heard his radio signal-in but did not hear the copy; didn't need to hear it either. Still running to beat the blue devil, Tony turned right and continued toward the front doors of the school. He thought he was going to get into the atrium, then into the gym, hopefully losing the law men in the crowd and the noise. But then, at the last minute, he saw something.

The row of men's room windows, which were just to the left of the main entrance, were cranked all the way out, as open as they could be. This was it, all three sets of doors were closed, and the windows were open. Tony veered toward the windows, picked one, ran for it and jumped. He just did make it high enough so that his forearms were over the edge of the wall, holding the sill inside. With all his available strength he hauled his hips over the sill and ass through the window, landing on his hands on the bathroom floor. The cop that gave chase couldn't have been too awful smart, for instead of just going around to cut Tony off on the inside, he tried to catch Tony going through the window before Tony could make it over the wall.

Tony knew officer friendly would be coming after him, so he got into one of the stalls to get rid of the little bit of personal matter he had in his jacket pocket. Slipping into the stall closest, he threw the bag into the toilet and flushed. He then yanked his pants down as quick and as far as he could and sat there, shaking like a hound dog shittin' razor blades.

No surprise, the cop came in completely out of breath and really, really pissed-off. He cleared the room and then went straight for Tony. He probably recognized the boots. Grasping the handle to the stall door, he gave it a tremendous yank that sent the door open his way so quick and forcefully that he knocked himself in the forehead with it.

Jeez, it was hard not to laugh out loud at that dumb-ass motherfucker. He demands Tony come out of the stall immediately, without flushing it, which, as a surprise to him, Tony does. He jumped on Tony, wrestled him to the ground, did a quick search, and then stood the young man back up. He looked in the latrine and saw only the yellow urine Tony had managed to squeeze out just after flushing.

He had pulled from Tony's jacket pocket a bright brass chamber pipe along with a pouch of Bugler tobacco and papers. The Bugler Tony took up smoking over his favorite Camels, for times like these, when he would need an excuse for carrying rolling papers. The pipe, well the pipe was obviously paraphernalia, but the pisser is, that it had been virtually unused. Not a toke had ever been pulled through it. Tony just purchased the pipe in Hampton Beach that very afternoon. By now, there are two officers in the white house, scouring over the pipe, carefully examining it, but being brand, spanking new, there was not one iota of residue!

Paraphernalia was not illegal in New Hampshire. But knowingly in the presence of said paraphernalia was justifiable cause for the law to search and seize. You wouldn't go flashing it around, but it could be purchased at the local head-shop. Pipes, papers, bongs, hookahs… You name it. The shops were a dime a dozen. What they most definitely could get you for was residue. That's what the cops are looking for; resin. They opened the chamber. They pulled the screen out from the bowl. No residue there… One is asking all sorts of questions, trying to get Tony to implicate himself, but Tony was too good for that.

"What do you use the chamber for in this pipe in the first place," the man in blue asks.

"I plan to pack the chamber with mentholated spearmint to give the Bugler a more refined taste."

Tony denied having been outdoors that night, since game time, and they were forced to return his goods to him, and be on their way. They didn't leave without telling Tony how lucky he was.

"You had better watch your ass because we're damn sure going to do so."

Tony got back in the stall and sat there relaxing for a bit, and had a nerve induced BM. He needed to chill, so he decided to head toward the gym to watch the rest of the game. As he tried to make his way into the gym, having finally left the men's room, the same cops met him half way across the foyer.

"You know, James, we got your buddy Drew,"

one said, trying to cajole. "He told us all about it."

"Tweet, tweet," the other sang. "He's singing like a bird."

"Excuse me?" Sounding perturbed, Tony innocently replies as he pretends to be rushing back to his seat before the buzzer.

*

Cap died in an automobile accident a mere two weeks later. He was in his Volkswagen beetle trying to back down an interstate ramp upon which he had mistakenly exited. He backed right into the path of an eighteen wheeler coming fast up the ramp and was instantly crushed to death. Cap's rear lights, reverse and brake included, were not working.

"I'd like to say that fate has a way all by itself, but I cannot."

As that was his first offense, Drew got off with probation. The only other time Drew had ever been taken into custody was with Droid, the spotlight man, for sleeping in Market Square. They were both full of Genes and Librium, passed-out behind the North Church. They had been taken in for vagrancy. Droid threw-up all over the police station floor. They were each given a single, small, white wash cloth, and made to clean-up the entire mess. When their parents entered the station to pick them up for home, that's how they found them.

*

The last time the law ever got close to Tony and Pression was when an ex-cop turned informer named DeForest showed-up in Portsmouth. In the course of less than ten days he managed to make some kind of deal with almost every two bit seller in town.

Tony never, ever dealt with strangers, but there was one kid named Joey DeSmit who was always eager to turn something around - anything - for the couple of bucks that may be in it for him, or for the stash he might squeeze out of the deal. Even perhaps, just for the thrill. Dope is a head game.

While at home one night, there came a knock at Tony's back door. It was Joey. He had with him some guy Tony'd never seen before. It took about a second and a half to peg him. He may as well have had NARC tattooed in red, white and blue over his eyebrows, across his forehead: Tone just knew. The typical tell-tale signs: his hair wasn't long and it wasn't short - it was combed - parted straight - on the side; he wore high-water jeans - a little too short - with casual, shiny, slip on leather shoes; Navy Blue nylon crew socks; the button-up shirt with the flared collar; and the biggest give-away of all — he stood (and walked) with his arms bowed out as if he were still wearing his holstered service revolver and radio. He was way too friendly and smiled way too much.

A real ditzy-dick.

Joey asks if Tony could help him and his friend out, but Tony acted like he didn't know what in the world Joey was talking about. He is playing it totally dumb, but then asks Joey if he may speak with him for a moment in private. He took him into the kitchen, leaving the dick outside, and without raising his voice, hissing like a rattled snake, relayed an important, unheard message.

"I just know that dude outside is a NARC," Tony says. "And do not _ever_ bring any stranger to my place again!"

Joey pleaded with Tony to somehow work

things out; he really needed to make it happen. Tony is reluctant, but learns that the guy wanted seven keys that very night, on the spot, and Joey had the cash in hand. Tony tried exactly once to talk Joey out of dealing with the runt out in the car port, but Joey was intent. Like Pilot, Tony applies his own mental floss, sweeping clean his own webs, and finally issues forth instructions.

"Leave me the money," Tony began. "But, don't tell him you did. Got it?"

"Okay…"

"I want you to leave the premises, take a ten minute ride, and then circle back and pick up a garbage bag that you'll find on the track-side road. Got it?"

"Yeah…"

"It'll be just after and behind the next house down."

"You abso-fucking-lutely say nothing more to that other guy, and, lose the motherfucker before you come back. I don't trust him one bit."

"Okay Tony." Joey thought Tony was being paranoid.

Paranoia, for Tony, has always been a seedling for survival.

That visit happened on a Wednesday evening. The following Friday, at 6:00 AM sharp, over two dozen warrants were issued and damn near as many arrests were made all around Portsmouth. Cops were beating down doors and rousting all the poor suckers out of their beds – showing no mercy. The FBI were also making arrests at the high school and up at UNH throughout the day.

Pression had received a tip the night before from a waitress she knew who worked in Rosa's, a bar just around the corner from the police station. That evening, Tony had arranged for everything at home to be taken out of the house and buried in the woods, just in case. They never came for him, but DeForest, the NARC, knew who Tony was. Tony knows that he knew that he merely nailed him that night when he and DeSmit unexpectedly showed up.

Joey was only one of many that got burned. Hogweed got busted too, as did a multitude of other friends and acquaintances, but Tony and Presh slipped by. It was a shame that most of the people who were busted that morning were actually more user than they were dealer. The biggest dealers in the county – Neil, Bernie and Tony – never got hot, and never got caught.

*

It's Friday morning, and Joey's dad just left for work. An executive with The Bank of Boston, he commutes to the city focused every day and returns home drained every night. Mrs. DeSmit never had to work outside the home and enjoyed her upper-middle class arrangement there in Portsmouth, New Hampshire. On any given day you could find her in town shopping the finer apparel shops, or sipping beverages and buttering a scone at La Panier d'Pain, or one of the other gourmet bistros in town.

Tony and Pression once made a special trip over to Joey's house just to get a look at what was one of the few and first microwave ovens in town. His Mom had even cooked Thanksgiving turkey in theirs that year! Baked potatoes too! Oh, how wonderful progress and technology are, along with the promise of tomorrow and yummy nuked meat and potatoes.

The DeSmits and all those like them are the pioneering generation for those nicely settling into Portsmouth nowadays. They are the young professionals that are a little too self-centered to authentically raise a child, and too busy even to contribute to the good of the community, which is fast becoming another suburb of Boston. Golf, high balls, stocks and boating are too far a cry from the freedom fighting, salty dog ancestors of years gone away. A lovely simple drinking town, obsessed with a wicked shopping problem.

Their lives are just perfect there on Whipple Lane, just off of Middle. Until the morning raid, Joey's parents were no more aware of their son's smoking pot than they were his experiments with speed, LSD, sedatives and painkillers. Joey was the baby-faced, lone child of a couple that had arrived. Fortunately, their spoiling him had not fully ruined his heart, though friends infrequently were faced with tolerating the spoiled child misgivings embedded in his otherwise earthy personality.

*

"Open the bulkhead!"

That was all Neil said between Pression's own "Hello", and his hanging up. If he was calling from home, it would take him eight to ten minutes to drive from his Grandmother's nursing home on Rye Beach over to the house on Banfield Road. Tony went downstairs, locking the door at the top of the well behind him. Only after he ran a quick pick-up around the room did he, from within his own clean, stellar cellar, unlock the inner and outer bulkhead doors. There from within the thick expanse of Limbo he could only wait and wonder.

Tony didn't have to wait long; not even

those ten minutes or so he thought it would take Neil to get there from Rye. In moments Neil was through the doors. He had a brown paper bag from I.G.A. under one arm and unclearly motioned with the other for Tony to lock-up behind him. He managed to close the steel outer door behind himself in his own haste, but did not slide the dead bolts into place. Tony went up the short flight of cement steps and bolted the outer bulkhead door. He then turned, went back down the steps and through the interior door to the private sanctum, securing that passageway behind him.

Neil pulls out a six pack of Miller High Life and put it on the stage, where Tony's drums were set up for practice and rehearsal. Without words, Tony instinctively grabs a bottle and cranked it open, thanking Neil with a wink and a handshake for bringing the beverages. Neil grabbed another, twists it open and offers up a salute. They guzzled, they belched and they smiled.

"So, what's happenin'?" Tony asked finally. "Why the urgency, brother?" Pression was curious, too, but she was busy upstairs, locked out anyway.

whatever

Neil reached over and pulled another bottle out from the pack. It looked like a Miller, labeled, capped and clear. Clear!

"Alright," Tony questioned with a tired sigh. "What is it?" He had waited long enough.

"Demerol," Neil said with a smile and quiet excitement. "Liquid Demerol: Pure liquid Demerol."

Tony thought the brown bag was empty, but out next came what looked like a cigar humidor. It was a medium brown wooden box with a hinged lid. Quite ingenious Neil's little travel pack, with the six carton resting over and perfectly covering the thinner vessel at the bottom of the shopping bag. It looked like he had simply come from the I.G.A., where presumably he had just picked up a six to share with a friend.

Tony knew something was up the moment he saw the Miller come out of the bag. They never drank Miller! They drank worse than Miller, and better as well, but never Miller High Life. Maybe for them, the name brand was a bit too ambiguous. Neil bought the Miller for the clear bottles. How meticulously detailed, if not a thoughtful, Neil had been.

Very careful was he having glued the bottle cap on the top of the cork, steaming the label off the bottle of beer and wrapping it round the twelve ounce bottle of opiate. The fact that the liquid itself was clear and not pale yellow, possibly the biggest bottle-job giveaway of all, did not seem to enter. Neither of them mention it. Bet the arresting officer would have mentioned it, but not on that day, for Neil was home free at Home Port, home free in the little underground den, beneath the cares and worries of all that moved above them.

They didn't play with the stainless and tube works, because Neil's blessed box also contained a bag of thirty-two disposable insulin syringes. It was all too easy, and it was done in moments; and a few moments later, done again, and again.

Neil, for his stay with Grand Ma at her nursing home on Rye Beach, did the work that she and the other old people there, could not. Lifting people back into, or maybe out of bed constituted most his responsibilities. It wasn't long before he discovered the existential in-house pharmacy, but it was just recently that he had decided to move in on it.

The Demerol is old. It had been there for a couple of years, untouched and unnoticed. The two older medicine cabinets that Neil had realized hadn't been in use lay just across the hall from his own bedroom in a closed-off wing of the old New England Beach home. Prior to that day, they shot-up only crystal meth and coke, but they had lately become interested in the smack experience that everyone else had been talking about. No one in the clan had ever diligently gone about buying any heroin, but now, Neil and Tony had the Demerol, which was close enough. The drug culture is a chaotic mess within which the boomers happily participate.

Those in their immediate clan were from time to time shooting dope, but no one ever formed a habit. Habits did form influentially by Neil and Tony when Neil stole that bottle of liquid Demerol from his grandmother's nursing home. He and Tony hid in the basement for the better part of three weeks lining Demerol into their veins, and when they finally climbed out, they were hooked. They spent the next two weeks weaning themselves off the Demerol by doing smack and methadone. Self-medicating mad men, they meant no harm. Pression was disappointed.

*

The scenario played much the same as any police raid portrayal done on television. The police pull-up out of nowhere, smartly charge and surround the home, announce loudly and violently at the front door that they shall be let in, or will break in, by virtue of the warrant, in the name of the law.

"Everyone down on the floor with your

hands out – way out – and to the sides! Do it NOW!" The announcement alone, immediately surreal, has Joey's mother screaming in terror outright. It is both a bad dream and a shattering awakening. The landscape about her bourgeois life, within which she blindly roams, accuses, and passes judgment is about to change forever.

Joey wakes slowly, as usual, still slightly hammered from the night before. Before he had the chance to rub the sand from his eyes and hit the head for a morning piss, he was face-down on the hardwood floor of his bedroom, in his underwear, hand-cuffed tightly behind his back. He peed and cried as the arresting officer read severely for him the rights of Miranda.

Joey's mother, now seated on the sofa, cries, and struggles to focus while another police officer tries to explain to her the reality of the circumstance, and the series of situations and evidence that led to her son's arrest. The poor woman could barely comprehend. Oh, she heard the stories, the gossip about others, but it would never, could never happen that way to her child; not to her family.

Why, she had even been thoughtless enough to ridicule a neighboring family who had had to pick up the younger of their two boys at the police station, just this past summer. He had been charged with (being) knowingly in the presence of marijuana. It was that incident, and her unfair assessment and assumption, that rang through her mind as she sat there quivering, legs tightly locked in chastity, on her velour couch.

God is punishing me!

The only thing that could have possibly been any worse would be discovering her husband's own follies in imperfection and infidelity. She will have waited years before the truth be told on that front. Meanwhile, three other cops were busy ransacking the home in search. They were concentrating on Joey's room, the closets, the bathrooms and garage. In Joey's room, one of the officers tripped on, and then kicked aside a small braided scatter rug.

He noticed an abnormality in the wood flooring, and with one fisted, gloved hand over the other, he pounded repeatedly at the ends of each short plank. One was obviously loose, and he shortly worked it up to the point of release. Upon release, the strip of hardwood repelled end over end through the thick air in the room, as if in slow motion. It hit the flinching investigator's own shoulder and then dropped to the floor with an uninteresting, dead clack.

The officer all but ignored the lid, barely looking over at it as he hastily brushes the evidence back toward his right patent leather boot. The officer is excited. He already stuffed his hand into the void, with not a second thought about spiders or mousetraps, and in no time pulls out a leather stash bag. Joey's small stash of weed had long been found, as it had remained from the night before in the inside pocket of his denim field coat, along with his cigarettes.

The payload for the piggy was in the bag under the floor boards. There was a small stash of pills and a few tabs of acid in there, but the paraphernalia found in the bag would prove to be the star of the show. Joey, for some unknown reason, had become completely enthralled with syringes. Pression once suggested that it may be something to do with how he chose to deal with the good and spoiled child stigma under which he had been thumbed. He had accumulated a small arsenal of works, and the needles inside that stash bag held the most weight that morning.

The turn of events that followed tore Joey down. His parents decided to commit him after having learned the police had found multiple sets of syringes under his bedroom floorboards. They refused to believe his repeated cries of denial, which only drove them to patronize him agonizingly more, and more. If he were insane at all, he was driven the distance to that place by his own parents' unwillingness to listen and understand him.

Discovering the implements had an overwhelming effect on the arrest, Joey's family, and the immediate community in general. It was a curious outcome, considering the actuality that Joey had shot-up dope only a handful of times. The police expected to find the pot, and were not surprised that most of the freaks in town were into speed, acid and barbiturates, as well. The needles, suggested something much worse — opiates and meth.

Joey DeSmit took a liking to shooting dope, and what he perceived as a cool earmark that came with it. Even though he does not do it often, he insists he needs his own set of glass works. He always had the implements handy, just in case — the jug of water, the cotton, the spoon. He just liked to get high, but he liked even more the romantic idea of chasing the dragon, and the power that came with the preparation.

*

There at the Dinnerhorn sat Mr. and Mrs. DeSmit. They were eating their Surf n Turf dinners with the embarrassing drug debacle two years past. They didn't notice the vehicle, but witnessed the collision. A pick-up truck had veered off Route 1, and then swiped a telephone pole, before plunging nose first into the bay across the street. A muddy rudder. At once, virtually everyone who was in the restaurant filed out to the edge of the highway; some to help and some to gawk.

Mrs. DeSmit could have used the institutionalized help more so than her misunderstood son, after seeing his dead body being dragged from within the smoldering, steaming cab. Sadly, Joey timed and planned his suicide-over-dinner perfectly. He waited until his parents were seated and served, then drove down Route 1 to Holiday Drive, took it up to Peverly Hill Road, and then turned back North on Route 1. In an act that played out more like a professional stunt, Joey tucked the thirty-eight caliber up behind his left ear, waited until he was about an eighth of a mile from the restaurant, and then pulled the trigger. He had only been out of the ward for two months.

There were a lot of people from and around Portsmouth out to get asshole DeForest that autumn past, but no one ever got the chance. He disappeared just after the court cases were about close, and nobody has seen or heard of him since. Nobody ever did try dragging the Mystic River for his dead ass did they, because he's down there somewhere, inside of a grave seal stolen from Farrell Funeral Home. He in that seal is strapped shut and weighted down. What's more, he was alive on the initial trip down, but he is without doubt very, very dead just now.

*

Now, everybody knows that when you wake up every day to two or three grams of coke, and ingest five to six more throughout the course of the day, you don't go to bed at night without a little more medicinal attention. Tony chews up to seven Quaaludes a night just to wind down enough to get to sleep. Kenny was no exception, and neither were any one of the Fool Star's men, once settled in under his wing.

Regardless of the ensuing fuzzy head, Kenny has a way to keep it all together. He maintains all the way around. He invests well; owns property and dwellings all over Miami, and has a small fleet of vehicles from which he could choose to drive on any given occasion.

He stays happy. He and Tony were the only ones in that house that never let any drug steal their heads. They stayed, at all times, entirely cool. That was a welcome trait to Pression. If Tony was going to get high, he'd better at least handle it. As much as she had concern, she was glad her Tony was always her Tony, no matter what. Kenny loves rock and roll, he stays ultra-cool in utterly torrid situations, and he retains an excellent sense of humor. All of those are essential qualities if you are into what he is into, and, if you hang with a band as the Fool Star's is reputed to be. Those were the traits of survival if you intended to remain balanced and sane at the end of not-so-typical days.

The group enjoyed the big, old, cheap house that Big Daddy supplied in Homestead for the first month, but when Kenny invited them to stay in one of his homes there in a well-to-do subdivision in Cutler Ridge, they took him up on it.

Kenny alternated living between the house he essentially gave the band on Dominican Drive, and another house he owned just a couple of miles west. There in that plushy, exclusive, stone faced home on Dominican Drive, they planned to live, and live high for the rest of their stay in South Miami.

CHAPTER THIRTEEN

Word travels fast. Vonegan had done it again. This time, he raped a fourteen-year-old girl from Portsmouth. Her mother was afraid to press charges for fear the publicity would pain further the young girl and her family. The little girl was the younger sister of a friend of ours, and no one could stand the pain he and his mother were going through. The older brother alone could have killed Vonegan easily, for he was a stout little Yankee, built like a muscle machine.

"He was the one and only kid that had to

shave as early as seventh grade," Pression remembers.

"Sadly, he's on probation, Presh, his hands are tied," Tony says. "Besides, his mother pleaded with him not to get involved."

Yes, he heeded, but oh, how he wanted Vonegan. Eventually, he would have had him regardless, if Neil, John and Drew hadn't gotten to Vonegan first. They have charges of their own they are ready to press. Had Tony been home, it would have been all his, but in his absence, the old posse followed through on a plan – one laid out years earlier. The return trip to Jamaica was on! John, Neil and Drew reviewed the plan, but then, upon checking flights, found the best they could do in a pinch was Miami.

Altogether, that made better sense anyhow. It just seemed Miami Beach, Florida was the picture-perfect destination for a blue-haired old bag. The pieces fell into place just as they had planned before, back when Tony was still home. They loosened Vonegan up, they dosed him down with morphine, and they heavily anesthetized him. Once he was under, they made him up real good, and got him down to Logan and on a plane, fast, wheel chair service and all. You're right - money does swear, Mr. Zimmerman.

Without Neil, the stunt could have never worked. Not only did he provide the implements and credentials, but also with a fresh haircut and an inherently sly way about him, Neil did all the smoothing at the airport. He was very persuasive and non-obtrusive, and matter-of-factly all about business. The dope, the clothes, the make-up, the wig and the wheel chair all came from Neil's Grandmother's nursing home. So authentic was the old woman Vonegan.

The instructions given US Air called for an attendant to wheel her to baggage claim, retrieve her bag and then leave her for a personal escort that would plan on being there at arrival time. The attendant was to place a placard across the old woman's lap that read "**Bent.**"

Thoughtfully, the three comrades packed Vonegan a bag full of old ladies underwear, some outerwear and some make-up. Vonegan woke briefly once, but he was unable for the next thirty-six hours to move or speak at all. All he can do at this point is look around him a few seconds at a time – few and far-between – to sights quite a blur, then, he's out again. It would be another day and a half before he would regain at least some of his composure, if you call Vonegan's behavior at all composed to begin with.

He does not know where he is and barely

knows who he is. He can't keep his eyes open for more than a half a second at a time, with hours between blinks. He knew he was comfortable, but has no idea he is in a wheelchair. He has no idea he is in drag. People walking by tried unsuccessfully to pass without staring, most looking sadly at the haggard looking, old woman in common sympathetic disgust.

"Bent."

By the time airport personnel had arranged to bring Vonegan to the nearest shelter for the homeless, he still isn't conscious enough to respond, let alone object. Once there, he slept through the entire night. Vonegan slept soundly until at ten-ten in the morning, a beautiful Cuban volunteer from the shelter approaches the feeble looking old person. She knows the old woman is not dead because of the tremendous snoring evoking from the openings to the cranial cavities of the elderly being. The young, dark woman tries gently to wake Vonegan, but is unsuccessful. She held the strange looking hand in hers and repeated just above a whisper: "Ma'am, Ma'am, time to wake up dear."

*

They were all invited, the band, crew, and anyone else they wanted to bring, within what would become clear, obvious reason of course. Invited to what was definitely the wedding of the year, Pression joked that if People magazine was there to cover it.

"...the bride wore a black fringed leather vest and denim slacks with high brown boots with brass spurs and silver toe shields, over nothing.

...and the groom sported a black tee, black

Levi's, black boots and a black bandanna for neckwear."

Press or no press, Tony and Pression have since heard it, and have referred to it themselves, as the welding of the year. It was heavy stuff, all iron, chrome, steel and tattoos. It was original heavy metal. The band knew the bride and groom, from Homestead. Rob and Deb made an adoring couple amidst all the guests and fanfare, handsome and beautiful as they are – and Tony and Pression do find bikers beautiful. Even the minister was a biker. This priest would be one of the few around that definitely was not ever into screwing the young parish boys.

"…needless to say, the holy man wore black as well, with some kind of cross and chain across his chest…

…And probably held close a bit more. Like a nine-millimeter, for instance. You know,

those folks were into blue steel accessories long before they became fashionable."

Presh can't stop. It was funny! Tony can't stop laughing. But then he saw Floyd and involuntarily stopped right away – as did Presh. This is the first time the group ever actually met Floyd in person. Oh sure, everyone had heard of him. The group had all heard of his infamous and otherwise dubious acts, and his enforcement of the law - his own.

He had his own corner booth in the back room at the Homestead Big Daddy's. Tony never comments about any of those stories, rumors or whatever, but what he does know immediately is that every word ever heard intended to describe him physically, as unbelievable as those accounts sounded at the time, are undeniably true. Floyd is an easy seven-foot-one, and over three and a quarter feet wide at the shoulders.

"*…and the great Floyd, also in black denim, tee and boots, with just the right…*"

Luke whispers to Pression, "Shut the fuck up already! " and laughs with her.

What Floyd carried with him also proved to live up to the legend. He had four fingers (that would be two of Floyd's) of white in a baggy, and to serve it up, a standard issue seven and a half inch buck knife, held personally by Floyd at all times. Floyd with a knife to your face, even if it is loaded with flake, is a scary scene.

The group had just pulled the RV in to the field, and Gene was parking it. Before they have even a chance to jump out and stretch, to join the goings on, Floyd and a couple of his mechanics are stepping on in to the RV.

After a one sided introduction, big Floyd brought out the bag of white, and served it up personally over the tip of that buck knife of his, around, around and around, and then around again. Tony could see the boys were lit after the first round. Pression sat quietly without indulging.

The court acquitted Floyd on three counts of murder. He is up for two more in the near future. He is deep and connected. Floyd tells Tony that he is damn good, the band sounds good, and to keep on rocking. By the time Tony got out of the RV, with what felt like his scalp peeling back on him, all that his mind could pull forward was the thought, "Gee, that Floyd. He's a pretty nice guy!"

"It is well beyond me," Pression jokes, once Floyd and his small army leave. "Whatever made anyone trust that man to hold his weapon right under each of your noses time after time?"

*

There is a commotion out in the pasture. Completely hilarious, there are five or six huge and hulking dudes chasing a chubby little goat all over the field. It strikes Pression comically that it took so much effort from those iron horsemen to catch a piddley-assed domestic farm-billy. Tony explained it was all in fun; using any kind of firearm on that fucking goat just seemed too easy, you know.

The good old standard issue buck that all seemed to have hanging off their belts handled the culinary rudiments nicely. Our master game hunters bled and cleaned the animal right there where it had been tackled, then they dragged it over to the pit, skinned it, and reamed that poor dead carcass primed for the spitting. With a makeshift rotisserie, they proceeded to roast a feast over which the fucking Frugal Gourmet may well have been proud.

The burnt beast didn't taste too awful bad, though it was tough. Nobody did give a shit anyway, because all anybody ever really wanted was just another hit, another toke, another beer and another pull off the Jack Daniel's or Jim Beam.

The festivities throughout the day could not have been better. There was target shooting, drag racing, wrestling and don't forget goat chasing. Target shooting meant behind the back shots and over the shoulder shots, some using nothing more than their old lady's make-up mirror. There were no fancy targets either. Men were shooting beer cans out of their partner's hand, and shooting cigarettes out of mouths and from between fingers.

They'd all seen it done in the movies, or on loony tunes, but this was live, crazy and dangerous. The Fool Star called it fun. The bikers used a nearby clear straightaway for drag racing. It remained, for the most part, un-traveled most of the day. There were stationed a couple of finish line lookers, as well as a traffic cop. This family remained closer than blood in vein. There were a few friendly interventions from the real officers of the law, but there were no arrests. There were no injuries. It was fun. It was funny. It was LOUD. It was fast. It was crazy. It was a party.

*

One thing that has always irked Tony is prejudice toward bikers. It does not begin and end particularly toward the men either. Someone inevitably has to have something negative to say about the women, as well. Guarded are the feelings of the righteous society, that men and women are merely, and secretly envious.

Go down to Short Hills Mall and spy the nice looking women with their silver and onyx slave bracelet, the short denim skirt, the work shirt. Said shirt opened to show off those lovely tits, but oh, sorry, just enough of those tits that they want to be seen, and no more. They have their riding boots, the expensive tightly undone look on their heads, and the newest rage in make-up: the no make-up look.

What's the difference? The jewelry's polished. The skirt is pressed. The shirt is crisp. The tits don't sag. (Enter Playtex - it's the wonder-bra, boy. Without it they do.) The boots, my friends, have never ridden on anything but up and down their husbands' sorry asses. Ring up fifty fucking dollars on that perfect upstairs bed head look; add more for the makeover at the local Bloomingdales.

Those are the differences, and are the only differences. Scooter trash, executive, professional, homemaker or Minister's wife, they all like to fuck. They like it and want it bad and good, and hard, and fast, and slow. And, oh gwawd Madge – the clit! The difference is, that the free spirits, the scooter trash, none of them, bother bullshitting anyone about it. If they want to show you their tits on Daytona Beach, for example, you are going to see their tits. In most cases, if you want to get a gander at those things, all you have to do is ask.

They're just tits fercrysake.

*

Like any band on the sacred mission, the Fool Star's is constantly on the lookout for a way to break through – earn a recording deal. They are generally aiming high but shooting low. They recognize and agree they didn't necessarily need a major label deal, as an indie would be great too! It would be nice just to be able to finance a little studio time.

Homestead has, by now, become a second home for the band. They realized a tremendous and devoted following there. As a result, they are receiving many offers. Good friend Kenny is always on the lookout for the group's welfare and development, and schemes right along with them when they sit around brainstorming their way to the top. Even though many of the storms in their brains at the time were direct results of the brain food ingested, they were driving forward even with perhaps only one eye closed. Traveled as they are, they manage at least to keep the fog lamps burning all of the time.

On one of those occasions, Kenny brought up an acquaintance of his, named Sally Clarke, he said might be interested in, and could definitely afford, investing in the group. She was a friend who was also the wife of an ex-partner of his. Sally, he said, is into many interesting investment schemes already, such as horse breeding and racing, boxing, coke dealing and other assorted money making endeavors. She might be interested.

Without much thought about implications, that's all the Fool Star needed to hear. The group agrees that Sally could be a perfect candidate to approach. She just might want to join them on their mission, and thus, want to sink some bucks into the band, especially with Kenny accompanying them now, too. The Fool Star looks upon it as investment – risky, yes - but hoped she would too. Yes, an investment, that is, if his band made any money off the initial funding she would provide. An investment, that is, if she decided to give it to them in the first place. If… If… "If" – The middle word in life, Colonel.

Kenny brought Sally to the club to see the band perform, and back again later to meet them and the crew, to talk. There eventually came a number of get-togethers with her, and it doesn't take long for the Fool Star, along with the group, her and Scar to come up with a plan-of-action. It was a simple POA. She would give the Fool Star's corporation (the S-Corp Tony established) six-five-thousand dollars, and management would make her the Executive Producer of the album. Points come with the title, of course, as well as a flat-fee.

The band would use the money to produce as many finished recordings as they possibly could, assemble an album's worth, and then use that recording as a demo. Using advance money, they would contractually plan to pay Sally her money back with interest, on top of her point on the deal. No one talked of the possibility that there may not ever be a deal. That there would be was understood, assumed. Sally likes the idea as much as everyone involved does, and she was as excited to be a part of it, like, 'With the Band.' Tony immediately draws-up the plans that would get the group off the platform for a month, and secure some solid time in Studio Center.

"Here's your money," Sally says happily, "Honey!" She hands to Tony two size ten shoe boxes – a bit frayed at the edges. She delivered the money within a week. It was not in the form of a money order for sixty-five thousand. Nor was it a cashier's check for sixty-five thousand. It was not an electronic deposit advice for sixty-five thousand, and it was not a personal check for sixty-five thousand dollars. She hand delivered to Tony exactly two size-ten shoeboxes full of cash. Dirty cash. She handed it to Tony, and he to Scar, a fucking shoebox, full of tens, twenties, fifties and hundreds.

This was not a first for Tony, as he'd certainly held in his hands that vast an amount before, but by the way the rest of the group were all - excluding Kenny of course - taking turns holding on to it, feeling it, and smelling it, Tony suspects that nary any of them had. It didn't much matter to the group how the money arrived; it had come. A crony from the studio opened an escrow account and would throw this pile into it that very afternoon. Yeah, that's right. It was a pile. Standing it on end, it was a good eighteen inches high.

Pression could just imagine Sally that morning, digging the stash out of her mattress, or better yet, the coffee can in the back yard. Sally had a Rottweiler whose domain was wherever it roamed, but it hung out in the back, under a tree most of the time. Cash, that was what it was all about, and it didn't bother Sally one bit to share and invest, so why should it bother the group? This is a dream come true for Pression as much as it is for Tony, because she knows how much it means to Tony – the lovers circle be unbroken.

Amazingly enough, out of all of those bills in the boxes, only one turned out to be counterfeit. One fucking twenty out of the whole damn batch was identified counterfeit.

One might tend to reason, for good reason, that there should have been more than just one bogus bill in that stack. The authorities questioned Scar about the counterfeit bill, but neither the incident nor the bill amount to anything detrimental. Luckily, the group slides right through it, like a snake in a wagon rut.

*

Out of all the articles one can almost surely predict are in any given woman's handbag, there were three things you will have always found in Sally's: Cash, Sniff and Ludes. Therefore, wherever the band happens to go, Sally joining in, or wherever Sally decides she wants to take them, it always turns out to be an excellent adventure. She assumed the surrogate mother role over all of them, and they all play, or rather are, in whole and truth, the spoiled children just fine.

A typical night out to watch a performance, Sally would, just like any other woman, pack her bag. When the bartenders heard that Sally was coming, they would fight to tend her. It was no wonder, for it was Ms. Clarke's classy good habit to tip well. If she went to the bar, the least she would lay down would be a twenty. She wasn't one to go to the bar and order just for her, so the bill was often over twenty dollars. If that was the case, down went another twenty, or more likely a fifty. Sally didn't believe in taking change. The entire balance always went to the barkeep. And if that were not enough, down went another twenty! Sally knows what is going on with the help, so she purposely travels from one bartender to the next, just to be fair and to share the wealth. She, in a word, is cool in that way – the way of the world – money, power, love, peace and sex. She doesn't flaunt it, or doesn't mean to anyway. It was like when someone wealthy, or famous, or both, is in a public place, everybody else there becomes, somehow, very aware of it.

On one occasion at Kenny's, Sally took the crew grocery shopping. She had by then moved-in with the band and crew. It was to be merely a trip to the local Public's Market. She and her husband were divorcing, and she asked if she and her son could live there with the band. They never gave it a second thought, and could never have refused, anyway. The band is rehearsing, but the crew, Sally and Kenny all went in the band's Suburban to the shopping center. The band lost track of time and didn't realize how long the crew had been gone. They got to jamming, and as usual the magic carried them away and time became simply two hands across a face, four numerals on a monochrome screen, invisible measurement of pain, nothing more.

Having fun with Sgt. Pepper, they noticed the crew coming in with the ever-familiar brown bags with green printing. The plastic ones were for frozen food. One after the other, then back out again, and back in with another, and back out again, and back in with another, and then back out for yet another, ad infinitum, the crew continued to tote. They should have known by then what to expect, but Sally surprised them yet again. It was more amazement than it was surprise.

"I envision the workers being not unlike the long trail of ants on a sidewalk in the summer," Pression tells Tony. "Whenever there is a sizable morsel, a steady trail, marching the goods to the colony, and then making their way back down for more, repeatedly."

"Ants they are, the teamwork, the steady

rolling line, the little legs moving, the incredible show of strength," Tony interjects. "While ants can carry five times their own weight, our crew could carry about twice theirs."

The groceries had arrived! Someone counted the bags in all; the ones in the kitchen, covering the counters, the floors, the butcher block; the ones in the laundry room, covering the washer, the dryer, the floor; the ones in the hallway, on the sofa table, and on the floor. All over the got-damned house were strewed one hundred forty three bags of groceries.

Our gal Sally, she'd done it again!

Granted, they had two huge refrigerators and a freezer big enough to keep Haystacks Calhoun's family on ice; Tony really doesn't think the mighty shoppers were thinking about where they might store all of that stuff once they got it home any way. It was just another day at the store with Sally. Outings were unplanned, quite by whim. Sally was very casual about it all. As if implicitly to ask, who doesn't want, or need, to shop for whatnot occasionally?

An especially enterprising trip with Sally had been one they made to the music store in Miami. Sally went along on that particular outing and for the life of them all, they didn't know why she did, but were in the end, damn glad she did. What starts as a typical little doodle down to the store for some strings and picks, some sticks and heads, ended only when the group had all walked out of that store with each a special gift from Sally. Dollar for dollar, Tony and Pression didn't know what she spent that day, but it was, easily, a twelve hundred dollar item for each of the band. And, crew. Five band members at twelve hundred a piece is six grand. Sally bought Dolphin a vintage Martin mandolin. Gene received a top of the line Gibson banjo. Allen got some kind of midi something or other for his keyboard bank. Sally bought Dee the antique Fender Jazz bass that happened to be on display in the store window. In addition, Tony got a new cymbal set, new microphones and a few pieces of miscellaneous hardware for the drum kit. Their lives had turned into Disney World by then, but Sally took them on vacation to the real Disney World in Orlando, regardless.

"Just for the pure joy of it!" she hollers. If there's anything better than Disney World, it's Disney World with Sally Clarke. Because it's the land of dreams, she made sure dreams come true. You may venture to say that Robin Leach could not have kept up with this group. They had to arrange for a Disney staffer with an extended golf cart to truck purchases out to the parking lot periodically throughout the day. Clothes, souvenirs, costumes, hats, plush goods, masks, masks, and more masks. Oh, the band loves the masks. Like other trip-meisters from their generation, they enjoyed goofing with the audience – stage or highway – from time to time, and masks did sometimes just the right trick.

Sally enjoys her horses. She has an interest in breeding them, buying them, riding them, racing them, showing them, selling them and betting on them. Sally, being an equestrian, has a favorite western wear joint, as well. She was determined to have the group join her on a trip there someday, and one day she follows through. She has them drive her to the shop, and although it isn't like the day at the music store, it comes, relatively speaking, close. The Executive Producer bequeaths to everyone that day new boots, new hats, new vests and new spurs. The bill is not quite six grand, but Yee-fucking-Haw anyhow!

"On the yacht down there in Key Largo

You said you had a very weak stomach.

But it looked like a strong one to me:

It threw food over the side of that vessel

Further than anyone else on
the deck that night."

PART V

CHAPTER FOURTEEN

If there's been painted an all too perfect picture of Ms. Clarke, take heart in knowing that there was one aspect of the relationship with her that, even though just the one, was a major entity and terrifically negative force. It was the kind of slight and insignificant difference that flies under the radar, yet large enough to change history; like an assassination, or a flood, or a war.

Rusty. The name alone evokes an image of the quintessential all American boy. Red, curly hair, freckles speckled over a pug nose. He's just a wee bit shorter than the average, cap atop slightly askew. He wears torn dungarees with a bandanna in the left back pocket, comic books in hand, sporting perhaps, a black eye. He's the catcher on the Little League team, batting ordered somewhere right in the middle of the line-up. The Black Converse All-Stars, right shoe untied, Rusty will certainly not notice before his mom does. The Rusty about whom written here may have once been reflected all over the preceding in this paragraph, but no more.

If first impressions, however too early to tell, do mean anything, ours of him should have scared the hell out of the band. They had, by that time been involved long enough to know an asshole when they saw one. After all, just as they were, they too, were everywhere and they stink. They might have been, one might suffice, at that point, too numb to notice. What they got out of the experience initially was a hell of a scare. Afterward, they had themselves a good, long laugh and recognized it as the first of many reasons to hate Rusty.

No matter where the band plays, one can always count on a routine. The band plays a set, and the band takes a break; play a set, take a break, play a set, take a break. Bands are under contract to do this for some predefined length of time, (or for however long they wish to, depending on who is watching). The big shows and finer nightspots provided break areas or dressing rooms, green rooms for the group, but there in Homestead the group spent most of their breaks outside in the parking lot, always among a crowd. The Fool Star hung out with the locals either outside, or in the RV, usually getting high. So did the group.

They were out in the parking lot for a break on the night of that first impression.

The break time excitement to date had been the episodic, almost weekly occurrence of the Barrow brothers going yet once again to fisticuffs, wrestling bare-chested all over the lot. On that night, the twins had managed to slam each other right into our group's RV, breaking one of the side view mirrors right off of the cab. Bloodied as usual, both boys were quite a sight. Typically, soon after the hell broke loose, they were hugging each other again - a mass of derelict wire and muscle, long, matted brown hair and tattoos - planning on their next big pit bull gig. The twins looked just like the singer Anthony Keidis from the RHCP's, back when he had long hair. They bred, raised and fought pit bulls as a moneymaking hobby.

By the time the Barrow fight had ended, all would remain as calm as could be expected considering the venue. Then, all of a sudden, around the corner came a loud, maniacally driven, speeding yellow jeep. The canvas was down on the Wrangler J5 and there were two men in the vehicle. The driver was blowing the horn, shrieking and cackling with lunatic laughter. The passenger was half standing, swaying wildly, and screaming insanely. He had one hand on the roll bar and the other on a pistol.

Moonstruck chaos all at once filled the scene as the hot spur continued cracking off shots as they drove by. He fired shots into the air, but others hit the ground and ricocheted off the building all around the lot. Shots were fired everywhere in a barrage. The return sounded like a nine-millimeter, but the weapon could have been a three-eighty or perhaps something slightly bigger.

"Echo was a factor, and I am not any Joe Fucking Friday, mind you."

KaBANGang…KaBANGang…BOOMang…

Everyone out in the lot hit the deck and rolled under the nearest vehicle. Everyone except the band knew the identity of the shooter straight away. Although his reputation does precede him, the locals recognized Rusty's jeep right away. Sally's husband, Rusty! The crowd also recognized that this was nothing more than a typical Rusty incident.

"I have to admit," Tony looks to Pression and says in jest, "I was a little impressed and taken aback at the same moment."

"Yeah, well I felt suddenly transported to some Godfather – slash – Zachariah dream world, come true."

They stayed right where they were, hugging the asphalt for a few minutes, then scurried back into the bar once the dust settled. The whole place caught wind of what had gone down and virtually everyone there got a big chuckle out of it. That ol' Rusty. They cheer as the band came back in through the entrance.

"We've just been shot at," Pression says.

"Nonetheless, the band plays on, dear," Tony replies. "It was no social crises; it is Homestead, remember?"

Sally had become a regular at the club, and usually travels with the band wherever they go. As Executive Producer, she may have well been part of the band, if not an honorary member. She is a regular at whatever venue they happened to play, and a regular in the studio. She had also moved in with the group on Dominican Drive. That is what had Rusty in a paroxysm. He let his imagination get the best of him, and on came the green streak.

The band had no idea her true marital status in the first place, and they had no reason to question her arrival. Moreover, when they did find out, they just took it in stride. She stated that her marriage had been failing for a long time, and it didn't matter much to her anymore if it did. Therefore, she surmised and directed, that it shouldn't bother the band much either.

"Enough said," concurs the Fool Star.

Rusty had an entirely dissimilar view of the situation. Rumors were flying around that the group had really pissed him off, hence, the shooting incident at Big Daddy's Homestead. He had this notion that the group had seduced his wife into being some kind of rich, ultimate groupie for them, catering to their every whim; be it monetary, material, emotionally, and yes, sexually.

The Fool Star may have stepped on a few toes to date, but Sally's weren't ten of them. The group had no reason to use, or abuse anyone, period. Things turned convenient for them for a while, with Kenny's generosity and Sally's support. It was a love affair, of sorts, but not the kind of affair under which Rusty had mistakenly become obsessed.

Sally, at one point, actually did beg Dolphin to have her, but he, and no one of the group, ever saw Sally as a toy or an object. She was like a big sister, a fun loving, life-loving, rich, and elder sister. I'm sure she could have appreciated that, yet especially not on those horny, hot Miami nights. She shared a bedroom on Dominican Drive with Tony and Presh, Dolphin and two crewmembers, and shared the house with eleven able-bodied rockers and their assistants. They would together party nightly into the morn, but there was never any sexual connotation to be had. Albeit, not with Sally.

*

A second incident with Rusty would come only a couple weeks later than the first and it confirmed the band's thought that they might be in more trouble with him than they had first imagined. Dee and Allen went to run some errands with Kenny one afternoon. By then, Rusty was watching Tony and his mates, or having them watched twenty-five hours a day. On that otherwise seasonally sunny day in home sweet Homestead, it was Rusty doing the watching. The boys weren't yet a couple miles away when all of a sudden they heard thunderously close gunshots, sporadic and crazy. Kenny took a glance in his rear view mirror, another in his side view, turned quickly around to see again, and then turned back to the road ahead. One more look in the rear view provided confirmation. Sure enough, there he was, riding right up their ass:

"R U S T Y!" Kenny yells, in almost perfect unison with Dee and Allen. A few more quick shots rang out. Two of them hit the car at about the same time Dee and Allen hit the floorboard, sweating, swearing in ululation. Poor Kenny drives on as fast as he can go given the congested traffic. Trying to lose someone following who knew the area as well as Kenny did was not easy, but Kenny did his best to shake him. Even though Kenny would usually be the last person in the world to go for a visit to the Dade County Sheriff's Office, that is exactly where he was heading, because if Kenny had ten good reasons to stay away from the local police station, Rusty had a hundred.

The sight had to be worth a million. Here we have a right-handed Irishman, driving his huge Lincoln Continental, using his good hand to steer, waving a forty-four magnum haphazardly, firing as the spirit moved, out the side window with the left. He could not have hit a standing target under those circumstances, let alone a moving, speeding, swerving one, unless by luck. Nevertheless, he did stand that chance; he was indeed Irish, after all.

Over medians, over lines and against the traffic, Kenny, Dee and Allen finally arrived at the destination nouveau. They remain in the visitor's parking lot at the Sheriff's Office for an uncomfortable thirty minutes. It took that long to regain the stamina for them to chance the ride back home. They didn't request a police escort, although the fantasy did cross their minds.

*

Living at Dominican Drive was pleasant, productive and comfortable. The Fool Star woke to coke and snoozed to Ludes. Most all did. They used the back half of the great room as a rehearsal hall, and the front half as a living area. There are four bedrooms, one of which, the master, belonged to Kenny. One of the other bedrooms had two sets of bunk beds, the second had two queen-size beds and the third room had four single-size bunk beds. They fit five in the third room by one occupant sleeping on the floor. There were usually a few visiting stragglers, sprawled out in the living room somewhere. The band put up nightly a moderate multitude of houseguests. Their live-ins depends on who the current girlfriends are, but they also made many friends who happened-in-and-out over time immemorial. There were many visitors, but not all of them found themselves too incapacitated to drive away when the time came. Most did, however.

*

The band often times planned an activity for days off along with the group, but they were enjoying this afternoon at home. The band, crew, the girls and a few guests were sitting around, listening to music, watching a silent television and bullshitting about with flake. A knock on the door sent TL out through the kitchen and then through the mudroom to answer. The last person any one of them expected to have paying a friendly visit was Rusty, but low and behold and Lord give mercy, there he is standing in the rainy door yard under the car port.

He is dressed neatly with his hair held down in some kind of wet look that didn't help, and he is holding a colorfully wrapped present in his arms. Because the entire group was in such a pit of disbelief, they each took a comical turn peeking around the corner of the kitchen, through that entryway, to verify that TL's vision was indeed the reality. That one measly, little gift wasn't even going to gain any forgiveness from them!

Rusty begged to let him in, every one he saw looking around the corner at him. It was really quite strange. He seemed to be groveling.

"My first plan of action," says Tony, "is no action. Maybe if we ignore it, it will just go away."

That didn't happen. Rusty kept knocking on the door, pleading for someone to come let him in. He was calling out for Sally and his son.

"Tony," Pression asks, "Please go see what he wants."

While Tony was out speaking with Rusty, Sally admitted to the others that the following day would be their son's birthday. She explained that Rusty probably just wanted to give the boy the gift. Our second POA was to convince Rusty to leave the package on the doorstep. They would guarantee delivery for him. He pleaded with Tony that he wanted only to sit and spend some time with his son for his birthday.

"I promise I mean no harm to any of you."

Sally endorsed the idea, stating she thought he sounded sincere, and so the group did what it didn't want to do: They let him in.

It wasn't that casual or relaxed, however. He was practically made to strip search himself out there in the dooryard. TL and Hogweed, the extra-large part of the crew, went out and patted him down. They disarmed Rusty of a .38 Special, and accepted a promise from him that he would behave. Then, they escorted him through the door and into the house.

Rusty's presence brings naturally with it, tension. It had become thicker than elephant shit when he entered the living room. Nevertheless, things were going along all right. He sat with his son and his estranged wife for twenty minutes. Everyone else cleared the room for a few minutes to give the dysfunctional family some time to themselves.

Given experiences, the crew was reluctant to leave Sally alone with him for too long. Some of the guests left the house when we left the room, but the rest of us returned to the living room in short order and found seats all around. Rusty had many questions for the band. He wanted to know where they'd been and where they thought they were going, plans for the future. He hinted at wanting to know the details of any deal we might have made with his wife. He wanted to know the sleeping arrangements in the house.

Suddenly, there he was as we had come

to know him. Rusty was up and running wild through the living room, going berserk slashing at everything and everybody in his way. He had somehow managed to pack his buck knife in - right past security!

"Follow me," Tony screams. "Now!"

He grabbed Presh, Sally and her son and got them quickly into their bedroom. Dee and Allen followed. Once inside, Tony locked the door and they all helped jam it with a divan. Meanwhile, the others scurried into and locked themselves behind the closed doors of the remaining empty rooms. Rusty was going nuts, and if he smuggled his knife in here with him, there was no telling whether he might have sneaked a pistol in as well.

There was a couch in the hallway outside of Sally's and Tony's room. Rusty put himself behind it, and easily on its castors positioned it so the end opposite him pointed directly at the door. He then began ramming the door behind which Sally, her son, Presh, Dee and Allen and Tony were sheltered. Rusty screams maddeningly at Sally to come out, and threatens her and Tony repeatedly. Sally and her son cowered into the back corner of the room, but Dee, Allen and Tony held the door steady.

"Visiting hours are OVER asshole," Tony yelled back at Rusty, "Get the fuck out of this house, or I'm coming straight outa here with shotgun in hand motherfucker!"

With that, Tony let a slug out about waist height. The explosion of the twelve gauge round was deafening. Sally and Mark are sobbing in the corner. Tony fired the second barrel at waist height again and blew a hole through the door over ten inches in diameter. Rusty was hit with both shots and bleeding badly out of his abdomen. He stepped away.

Unfortunately, Dolphin never found a place to hide. He remained on the floor behind the couch in the living room that separated the front from the rear. He peeked over the back of the piece, and once Rusty caught sight of him, another episode unfolded.

Rusty chased Dolphin all over the house and finally tackled him roughly. Rusty fell directly on top of him. The knife Rusty was reeling came down hard just to the right of Dolphin's head, taking a small slice off the bottom of his ear. The wound was dangerously close to the jugular vein, however, and Dolphin knew it. After a wicked, slow-motioned second or two, while Rusty seemed to have lost a bit of his drive, Dolphin was able to roll away.

Once the couch ramming had ceased in the hallway upstairs, TL and Hogweed slipped from their room. They watched fearfully and apprehensively as Rusty chased Dolphin around the living room, and when they saw Dolphin roll away from an extremely close call, Hog and TL took advantage of the moment and overtook Rusty easily there on the floor. Rusty was struggling hard to regain his feet and his weapon. He was screaming as though he were a woman possessed as they bodily threw him out, literally, into the middle of the street. They had no reason to be the least bit careful with him. Watching cautiously from the window, they saw him get into his car, relieved that the incident had finally ended.

Rusty sat in the street for a moment, and then climbed into his Lincoln. He appeared to be quiet and contemplated. He was quiet all right, but not contemplated.

Fucking contemplating.

"Everyone to the back of the house!" Tony orders.

Rusty started revving the engine in the Lincoln as if he was waiting for the tree to fall through to green on an NHRA strip. All of a sudden, he threw it into reverse, hit the street and without coming to a stop, ground it into drive-1. But he wasn't heading down the street; he was heading toward the front lawn! He in the vehicle jumped the curb and ran over the dogwood tree in the yard, before ramming the first car he came to.

Some of the band, crew and guests had to park some of the vehicles on the front lawn because there simply wasn't enough room for them in the driveway: The RV was parked there. Different parking arrangements would not have made a difference in this case. Rusty rammed the hell out of Phyllis' brand new Toyota Celica. Phyllis was Dolphin's girlfriend from Atlanta. This added another ugly layer to the way Dolphin's day had thus far developed. The sound of the cars crashing together was utterly vexatious. It sounded like a complex sonic equation of a ram, plus a boom, plus a crunch, multiplied by an explosion. Again, and again, Rusty kept on backing, and ramming.

Phyllis, bless her heart, was literally losing her mind. In a true textbook scenario, which included pulling her hair out, running rampant throughout the house and back, she was truly a woman run mad. She was moaning, sobbing and screaming as though she were witnessing her only daughter dragged off to an all-girl prison.

There was one more hellacious ramming. That last one was the one that knocked Phyllis' car into and completely over the garden wall in front of the house, and into the house itself. Her car stuck out of the house, lodged in between Kenny's bedroom wall and the crawlspace beneath. It was an ugly and atrocious sight, a mess, but one that had apparently satisfied the wild committer out there. He drove away laughing and screaming unintelligible into the dusk.

The local police precinct received several calls from Dominican Drive besides the Fool Star's that afternoon, so the dispatcher sent the units over quickly. The police arrested Rusty shortly thereafter.

*

Shortly after the car-ramming incident, Floyd paid the band a visit. One of his boys was in jail. Floyd was the only one standing between Rusty and the man in Columbia, and the woman in Miami, so he was concerned over the situation on Dominican Drive. He decided to visit them after he heard that Rusty was losing his mind over the matter. He thought his visit might help Tony and his people better understand Rusty, or at least explain Rusty's erratic behavior.

As he readied himself to depart, a brand new state-of-the-art Toyota was parked at the curbside. Just as Floyd walked out the door, he said "I'm sorry Rusty ruined the Toyota. I have replaced it with a Land Rover, free of charge and paid in full. I want to make sure to do as much as I can to please you all after that awful ordeal. I hope she enjoys her new ride!"

Tony knew Floyd had come on a mission of peace, because he recognized Roy following Floyd, as he always does, carrying with him up the driveway a large glass pipe and torch. They never came into the house beyond the entryway to the drive, which doubled as a laundry room and mud-room just off the kitchen. No one else cared to question why, but based on Tony's own shrewdness, it made perfect sense to camp there: Escape plan.

That first visit was a monumental one; because it was the first time anyone in the group, besides Tony, had tried smoking coke. Most of the others took one hit each, and took no more. A couple of them took two and stopped. It felt so nice, so good, and so warm that it absolutely scared the shit out of them. The rush.

Smoking coke is very close to lining it, but in addition to the warmth, there is a kind of hypercritical excitement. The heart pounds, the head peels and one can almost feel the blood racing through the body. The ears buzz. Dee was just two hits into it before implicitly getting Floyd's point. He had at least the wherewithal to have come out with, "Man! No wonder Rusty is so fucking crazy!" Dee, of course, was right, and that was exactly what Floyd wanted us to understand.

"Cheeziz Tony, how do you do it?" Dolphin asked. "You just maintain, like you haven't done a goddamn thing."

That was not the first time Tony heard that. He's always thrived on extremity. Subtlety and comfort depress him. He has found that nervous tension causes a heightened awareness inside. He discovered that at a very early age, first dabbling with astral projection. He found that on those occasions where he felt very nervous, or maybe high on meth, the inner self tended to rise easier, with far less conscious pseudo-concentration than usual. Therefore, while the others let the tension of an eight ball up their noses and another two or three grams in their lungs nibble away at their sanity, Tony just sat there, satisfied, thinking, wondering and feeling thoroughly entertained. Poor Dolphin looked so wired after just two pulls that Tony warned him, "Don't go picking your nose for fear you may poke out your eye out! Heh heh." Pression elbows Tony and smiles at his remark.

The band indulged in many recreational drugs along the way to Miami. Since moving in with Kenny, however, they had taken to snorting coke (and in Tony's case, smoking it usually with Floyd), smoking pot and chewing Ludes exclusively. Up until Tony started smoking coke with Floyd, the most dangerous activity he had partaken was when the Hog and he would steal away for a night or two at a time to shoot some Dilladin. No one else knew about any of that, and if the rest of the group ever found out that he and Tony were using works it would have shocked them seamless, and scared them to death.

A few years before, the Fool Star bought the recipe for brown crystal meth from a Tampa fan aptly nicknamed Mad Dog. Mad Dog lived daily on that speed and on M.D. 20-20 by the case, hence the Mad Dog moniker. Red bandana, and all. The band never knew that the brown speed we bought was intravenously great. Luscious as the brown speed was, it burnt hell right into your nose, but it was as warm as mother's milk going into your vein. Either way, the high was immeasurable.

The FDA finally wised-up, but for the longest time the Fool Star bought from the local drug marts a certain brand of inhaler, other chemical ingredients, boiling them down, mixing the derivative with a crystalizing agent, stirring above a stove burner, and creating some of the most inexpensive and best meth-like speed ever done. The stuff was a mystery to all, including law enforcement.

The Tampa police stopped Pression, as she was driving home from Lakeland, where the band was playing. They found a half a gram of the brown stuff strewed after being spilled in barely visible powder at the bottom of her brown leather bag. They had to let her go because they couldn't figure out what it was from the bottom of her bag. That was just as well, because she was carrying what was Tony's, not hers; it had spilled. Pression had been clean since they were teenagers.

Floyd was somewhat impressed with Tony, because he was the only one who kept up with him on the pipe. After that first visit, he began stopping by to pick up Tony, and take him out to get high, leaving the others behind. Tony got the impression that, in all his massive glory and importance, he was secretly thrilled to hang out with a guy in the band. Tony's tracks were laid at Studio Center. And that's where the bonding started.

CHAPTER FIFTEEN

Although their unofficial home was the house on Dominican Boulevard, the Fool Star had to get a place up in North Miami, a little closer to the studio they had secured. So, with their sixty-five thousand dollar box of money, they bid "So long for now" to Dominican and moved up to Biscayne Bay, which was just a seven miles south of Studio Center. It made perfect sense, since they leased the studio for twelve full weeks, with an option to extend. The lease came with an engineer, assistant and 24-hour access. As well rehearsed as the band is, recording an album surely could take much more than that.

They also had to build time into the plan for the mix downs and Mastering processes.

*

On the first night in North Miami, they decide to go to Tony Roma's. This is a first for the band. They were all anxious to go because Tony Roma's was, at that time, world renowned for their baby-back ribs and onion ring loaves. They would partake in both, along of course with some adult beverages. They passed a telephone booth on the way there with a poster ad on the bottom half of the enclosure.

"Look who it is." Tony whispers to Pression, who took a glance at it. And, there she was. She was looking as good as she had ever, in a spaghetti-strap short gown and heels, champagne in hand. Everyone looked, noticing Tony's and Pression's own unthinking reaction, and instinctively next, everyone all looked over at Scar. Halfheartedly trying to behave sincerely, the group was also openly excited at recognizing someone they knew in the business that actually appeared to be getting somewhere… anywhere.

"It doesn't look like a billboard to me," Scar says, blowing it off seeing his ex-fiancé on the side of a telephone booth. It was an off-hand and defensive remark, but just as he spat it out, and just as Gene turned the corner to get on to Biscayne Boulevard, there she is again. This time she is forty-two feet high and fifty-six feet wide. This time, she lay there seductively, again as sexy as legal, selling Miami Beach the spirit and cheer of the season.

"I fully admit she makes _me_ want to buy the store," Allen remarks, smiling.

And that's when he lost it.

The floodgates opened, and Scar cried aloud. However, he isn't just sad. He is mad, jealous, humiliated and embarrassed all at once. Everybody had to sit in the rib joint parking lot for over twenty fucking minutes, waiting, while he gathered his wits and got his shit back together before they could go in. Truth not need be told that he drank quite a bit more than usual that evening, even though as much as usual was usually more than enough anyway. Delivered home, he spent the rest of the evening laying in his motor coach in the Studio Center parking lot, crying, sleeping, puking and thinking.

*

The Fool Star and company is in Augusta, Georgia when Tony, beyond any doubt, figured out what kept that goddess covering Scar as long as she did. The band is playing a showcase venue called *The Whipping Post.* It is their last road date before the scheduled production would begin. The showcase and the money made the trip worthwhile. During the three-day long engagement there, the crew befriended a small bevy of young, negligent (along with two or three genuinely nice) girls, and had of course partied them nightly.

The second night there, the crew inadvertently set forth a bizarre method of weeding out the good girls from the bad. There must have been at least two women for every man in the hotel room this night. Most everyone is sufficiently smashed by the time they left the hall, so when quite suddenly one of the crew announces that in ten seconds the lights were going out, and that after that – "anything goes" – nobody expects much objection, especially since most of the ladies in tow on this night survived the night before. One could only assume that the others, the new comers, were from the same school.

The seconds tick by, likely slow for some and not fast enough for others. Then the lights went out, and when they did, the room grew surprisingly quiet, but the silence remained for only five seconds, or so. Suddenly, there was a let go of a jagged and shrill chorus of B-Grade screams and debutante-drillable protests. One girl in particular, who happened to have been sitting between Hog and TL, screamed – excuse the cliché – a real blood curdler.

Tony is there purely for the mind fuck, foregoing the more physical oriented festivities – for he has his Pression. She lets him out to play sometimes. He's sure that old Hog had dirty things in mind, and Tony knows that between them sat, certainly by far, the nicest looking girl from the hall.

when the lights go out, and the girl starts to lean toward TL, practically on him, and knowing that she knows that the band good girls, like Pression, it is apparent that the Hog was moving in on her. To this day, no one knows exactly what he did, or what he whispered in her ear, but oh, it set her off scared like a white doe in the woodlands. She was one of the three, maybe four girls present that night that flew out of there, bellowing in protest all the way.

The third night in Augusta, Pression accidentally walked-in on a shower party involving three of the crew, and two of their local girls. Now there were two obviously good sports all the way around! All Presh could think of was water sports. Imagine the sight she beheld of three big men from the crew in a relatively small, hotel shower, with two petite young girls, busily scrubbing, rubbing and dubbing.

"Listen," Tony explained to Presh. "Scar has not yet fully recovered from the blow to his empire, and I have an idea that I thought might help bring him back around."

"Go ahead. More…"

Following through with it, Pression asked the two lovelies she met in the shower to do a big favor for the band this night, when they expected Scar to arrive. She just wanted them to baby Scar through the night, show him a little affection and try to keep a smile on his face {wink}. Her exact words were "…just be real nice to him, show him a good time."

Nobody notices the three of them, Scar and our fair young maidens, exit stage left toward the green room. The band plays on, their final series of tunes for the night ending in crescendo. They come off the stage for a three-minute break before the encore, heading toward the green room, and there it is - Scar's meat. The girls have him slouched in the back left corner of the hallway leading to the dressing room. He is leaning into the corner, bent slightly, hands on his thighs, just above the knees, as if he were waiting for a ground ball. His pants were down around his ankles. The girls are on either side of him, both worshipping in their own dutiful way, his LBJ. He was getting much more attention than Pression had bargained for.

*

Stereotypical categorization of music was yet to come out much beyond jazz, blues, rock and roll, bluegrass, folk, country and classical. There was no "alternative." There was no industrial rock, arena rock, techno-pop or EMO. Competing with punk, new wave, disco and hair-band-metal is humiliating enough, let alone having to go up against rap, hip-hop, pseudo-country, and the multitudes of little niches carved out of the radio world then. The door today is much wider ajar for young musicians than it was yesterday, yet trend remains paramount to success, it seems. Finally, it settles into a category named by the decade from which it came: Grunge. It was better than "Alternative."

All the band can ever be is a Southern Rock band. That's just the way it is. They always felt they could break the mold, by virtue of their music alone, but never had there been management present enough to push it. Tony's band got a bad rap because of looks and location. Their many influences shown through their music most times, and so did their Live-Your-Life-Motherfucker-Attitude. It was not because the moniker they couldn't shake was the infamous "Southern Rock," they were always proud of where they were from, and the kind of music they played, whatever that was. Who's listening? Ask them what it is! It was everyone else in the plastic world of music, the business, adds to the complication. Unlike the practices of today, marketing a band from the south that didn't play Southern Rock was a marketing nightmare twenty-five years ago.

Scar stumbled his way through the responsibilities given him in the studio. It wasn't long before the band figured out why he went to the bathroom every twenty minutes or so. You have to have an ear to produce a record. You can't listen to someone else's work hoping to design and craft a uniquely different song. You have to relax, and listen to the song at hand, and reach into your mind and your soul to hear the potential in the sound that's there, that needs to be there and needs to come out; hence production.

Sometimes, all it takes is a listen to, everything else just flows, from the count on, but you have to have that ear to be able to capture those great moments that come along. You have to have an ear to capture the moments that interrupt the flow as well. One must also display a bit of intuition, if not shrewdness and practical understanding to pick out what might or might not be marketable, as there is hardly a formula. If there was, we'd all be rich.

Moreover, a producer has to have guts. Scar did not have guts. Our engineer had guts. Scar was a trend follower, and although Gary was a rock and roll guitarist, he had not yet produced a rock and roll record. Because "New Wave" was the latest flash out of the ass that was the music biz, Scar was compelled consistently to push the keyboards into the top of the mix. It was a constant struggle to keep the control room sane, and above the fads and beyond history. Here was the decisive factor for Tony. Both Scar and Gary were deathly afraid to turn up the drums. Tony argued with both of them on a daily basis that virtually very few had yet discovered the power of a pumped bass drum and toms, and no one was tripling the snare, and experimenting with other microphone placement techniques over the drums. But, Tony wanted to. He could hear it! Not merely because he was the drummer, but because he could hear what was missing in every song he ever mixed with the two of them.

It had been missing in every other song heard to that point. Very few bands had a decent drum sound. Without fat drums, it's enough to make you suck. Nowadays, fat drums are the standard. You don't have a record unless the percussion is fat, but Tony knew it back then. He could FEEL it. He could hear it coming and he knew what he wanted to sound like on record, but Scar and Gary couldn't give it to him.

Tony could not blame Gary, because the only gold records on his wall were from the disco craze. After all, he would do what Scar told him to do in that control room. The old cliché rings true and harsh. You get what you pay for. Tony did blame Scar, damn it, for he should have backed his drummer up, the band up, instead of driving asleep at the wheel.

"That's why I said that Scar was a poser when we met him," Tony said to Presh.

"And just think, Tony, he'll be something worse when you leave him."

Scar enjoyed the regional success the Fool Star helped achieve by this time with the band, and he knew he was on to something good. He figured he could use that success to fuel his nearly defunct, old booking agency a bit. Mistakenly, he allowed himself the luxury of thinking that he was actually responsible for the success the band was enjoying, but he was merely riding their coattails. He was a poser when they met him, he was a trend follower and he wasn't a true breakthrough producer or rocker. He took on a few additional bands from the Miami area, and called down a couple of his old acts from Orlando. He collected twenty percent from all the happy rock acts he took on for Big Daddy's, and that kept him happy.

"As far as we are concerned," Tony says. "Scar's business is growing in the wrong direction."

"What pisses me off is that he is not performing for you exclusively any longer." Pression said. Funny, like she was in the band. She's in Tony's band.

"He is not doing what we had hired him to

do. He is squandering the resources," Tony went on, "in our view, and has fallen back into his comfortable booking agent role."

"We didn't rent him the office space in Studio Center so that he can build up his booking agency. Booking on the side may have been cool, if he had only performed his job for us. That's all we ever asked from anyone. Do what you say you will do."

Scar would maintain that he had indeed started to manage and book a couple of other bands in his spare time. He hadn't completed his job for the Fool Star's band yet; therefore, they would maintain that he had no spare time with which to spend. From that point on, things were not the same between Uncle Meat and Tony's band. Scar missed many good opportunities to shop the group with influential labels because he didn't keep his eye on the ball. He also, upon working with more and more bar bands, started in again with that trend-following, bullshit mentality that the Fool Star had tried so hard to break him out of; suggesting perms for their hair, wearing "Florida" looking clothes on stage, and even mentioned once that they should enter the stage to "Good Vibrations", the Beach Boys' masterpiece. He wanted them to pass Florida oranges out to people we met in the audience and back-stage. Shaving, of course, also came up.

Is that what he did all day long in that fucking office they rented for him? Were those his big ideas for them? When his band played on stage, they played for keeps, for fun, for each other, and everyone interested in listening. The Fool Star's band didn't just play the music; they made music. They were extremely serious about their sound, performance and production.

No interest in gimmicks, they were merciless upon themselves. It was Scar's good fortune to have been right there with them when the group fell into the good shite, the hit records, the money, and his misfortune to have blown it all away. He fell into the pit of ignorance usually reserved for those who the outfit could only call, with no disrespect to the musical times, disco-lickers. The Studio Center album came out all right, overall, and the group got a lot of mileage out of it, but they could have gotten more. Scar especially could have done more. When the band let Scar go, he stayed on at Studio Center for a short while. He had a plan.

"Miami Vice was an interesting idea for a show, but a play on those words will paint a much truer and colorful picture."

PART VI

James A. Landry

CHAPTER SIXTEEN

Moving to Key Biscayne raised the bar of standard but did little to raise awareness. The glamorous island life, bluntly stated, was perfect for the likes of Fool Star, Pression and the band, help and friends. The last time they came to North Miami they stayed several miles up Biscayne Boulevard in the *Voyager Inn,* historically noted both famous and infamous. The Voyager is famous for the claim that Barbara Streisand was, many years ago, first discovered there, in the hotel lounge. It is infamously known as the hotel where the XXX movie classic *Deep Throat* was filmed. This trip to Miami was bound to be different, because they had money to make it so.

A famous celebrity acupuncture specialist owned the house rented by the band. She was a globetrotter, who traveled more than dwelled, presumably mixing house calls with vacationing. Renting her home on Key Biscayne during her absences brought her an extra fifty-one hundred a week. She certainly didn't need the money, she was rich already. She had her acupuncture practice, but several years prior, her dead husband left her a bundle.

Although the home was handsome, expansive and exotic, it was relatively modest compared with others in the neighborhood. The Bee Gees' Gibb family live just a few houses down on the left, and Eric Clapton has a cape on Ocean Boulevard, just north of the bay. The Eagles were in town, for a session with Bill Szcymzic a few miles away in Coconut Grove, and they were staying right down the street from the Fool Star's group on Key Biscayne. Their place is the first home on the left after crossing the causeway to the key from Miami, at the Miami Mall on Route 1. It is a sprawling and spectacular one-story home with a built in pool in the back. Beyond the pool stands a seawall, which was all that lay between the beautiful bay and the inhabitants of the large home. Some of the group jumped the wall from time to time and swam over to a small island maybe fifty yards across the bay.

A wealthy Columbian family lived in the home right next door to the group. Of all the neighbors on Key Biscayne, the eccentric and only son of rich parents next door was the friendliest and most fun. He is like a character right out of the movies, maybe The Great Gatsby, forty years old going on fourteen. He dressed daily in a silk smoking jacket and kept a flask of vodka forever strapped onto his calf. He constantly sang as he walked aimlessly through the neighborhood and around the adjacent gardens and lawns. Tony liked to call him Heff.

Lou Heffner.

Christ! I guess I'd have been whistling and singing the days away too, if I had his life of ease.

When he learned it was a band moved in next door, he came running over to the house right away. He had his accordion strapped to his chest and was eager to play. He played and played on for over an hour, and the band agreed he was an excellent accordion player! He knew all the traditional and well-known show tunes, as well as many cultural and popular classics. Impressed by his virtuosity, the band twice invited him to the studio to lay down tracks for a ballad the band was working on. His accordion tracks actually made the pivotal difference on the record.

The group always made plans for nights off: a movie, maybe a show, and a drive down through the Keys, or checking out the competition in town. A diversion with Sally was always fun. Shortly before moving up to Key Biscayne, Tony had been walking around South Miami completely numb, because of all the Coke and Ludes he had for months been ingesting. Literally numb, he could no longer feel himself. He had also become somewhat delusive. For example, He refused to drink Evian water because it spelled 'naive' backwards. That was significant, because back then Evian was the only bottled water nationally distributed.

On a band outing to the movies to see *Apocalypse Now*, he passed out shortly after settling down into his seat. He never even saw the beginning of the movie. Pression woke him up, with popcorn and beer spilled all over his lap, just in time to hear Dennis Hopper tell him that *"If" was the middle word in "Life."* His eyes stayed glued to the screen from that point forward. He, Brando as Kurtz, and the movie itself had a queer, moving effect on Tony, as he went for days thereafter repeating the Hopper line in Mantra, thinking hard about nothing, thinking hardly of some things... and <u>not</u> getting high.

Tony knows he is sick, but he is determined to last long enough to regain feeling of himself once again. The numbness had begun to hurt his instrumental performances. He, quite literally, could not feel the sticks in his hands, and had no idea whether the tempos were close, let alone correct. Three weeks of sobriety brought him calm and cheer. The first two weeks were painful. Pression was getting real tired of Gene turning around mid-song and yelling at Tony that He was a fucking pussy! And to, Speed it the fuck up, you cunt!" By the time the group moved to Key Biscayne, and began working on the album, Tony was once again in top form. Although he was not able to lay off the white completely, he did lay off the Ludes entirely, and that made a lot of difference. Using the rests – just like in music.

*

Rob and Deb are a fine couple, good people and devout fans of the band. They are both slender and strong. He has a nice, custom Sportster with a slight rake and a little extension on a Springer front end, and always that fine old lady holding up the back end. The Fool Star met a multitude of folks at their wedding the year before, but they were the big stars. The group, by now, recognizes most everyone from Big D's, Dino's or the After Hours in Homestead.

Rob had a good, lucrative black market fencing business. The previous year, the Fool Star purchased a number of pieces from him for the crew vehicles. He always has quality merchandise for incredibly short dollars. He specializes in electronics, such as name brand stereo components, televisions, car stereos and the like. Not surprisingly, Rob and Deb also have a little going on with the white stuff. In South Miami, after all, who didn't?

*

Sally moved to Key Biscayne right along with the band, and pretty much had run of the house. She regularly accompanied them to the studio, and after a time, felt comfortable enough with the help there to befriend a couple of them. About eight days into the project, she fell for one of the studio hacks. That was good for her, because she had been waiting for some loving for a long, long time.

Presh and Tony shared the master bedroom, king-size bed and all, with Dee and his Asian girlfriend. It was sometimes awkward, Tony and Pression laying there pretending not to hear or notice her cooing through some Eastern language no one understands, as he did his best to perform the best he could under those circumstances. Third day there, Dee and his significant other were not around, and Sally didn't see Tony and Pression there either. They were in the vanity, just off the master, where Tony was cooking some white. No one, beside TL and Hogweed know that Tony was getting into distilling it. All Pression knew was that it made him wanting. Getting high like that was something they all had sworn off, quite a while before, but Tony wretchedly fell back into when it became too easy and convenient not to say no. Tony had already completed recording his own basic tracks, and it would be weeks before being called back into the studio for the sweeteners.

"It's Sally," Pression urgently whispers. "She brought company."

"Shit-Fuck."

Suddenly, Sally and her studio gopher storm into the bedroom. In sight and sound, Tony felt thrown back into one of those old non-graded, comedic X-rated loops. The door slammed behind them, as they ripped each other's clothes off, laughing, hooting and hollering, and together growing more and more wet and sticky.

There was a Polaroid camera on the valet

counter where Tony was sitting, and he just couldn't resist the temptation, the risk. He had just smoked a gram and his heart was racing.

"Hey," Pression doesn't holler. "Let me take one!" Pression decides mischievously to snap a couple shots of them in action, too. Tony cracked the louvered door just enough to allow the lens to peek through. She aims, and caught him as he jumped up and down, facing the camera, stark ass naked. His hydraulics were so pumped that the pipe was sticking straight up, literally plastered to his belly pointing directly to his navel. Just before Sally grabbed him and threw him to the bed, Tony snapped another. Sally then wasted no time jumping his bone.

"Give me that." Presh kept shooting, giggling softly. They were so caught up in their own moment the flash went unnoticed. Nor did they hear that unmistakable whirring sound as the Polaroid excreted the instant photo. Tony and Pression knew they needed to get out of there, but they knew that very moment was not the right time. Looking through the louvered doors again a few minutes later, Tony sees Sally riding the young operate as though he is an English saddle, not frantically, but slowly up and down, as if on a jolly afternoon trot. The actions were moderate and steady, but both Sally and her boy-toy were extremely vocal and loud.

"watching the scene from behind the wood-framed skybox offers up a truly sexy shot," said Tony. It felt perverted, but hey, who was it that said, "Seize the fucking moment!" Carefully, Tony opens the door again, a little wider this time, and squeezes off another shot. The flash and noise went again unnoticed. That shot caught Sally's rear end in the up position, just ready to slide back down the little white pole.

"On your hands and knees, Presh."

"All right."

"Ready," Tony asks. "Let's go." They were able to crawl out of there, across the bedroom floor, hugging the wall and out the door. Sally and gopher never knew Tony and Pression were there, or that they left. Nor did they ever learn who the horn-ball culprits were, who posed as a photographer that afternoon they thought they were alone. In the spirit of a roadhouse band of pranksters, the photos eventually made the rounds, passed around and enjoyed by all.

Also on that third day, Floyd drove himself up to Key Biscayne. He parked in the drive and came to the rear mansion door. Tony was still on his hands and knees, having just come from the master bedroom, camera and snapshots in tow, when he heard the knock at the back door. Floyd announced imperatively that he wanted to see Tony, see him now, and added that it was private. Tony went out to the lanai; Floyd grabbed him, and hustled him off and into his van. After speeding along for several minutes, Floyd said there was something he wanted Tony to see. He was driving toward Homestead. Floyd was extremely upset over their mutual friend's arrest. Both loved Kenny Bennito! Tony offered that he was also still reeling from the news about Kenny.

Christ! I was also still reeling from my Master Bedroom Vanity activity!

"Hey, we were talking," Tony tells Floyd. "And the group's first thought was that Rusty somehow framed Kenny. But then, that seems so… obvious."

"I know who set Kenny up," Floyd said deadpan.

Tony's stomach turned as he began to put the pieces together.

"I want you to see what I do to informers, traitors and rats." he added.

He was taking me there.

Tony could not stop farting.

*

From the corner of the soup-house room, Roy watches as the volunteer tries waking the old woman. He senses something odd, something peculiarly funny about the scene. The elderly woman's nails were painted, but the hands looked younger, and, they looked rather manly. If one looks closely at the person, as he is this morning, the woman actually had the ruddy face of a younger man, even through the worn foundational make-up. Is that a five o'clock shadow?

The volunteer's gentle vocal coaxing triggers Vonegan suddenly awaken with a start. He opens both eyes without a problem, and felt he had a little more control over his movements and senses. He had wet his pants, he realizes, but doesn't realize he is in drag. There was something on his head, a hat perhaps. His fingertips felt heavy. He felt bundled up and he felt very, very hot. He was sweating profusely, and worst he could smell himself.

As the young woman attending to him repeated calls to remain calm, he realized something was dripping down his cheeks. He swiped at it with his left hand, making a smear about his face, and looked down at the substance on his fingers. It looked like powdery mocha ice cream. He was actually looking at a mixture of mascara, liner, foundation and base powder. He started to freak. He started to shriek. He still had not the strength or capacity to move from out of his seated position just yet. Oh, but he was trying!

Roy jumped from his corner, along with two male attendants that were behind the kitchen counter. Roy was just a little person, an ex-jockey, but he was quite husky. The other two guys were huge black men. Between them, they were able to hold Vonegan right where he sat. Vonegan wanted to go wild but the two kitchen men holding him down did not permit it. They each outweighed him by an easy seventy-five percent. Roy patiently and unassumingly looked on, and offered comfort by repeating to Vonegan, "It's cool. It's cool. Calm down here, brother."

At that, all those around looked at Roy somewhat dismayed.

"Brother?" For he just called the old person *brother.* Roy picked-up on this right away and responded smartly by picking the wig off from atop Vonegan's head. Everyone there jumped and gasped at once, as though it was alive, and Vonegan himself almost got up and started to run, to where he couldn't have known, even if he were able.

Finally, Vonegan looked at Roy.

"OKAY, Okay, I'll calm down," he said. "I'm having a hard time remembering exactly how I got here, but I think it's coming back to me little by little."

*

Roy had been hand-picked by Floyd after meeting at the track on a winning day. By that time, Roy stood washed-up as a jockey and the owners demoted him to a groom, otherwise known as a stable boy. Roy works full-time for Floyd now, and his job was pure and simple. He did anything and everything that Floyd asked or told him to do, period, point blank.

With the job came insurance — the kind of insurance only Floyd could provide — plus, a little bit of cash and an endless cache of dope. What a peculiar couple they make: Floyd a colossal, hairy, mammoth of a man, and Roy, a balding, stout rather dwarfish little fellow. Nevertheless, Roy's eyes were as cold as Floyd's, and that was the attraction. That was how Floyd pegged him, by a look in the eyes between them.

The attendants let-up on Vonegan just a bit, but he could do little more than look down at himself in disgust, picking at the women's clothes in which he had been attired.

"I'm not a woman," he announced. What had become apparent when Roy removed the wig, became unmistakably confirmed the first time Vonegan opened his mouth. What a grotesque sight he is, sitting there, wet, make-up running, de-wigged, wretched and wrecked.

"Let's see what's in your bag," Roy suggests. "Uh, mind?"

"I didn't know I had a bag," Vonegan replies. "Go ahead."

"Ain't nothin' but a change of women's clothes and a box of make-up, dude," Roy tells him, then asks, "Who are you?"

"My name is Dicky Vonegan, and I am from New England," Vonegan says. "Where am I?"

"Miami," the woman volunteer replies, "At the St. Henrietta's Shelter for the Wayward and Homeless." She seemed so meek. "SHSH, get it?"

The group explained how Vonegan had shown up on a flight from Boston, and showed him the **"Bent"** placard he had been holding in his lap. They explained that the airport staff brought him to the shelter when they found they had no additional contact information, and thus, nowhere else to send him. He slept for almost thirty-six hours. This sickens Dickey down to the bowels.

"Where's the head?" he asks Roy, the urgency resounding in the tone and timber. He looks like a tired B-movie actor making his way to the dressing room, as Roy leads him to the restroom. Once there, Roy suggests Vonegan shower, and in the meantime, he would fetch some clothes from the thrift store across the street.

"What size are you, Vonegan?"

*

Floyd and Tony arrive in Homestead heading into the neighborhood where Rob and Debbie live. Typically, Roy drove Floyd wherever he went in the big, black van. Absurdly, just then did Tony take notice that Roy was not among them. As they approach the house, Tony notices its drapes are drawn. There were no vehicles in the drive. They pull in.

Tony almost fainted when he walked into the house. The smell is urine, sweat, feces and blood. Floyd walked Tony through the kitchen and into the living room. There stood Roy and another fellow – completely bald, bearded – whom Tony hadn't seen before. There was something familiar looking about him, though – something in his eyes. Tony pays no attention, as the uglier scene is Rob and Deb. They look like they had been worked over in torture, executed and quite literally probed for answers. They had each been poked, not actually stabbed deep, deep, just deep, but poked, a number of times, no, many, no, hundreds of times. Each poke maybe an inch or two in deep, with a prick-prick here, a prick-prick there, everywhere a prick-prick, punctured repeatedly, presumably with an icepick. Blood was exuding, dripping or running from every knife wound, depending on the depth. Presumably, they would be left there until they finally did bleed to death. Neither one is conscious.

"More mercy was shown to that old goat upon which we feasted at their wedding," Tony says. "That was shown Rob and Deb, it looks like." They were unconscious, barely but raspily gasping for breath, and slowly but surely dying. There lungs were rattling. As Floyd, Tony, Roy and the other guy all stood there, staring down at the pale, impaled couple, they listened as Floyd spoke of the dying having been suspected of turning informants.

"It has been confirmed," Floyd learned,

"sadly late as it is that Rob and Deb are the ones that fucked Kenny B."

"For sure..."

"Yeah, Tone," Floyd replies. "For sure."

"I told you I was up for it boss, now get me the fuck out of those stables!" The stranger said with a wink.

Both Roy and the other man had 9-millimeter pistols tucked into the front of their pants. Tony could only hope one of them wouldn't shoot off the genitals just below the barrel!

They all went to the kitchen and sat down. One night, Rob and Deb were right there with the Fool Star's band, as usual, partying, along with everyone else. Three days later, they were dead. Rob and Deb were found dead in their three bedroom south Miami cape, each tied-up in a kitchen chair, sitting in the middle of their living room. The first of those three days, Kenny got busted. After years of dealing big time, undetected, he was caught doing a small time side deal as a favor - a favor for Rob.

"Roy, pipe," commands Floyd, "I think Tony needs a hit!" He laughs.

Roy went out, and then returned with a torch and a pipe. Tony kept his head down and remained silent. Finally, he said, "I can't believe Robbie and Deb would do such a thing to Kenny."

"Fuckin'-A right they did," replied Floyd. "I been watchin' them for weeks. I was just a little too late to rescue ol' Kenny Bennito. FUCK!"

Floyd and Tony sat there for twenty minutes passing the pipe back and forth, Roy providing the heat, and they were toasted. Looking up,

Tony saw the stranger staring at him. Their eyes met.

"James," Vonegan hollered. "You barstid!"

Then, as he tried to stand to go over to Tony, Floyd raised his thigh-sized arm, knocked Vonegan on his ass and commanded him to stay put.

"You know him Tony?" Floyd asked.

"I think so Floyd," Tony replied. "Or, at least I used to known him." Tony looks back at the man on the floor, and asks him, "Vonegan, is that you?"

"You know it is, James." Vonegan said arrogantly from the floor. Floyd motions for Vonegan to get up.

"He's one of the assholes that sent me down here!" Vonegan said to Roy as he climbed back into his chair.

With that, Floyd and Roy laugh heartily and hysterically and laughed more until Tony thought they would burst.

"Bravo Mr. James!" Floyd said finally, after coughing, catching his breath. "Nicely done indeed, partner!" He cannot stop laughing.

Vonegan told them the whole story, or at least the parts he was able to remember and put together, about being dosed down and shipped out. Roy filled in the blanks. Tony admitted that he was in on the design and original plan, but his posse carried out the winning operation in his absence.

They all got in the van and first took Vonegan to the stables, then brought Roy to his apartment. Along the way, Floyd had Vonegan jump out and switch license plates. Tony knew better than to strike up a conversation with Vonegan, and didn't want to anyway. Vonegan kept his mouth shut, too. All the while, Tony was thinking how ironic it was that Vonegan ended-up working for Floyd. It was perfect.

The boys never missed Tony. He told them he was just riding around with Floyd. They couldn't tell Tony was cooked. Tony didn't mention to Droid or Hogweed that he saw Vonegan that afternoon.

*

Eleven weeks of luxury ended, and the band moved, once again, back into the Voyager Hotel. They moved there instead of back to Dominican Drive in South Miami for three reasons. One; their next leg of gigs are booked at near-by North Miami Big Daddy's, Two; they want to stay well away from Rusty, who lives in Homestead, and Three; they needed to remain close to the studio because they were still putting the finishing touches on the album. The hotel was right around the corner from the studio, and a short drive to the North Miami Big Daddy's.

Tony and studio management did not want to believe it was happening, but they were, in the end, forced to cope with threats received from Rusty. Rusty's flair was tempered for a time by Tony and Pression's friendship with Floyd, and by the consequences he paid for his rampage on Dominican Drive. Nevertheless, he was back with a vengeance as soon as the group moved away from Key Biscayne. The latest rumor was that he planned to kill them all at the studio. He sent word to the group that they had better beware, because he knew where Studio Center was, and he knew they were in there.

Although the outfit carried a rifle and a shotgun with them, they want to be ready for war, and they know just who to go to for that. Little Rat (just because he was a dite shorter than the other Rat – Big Rat), is a good friend from Miami, and he is an arms dealer. They met him at the Big Daddy's in Homestead, partied with him at Rob and Debs wedding and had been to his home for dinner and parties several times since. Rat was happy to provide on loan a couple AK 45 submachine guns, and a couple thousand rounds of ammo. He threw in a few grenades and several pistols. Tony passed on the RPG launcher for now.

The band and crew took turns sniping from outside the studio. The watch would sit hidden in the bushes just outside the private entranceway, and stake out any vehicle that came into range of Studio Center. Still coked to the max, they thought it just another day at the office.

Tony was getting close to the point of asking Floyd to step in, but was reluctant to do so because he did not want to put him on the spot. Rusty continued to be, after all, one of Floyd's under bosses. With Floyd in a difficult position, Tony wanted to be able to work it out with Rusty the best way he could on his own. Of course, Floyd also knew that, as did Tony, Rusty was losing his mind, and if Rusty were to get too out of hand, Floyd himself would step in on his own behalf, regardless.

*

Kamyani Kamyata is the manager the Big Daddy's North. He was an exciting young entrepreneur, as well. He was a tall, muscular island man who, through his mastery of martial arts, had a tendency toward keeping, by Miami standards, a tight club. His was nothing like the Homestead Big Daddy's. Kamyani didn't quite know how to handle the influx of bikers from the South that followed the Fool Star's band into his club, but he somehow did.

Money was made, all got along. He felt so strongly about the group that he produced his band's John Lennon tribute record "Just like You." They went to the studio within days of John's assassination, and laid down a song that Dolphin and Tony wrote. It was a dedication to Lennon, his legacy and his memory. Once completed and pressed, they gave the records away as gifts to all, until they ran out. Tony sent one to Yoko and Sean, in care of Elliot Mintz at The Dakota.

*

Christmastime was near and the band heard a rumor that Kamyani was pushing for Big D to invite the band to the annual party. Big D had never, ever invited a rock band to his favorite annual gathering. This was the office party of all office parties. Kamyani pushed back for it, and by the end talked Big D into inviting them. When they were actually confronted with the idea, they all had to promise to behave. With that, they accepted the invitation graciously. Neither Kamyani nor Big D could have known then how the party would end. The group still wasn't clean, but no one is clean in Miami.

The party is always held in the Central Miami Big Daddy's. The place was elegantly decorated, and had a sunken dance floor that lit up with the beat of the music, bi-leveled service areas, chandeliers and classic looking bars of mahogany, brass and copper. The group sat at the upper level bar, in the far corner. Although they moved freely about the room, that was camp. Had they been directed to sit anywhere in that room, that night, it would have been exactly where they had decided to seat themselves, well and far away from all the distinguished guests and VIP's. Big Daddy took notice the rock group took the back corner.

The group snorted off the bar, Tony cooked the cake and they all sat their sipping Kamikazes all night long. Occasionally, someone'd chew up a Lude. The Fool Star and all were the only ones there without suits and ties, leisure suits. They dressed for the occasion, but suits and ties were not part of their wardrobe.

Neither were socks and shoes for that matter.

"Hard times we've experienced probably have
a lot more to do with who we are today
than the easy times did, don't you think?"

PART VII

CHAPTER SEVENTEEN

OH FLOYD

XXX

Floyd and Roy first eyed the fair beauty at Big Daddy's Homestead. The little bitch was hanging all over one of the band's crewmembers — the spotlight guy. There is an unwritten rule among men that says you don't fuck with another man's cunt, and Floyd would not break it. He was a man. He could wait. And wait he did. Floyd waited a long, long time before carrying out his actions.

Time gave him opportunity to devise. Floyd is planning a party – a Snow White party, but the party was in Floyd's pants, though, and nowhere else. He had so much time to think. The band already left Miami, in fact Floyd saw them off with several hundred others.

Julie, who fell in love with Homestead and Miami, stayed behind. She promised to wait for Droid. But, now the young girl is free, and so is Floyd. Without knowing it, with only the mere thought crossing big Floyd's mind months before, Droid's girlfriend was already in trouble.

*

Droid met Julie in Daytona. She had come from Wisconsin on Spring Break, but extended her stay beyond the week by rooming with Droid through the next. Apparently disgusted with life in her cold and northern hometown, hungry to see the world, Julie latched on to Droid like a deer tick in the spring. What could be more attractive to a young girl than life on the road with a rock and roll band? Droid was a man all alone again, on the road, and he rejoiced in the infatuated, passionate relationship the two conjured up together. They grew serious enough, or so he believed, for them to arrange her moving in with, and traveling with him and the group.

Droid had one hang up that nobody could ever get him to break. He remained too relaxed. He's the kind of person who thinks everything is cool as long as he feels it cool. Instead of, like a Meer cat, poking his head up occasionally to see what the rest of the world is feeling, he's liable to bask alone in the spotlight as long as it remains warm over him and him alone.

It's always been difficult to define virginity.

Does it mean one is non-orgasmic-active, or does it mean one has not participated in intercourse – been penetrated? Although Julie was technically a virgin in either sense of the word, when she met Droid, she was merely a curious, violated kid who had yet to achieve a simple orgasm or reach any climax at all, ever, through her few previous low-down encounters, or by her own hand. She didn't know how. That is a virgin – one who has yet to come.

She experienced her first orgasm with Droid, and shortly learned the power and the beauty of oral sex, the clitoris and multiples. Oh… The experiences had Julie in a way worshipping Droid. It was nice to see him finally behave as though he had gained some control of himself, and his life, for a change. Droid and Julie were inseparable. For months, they romped together with the band, from town to town, and state to state.

However, it wouldn't be long until Julie discovered as well, the power of sex with drugs. The more she hung with the group, the more and more people she met and got to know. Everyone who ever met her adored her. She was indeed sweet, young, shapely, Wisconsin poontang. She never met a man who didn't want simply to have her at the moment of meeting. Droid was aware, but felt safe – he had a lot of friends in Miami to watch out for her – but he missed it when she crossed her fingers and gave him the wink.

She actually began to act upon her whim and urge while the band was still in Miami. There were just too many cool people, with lots of money and lots of coke! It wasn't long before Julie was out in the back lot mid-set giving out a blowjob for a nose full of blow. However, it wasn't all about the coke, for the group always had plenty of that. It was the attention. The excitement.

She dick-teased her way from one short-term arrangement to another once the band left.

Droid found out about Julie just three weeks before Christmas, in Miami. He wanted to be devastated, but he couldn't be. For one thing, he already suspected she had been fucking around on him, and for another, he was too numb to take real notice. When the band fled Miami that December, Julie had Droid leave without her.

Our Wisconsin dairy maiden pure

Was now a South Miami Coke whore.

*

Floyd kept some sophisticated implements in his belonging. He had a full size Gatling gun mounted in the rear of his van. He could literally back into any situation, let the doors fly open, and just start cranking! He kept a small arsenal under the benches in the van and in his house as well, including explosives, grenades, automatic and semi-automatic weapons, and, a swell knife collection.

He had a Dante-like basement room, and an Elvis-like bedroom. The man was eccentric. He was way up the ladder, living way out there on the fringe. Living the dream and knowing full well, he remained just one-step away from The Columbian.

Vonegan worked hard to seduce the girl through the horrid promise of the white stuff. If choice made, between Floyd, Roy and Vonegan, then Vonegan would be the likely candidate. Vonegan, however, was not exactly appealing to Julie just then. Nevertheless, as soon as she heard that there'd be other beautiful people, and plenty of cocaine at Floyd's, she caved.

Grasping and spilling her fifth kamikaze

of the night, she followed Vonegan out to the parking lot. He escorted her to the van, belted her into the seat, and drove north up Route 1. He had her now. All he had to do was deliver her back to Floyd's place – untouched and ready to party.

She was a goner the moment she set foot in the door. Had she fled, Vonegan would have pounced and forcibly brought her down, but she didn't, so that wasn't necessary. Nevertheless, they were ready. She felt it particularly odd that this was a party, yet she could see few other visitors there. Roy came out from the kitchen to greet the girl. Both Vonegan and Roy were being extremely polite, so as not to scare the poor darling. Julie ate it all up, and it made them feel good to be so nice, even though being that way came by way of direct orders from their boss.

Roy set up a couple lines on the coffee table and assured her that other guests would show up soon. Roy and Vonegan had arranged for the few that were there purely for show, and to not stay late. Only Floyd's boys knew how short-lived and temporary the part would play out for the extras. They happily did as told. Pass the mirror this way, please. Oh, how about the pipe?

Talk brought another three rounds of sniff to the threesome. Roy had been mixing Rumrunners in the kitchen – a Key favorite – and Julie enjoyed more of those as served, as well. The next go round brought with it sharing the pipe. Roy and Vonegan each took a tug. They had no trouble talking Julie into sucking the pipe with them. She took to it well and begged for more with each heart-wrenching toke.

That's just how it is. Once you get it the

first time, you chase it forever more. After basing twenty minutes, they gave her a couple well-deserved Ludes. The Ludes took affect within moments, really softening her down. Soon, they knew they would have her where they needed her - where Floyd needed her. Part of the Plan never rang so despicably true. The extras left.

Floyd lay patiently, waiting in his room. He masturbated twice at the thought. He read Easy Rider and Motorcycle magazines. He kindled up his own torch and cooler pipe. That evening, by ten-thirty, Julie, on top of ingesting line after line of cocaine and ingesting several Rum Runners, had done eleven hits off the pipe and had eaten six Quaaludes. It was time. She was nodding. Now it was Vonegan's and Roy's turn to wait, and wait they did, for all of ten short minutes. Then, she was out.

They carried her to the basement room. It had been pre-set with all the implements; hood, rope, cuffs, branding irons and alligator clips. They undressed her, cuffed her to the round stockade and tilted it back so that she'd be in more of a relaxed position. It was all Vonegan could do not to molest her himself, but he had been warned by Roy not to try it. How he wanted to tweak those little nipples and finger that twat. Their job was done, for now. For now, she belonged to Floyd, and he couldn't wait to tell her how he felt about her — to show her.

*

Floyd kept the poor girl enslaved with him for three long weeks. He kept her chained round the clock in the basement room, and shackled when it was time for sleep. With all the freebasing going on, there wasn't a lot of sleep indulgence. She kept right on doing the Ludes and sucking the pipe, because it seemed to her the only choice. It was one way she remained distant from the reality of the situation, and the thought of the potential danger it imposed.

Floyd liked to watch her when she pissed or shit. He adored her peeing into his cupped hands. He enjoyed wiping up after her, and especially enjoyed sponge bathing her every couple of days. He sodomized her repeatedly, and fucked her dry every day. He had her give him head, but only twice. His favorite thing was anal sex. He called it butt-fucking. He loved jamming his big-ass fingers into the girl, but he absolutely gorged himself pumping away at her rear end.

The girl's rectum was literally growing with every assault. As you may have guessed, Floyd's penis sized in well and well in proportion with the rest of his gigantic stature. At first, she bled. She bled from both places, but after a couple days, it stopped. She wouldn't discover until months later, and Floyd didn't even know he did this at the time, for he showed no visible signs or symptoms, but he inadvertently gave her perianal and genital warts and herpes simplex-2.

Thankfully, Julie thought after a week had passed, he appeared to like her enough not to want to hurt her any more than he would by virtue of his own humongous flesh weapon. He refrained, after the first couple of days, from using the alligator clips on her nipples, and when she cried at the sight of the branding iron, he put it away unused this time. She was silently thankful.

Julie had dreamt in the past, as most women will, about the big dick – of having it, just once, even. In her fanciest imagination, she never dreamt of anything the size of Floyd's. She was thankful he didn't demand head from her anymore after her first two attempts. Little did she know he didn't because there had never been a girl able to administer enjoyable fellatio to him. He was just too big, and he knew it. By the time her stay with Floyd ended, all fantasies involving the big one she happily sent to the back and then out!

Floyd liked his privacy. Roy would check-in every morning and get a list of errands from his boss. Floyd, during time he entertained company, would not leave the house. The two hands had more time off than usual during Julie's three-week stay with Floyd, but they kept busy running the daily dope, numbers and dollars for their employer. They happily stayed clear of the office for the time being.

Floyd loved the bathing, but he also enjoyed the feeding. He planned the menus for the following day in the evening prior, and left an order sheet for his boys to address in the morning. Roy and Vonegan would shop in the morning each day, and then prepare the meals for Floyd and the guest. They wrapped each portion up for easy reheating later.

Floyd enjoyed spoon feeding Julie, and wiping up the little messes she made around her mouth, and down her chest. Aside from the sexual assaults, he took care of her as though she were his little baby girl. Indeed, whenever he felt the ironic sorrow called up by the cross-wired emotion of the situation, he felt compelled to cover her head with the hood. Sometimes, he would just cover her eyes with a blindfold, for he just had to see that exquisite face as he felt the tightness of the young lovely one enveloping his big dick.

Julie was one of the long-timers. Floyd usually kept his girls no more than a week, maybe two at most. Some, he tired of within days. Nevertheless, Julie was different. He knew she would be, and indeed, she was. It was getting to the point where he could no longer avoid his responsibilities. He had been putting off meetings and such for over a week now, indulging himself with his cellar maiden. Into the third, unscheduled week, he was losing money. He couldn't put it off any longer. He never kept his little friends locked up without his company. He was very sensitive about that. He thought they deserved better, more. Therefore, when he could no longer afford to look in on, and care for Julie daily, he reluctantly decided to let her go. It was a sad day for Floyd, as he really did like that one.

*

Floyd called Roy and Vonegan back in on a Thursday night and told them to take the girl and bring her wherever she wanted to go. Floyd had told her that there would be no trouble as long as she kept her mouth shut. She took from him the token bag, some money and the ride, and did keep her mouth shut. She knew Floyd and his reputation. Roy and Vonegan knew better than to try anything funny with the girl. She was still Floyd's, even though he had, for now, finished himself with her and turned her loose.

Roy and Vonegan dropped Julie off at Dino's bar and grill. They sped away quickly as she slowly made her way to and through the entrance. Her head hurt, her stomach hurt, her crotch hurt and her butt hurt. She had a pocket full of Floyd's money, an eighth of an ounce of sniff in her handbag, and she was finally free again, but she still felt like shit. She sat at the bar munching on beer nuts and drinking cold Saint Paulie Girls. Every thirty minutes, or so, she'd go to the rest room to pee and snort a little flake. Julie sat in Dino's all night long, ignoring everyone but herself, and thought about how living with Droid was not that bad, after all.

CHAPTER EIGHTEEN

The band and crew met back in Panama City with the unscheduled Christmas hiatus behind them. Their first order of business was to decide where they were going to get work, and keep working, without the lost gigs in Miami. Even though the arrangement with Big Daddy's had been convenient, it felt kind of good to be out from under his thumb. The bigger problem is that the band's master tapes are shelved in the vault in Studio Center. They've never had a hard time managing to get work and play dates, but decent studios in Florida are few and far between. They wanted to get back down there to retrieve the master reels, but going back to Miami for any reason was definitely out of the question for the time being.

Tony began subcontracting the band with an agency called JAM out of Raleigh, North Carolina. The circuit through the Carolinas wasn't near as grueling as it had been the last time the band performed there. The itineraries were better planned, and the venues booked were usually appropriate. Additionally, the Carolinas were no longer intermittent stops along a much longer route. They constituted the core route, and seldom did the group have to travel outside of that core during the twelve months they worked there.

While on the road in Carolina, they met many bands and reconnected with fans, but they befriended fast two fellow-JAM groups: *Doc Holliday* and *Nantucket.* JAM had scored a major label deal for Nantucket, so that band bounced for a while back and forth between regional and national concert tours and appearances. Eventually, Nantucket would disappear, presumably off into the limelight, somewhere, but they reappeared soon enough, too soon, which told the Fool Star they had not fared all that well away from their home base. Nantucket had one hit song on their latest album, but coincidentally, and unfortunately for the Nan, AC/DC released the same song, at the same time and guess what. AC/DC scored the radio hit first with *It's a Long Way to the Top (If You Want to Rock and Roll)*.

Doc Holliday was also hoping for attention and treatment from JAM. Unlike Nantucket, Doc Holliday was not in competition with the rock and roll trend. They were more interested in continuing to blaze, and carry on the country rock tradition. So, they were not in the least disillusioned by the poor management behind Nantucket's untimely release. Doc's enthusiasm behind JAM had the Fool Star thinking of giving the management company an official try, as well, so he signed a short-term contract with the company and spent a year under JAM management. The management company was owned by a guy named Rhett Matthews and Phil Caine.

The Fool Star band booked The Attic, in Greensboro, North Carolina; a showcase for JAM. They reserved the two seats first row in the first mezzanine; the best seats in the house. The band was in top-form. At one point, Dolphin took a walk through the crowd during his solo. People were excited, reaching out to him, touching his guitar, the fretboard and all, strumming and just having a blast. Dolphin made it up to where Rhett and Phil from JAM were seated. They touched Dolphin, strummed and touched the guitar, laughing and having fun. After the show, JAM invited the all of them to a Bloody Mary brunch and gourmet grilled dinner at Phil's tomorrow.

JAM was excited to have Fool Star and his group on their roster, but the band soon realized JAM did not have the resources to support them on top of Nan and Doc. One thing they did do, and do well, is keep the band booked busy on the road. For the next nine months, they saw more of the Carolinas than General Lee!

JAM was another team that had corny ideas about marketing the group. They had already signed Doc Holiday and Nantucket, who were their 'Big Stars', so from the beginning, the Fool Star's band really didn't stand a chance at much more than sucking the hind teat. JAM was too small and unprofitable an outfit to be able to professionally commit to, and invest in more than the two bands they already had.

JAM did fund a road trip for themselves to Miami, with hopes of retrieving those Masters for the Fool Star. They were told, after a search through the vault left them unfound, that Scar had come in and left with the tapes. With a story that security bought, Scar walked into the vault one afternoon, and left with a quarter of a million dollars' worth of music on a series of three inch tapes in their tins. It is unsurprising to Tony that Scar ran off with the masters.

The ideas from JAM weren't much bigger than anyone else's the Fool Star had seen thus far. They failed to come up with any means to procure any additional studio work for the band. By the end of the year, the group returned to Panama City, once again discouraged, if not a little upset. Tony was, personally and lividly, pissed-off about losing the masters.

The Fool Star and his band returned to, and were welcomed home by a wanting crowd at Cowboy's. Cowboy's used to be called JJ's, renamed under new management. People in Panama City were eager to welcome them back, as they always treated the group – like royalty - big, whenever they returned home.

There is nothing like playing to the birthplace of the band. Everyone in the group was from Lynn Haven, which is right outside of Panama City, except for Tony, and although he'd been called a damned Yankee more than once, Pression and Tony were always treated like natives there. For that they remain ever grateful. The people in Panama City were plenteous, noble and grand – grand in every way – proud to the rebel.

The radio stations there played the songs that the Fool Star delivered, and people came out regularly to see them perform. The band had always had a good home base settled there in the Panhandle. Cowboy's and a few other occasional, local gigs took care of an income for a while, but the band was still working on trying to figure out a long term plan for the band to continue to be productive and to reach their goals. In the meantime, they released another single: an old, but previously unreleased song, which went into the Top Ten on the Regional Billboard Charts. That had helped get lots of work in the area. Everyone loves a record on the air.

*

The band's circuit had been huge. During the prior seven years his band played throughout Florida, Georgia, Alabama, North and South Carolina, Virginia, Kentucky, West Virginia, Tennessee, Louisiana, Mississippi and Arkansas. After playing two-hundred and forty-two cities, in fourteen states, and logging well over a quarter million miles on the odometers, they decided to try a different approach.

Although Tony wanted to relocate to an established business center, like New York City, Los Angeles, Austin, or even Nashville, he was outvoted. The group decided to concentrate on finding a 'House Gig,' or at least a circuit tight enough where they could commute home at night from each job they took. The plan had worked well in Miami, so why not try it again, elsewhere? Panama City is not the Mecca that it is today; they knew they had to set sights elsewhere. Unfortunately, and much to Tony's chagrin, the other boys were never keen on relocating out of state, so for the time being they looked only at the cities in Florida that might be lucrative. Besides Miami, they had spent a lot of time in Orlando, Lakeland, Naples, Daytona and New Port Richey, Tampa-St. Pete, Clearwater,

Sarasota and Bradenton, considering all possible candidates for a base.

They had burned out Orlando in the younger days. It was a regular stop for them usually two to three weeks at a time, two or three times a year. It was a very commercial town, with not much room to showcase original music. It was a town full mostly of commercial dance clubs. They considered the fan base there, but in the end decided against moving there. Fans drive.

They had been fired from the only decent theater venue in Lakeland after the manager breached contract and the Fool Star directed the band to walk off stage in the middle of a Friday night. A riot ensued after Dolphin announced over the PA to the crowd what the manager had done, and what the band was going to do about it. When they proceeded to pack-up their gear just after that announcement, all hell broke loose. Dolphin was arrested that night for inciting a riot, and the group hasn't been back to play Lakeland since.

Daytona was an excellent gig, but too seasonal. The clubs there were quirky, somewhat trendy and faddish, and for the most part, commercial. There was no studio action in Daytona either. Besides all that, they didn't want to live east; the Fool Star and the band preferred the Gulf Coast.

Between the five cities they considered, there was more year round work in and around Tampa-St. Pete. There were literally hundreds of clubs to choose from, and lots of rock rooms where bands were urged to play original music. Gene's wife and her family were from Tampa, so they thought that she, her family, and others the group knew in the area, might help them set some new roots down.

In the end, Tampa it is. Tony and Pression

begin once again to book the group, self-managing and essentially starting over. Glamour Rock was huge in Tampa at the time, so the Fool Star's band stuck out like a big ol' callused birdie finger. Being less pretty than the rest, or simply once again being the ugliest band in town, was a little tough on the ego at times, but they did not do make-up, masks, spandex or glitter. Despite the aversion, they stayed busy and were appreciated most everywhere. People liked to see a genuine act up there once in a while, for what was then, a change. They were still, without a doubt, the best sounding band around, and their production fit nicely the venues they played. Their light show was the best and they re-instated their other special effects and pyro-techniques. They remained a band tighter than an anorexic popcorn fart.

The band made the move to Tampa and rented a suite of apartments. They, for the first time in their collective professional life, set stakes down. And they were on their own. Tony manages and books the band, and makes sure Gene keeps the books current. They bought a sixteen track Fostex tape machine, used their own mixer as a console and set up a studio in Tony's apartment. The Fostex and mixer, along with an old four track Teac, was all they needed to produce quality mixed-down recordings. They also rehearsed in Tony's apartment. That's where it all came together; those sessions produced some of the best output ever.

The rooming at our newly settled homes was exactly like it had been on the road. Dolphin and Tony shared an apartment, and Dee and Allen shared one too. Gene and his wife, and the children they would soon breed, had their own place. Then, there was the crew. They had the largest apartment, but the most roommates. They also received the most company. Property Management put them in the largest apartment the furthest out in the back. Good move.

The most painful part of self-management was at the brokerage end. Often times and with the pain, Tony had to work through agents that held exclusive control over a venue. All that, and more made, more paid, so the Fool Star could pay them a percentage. Within time, however, Tony and Pression managed to book the band into the rooms direct, through the owners. Although that infuriated a lot of agents, it meant twenty percent more for the band on pay day, as well as more direct contacts for the future. After all, even the club owners recognized that they'd much rather work with the good ol' boys in the band over the sappy agencies that screw them but well on a nearly weekly basis. Nobody likes agencies.

For several months, the band worked a circuit that covered Tampa-St. Pete, Clearwater, Sarasota and Bradenton. During that time, there were good nights and a few bad, good times and bad, but for the most part, happy and productive. Settling down off the road, all in all, was good for everyone. Tony hired a music attorney and gave him a few thousand dollars to go to New York and Los Angeles to shop some demos, but he came back only hung-over and empty handed. Epic and Arista Records both offered a deal that did not include a point for the attorney, so he walked. He didn't even stick around to see what *would be* in it for him! That was a large disappointment for the Fool Star, and from that point on, he decided the business would be his… or theirs and theirs only. No more distant, unknown representative outsourcing at all. Willingness without willfulness could do it.

They experimented with the studios in town, but always returned to Tony's own apartment. At one semi-famous studio in Tampa, they made a deal to back up Dennis Yost, the lead singer from old *The Classics IV* - famous mostly for his recordings of *Sonny* and *Stormy* - for a solo come-back attempt. The Fool Star's band got to record one of their own songs – *I'm Goin' Home* – as part of the deal, but just like a trip to Atlanta to record a song named *Room 28* a couple years before, the tape never vaulted and made it only as far as Tony's cache, along with *Room 28*..

The latest strategy is to record their own demos and shop them out themselves. The recordings are good, but back then studio heads and A/R people didn't talk directly to bands. They wanted "appropriate legal representation," such as an agent, attorney or professional management. The business wanted face-to-face meetings over big, wet lunches, where the agent would show up like a wise man bearing gifts.

The solution is easy, as Tony is the manager, the owner, and legal representative and the spokesman for the band. He produced the Charter.

A reference would have helped, but the group knew no one that high up in the business. There would be no favors for them. Tony had already called every one he knew – old friends of his Dad's. The best offer he got, but the band turned down, was to write and perform the new *7-Up* jingle. The band would have also starred in the television commercial. Tony was voted down: The band turned it down.

Fuggum.

Another California family friend, Bob Parkinson, had called to announce he'd lost years ago all his contacts in the music business. He and Tony's father had been friends and partners. Together, until Tony's Dad died, they owned the Miss Universe franchise. Bob was sorry he couldn't help at the time.

The Fool Star's band eventually played a room called The Porthole. They had known of the room, and were eager to get into it because it was so close to home. The owner had contracted a house band several months prior, so the place was locked down until that contract ran out. The fact that they were open to auditioning the band, as well as the possibility of another house band option, made the group all the more eager to play it.

Tony booked it and they played a two-week engagement, and by the time it was over, the management there offered them the house gig. *The Porthole* in Tampa: It couldn't be better, except that it was truly the beginning of the end.

*

The number of famous rock stars on Florida's 'dead-celeb' circuit is amazing, and it grows by the year. Fool Star met and the group opened for many artists past – from Savoy Brown to Black Oak Arkansas to Rick Derringer to Fog Hat to GrinderSwitch to The Outlaws, The Producers to Mother's Finest, and more. Many musicians, eager to retire to the land of stink-weed, move or retire to Florida as well.

We befriended many stars in their days, but were impressed most with Robbie Steinhardt, from *Kansas*. He had the most distinct manner of taking a shot. He would down the shot, as usual, but then ream the inner glass with his tongue after each slug; like a slug. It was rather disgusting, if not comical looking, as if it were part of some kinky ritual. Maybe it subliminally sent out a magic tongue message to all the wayward girls within range. Regardless, he is a funny man and a happy drinker, and always has nice things to say about the group.

A career highlight is playing with Gregg Allman at PJ's in Daytona. He was far from a dead celeb. His mother lives down that way, and he frequented the town often. One night, he happened to be in the crowd at PJ's, and asked if he could jam with the band. The band had been duped once by a fake Jimmy Hall. He had made his way onstage with us only to blow it totally once there. He looked exactly like the star he claimed to be, and had instruments – harps – on a belt with him, as well, which added to the credentials. It was only when he hit the stage attempting to play and sing the notes that the Fool Star realized they had been taken.

Randy Bachman also made his way into PJ's one night. He bought the group all rounds and rounds of drinks, and invited Tony and Dolphin to sit with him and his date at their table. He refused to play onstage with the band, queerly they thought, but did let Dolphin play his black, gold-plated Les Paul Deluxe. Randy continued to party with us all week long. He had a limousine and driver, an assistant, and a beautiful blonde with him. Tony and Pression spent the days driving up and down Daytona Beach in the limo, and hanging out with him in his room, Tony all the time doing coke, smoking, drinking and partying. During his week in Daytona, he kept the group supplied with drinks, pot and cocaine at night as well. He even gave Dolphin the Les Paul Deluxe half way through the week!

He made phone calls transferring funds from his bank in Hawaii to his girlfriend's bank in Tampa. He made other calls to Burton Cummings, who he said was also in town for a video shoot they would do together for VH1. Except for refusing to jam, Randy was the real thing.

The band arrived at the club to practice Saturday morning, just in time to see Randy being wrestled to the ground and arrested by the FBI and Florida State Troopers. The group learned he was an escaped convict from Michigan State Penitentiary, and he knew he looked exactly like Randy Bachman. Tables and chairs were flying! The man was on the FBI's Ten Most Wanted list. He was a convicted felon – grand theft, forgery and double murder.

He escaped from the facility at lunch time, walked into a Detroit music store that evening, claiming to be Randy Bachman, and walked out with the guitar — no money down. He had talked his way onto a plane to Tampa, also in the name of Randy Bachman, and then, once there, swept the rent-a-car girl off her fuck-a-star feet — no money down. Walking into a limo agency, Randy, and girl now in tow, left within the hour in a limo, and full time driver — no money down.

He had borrowed five grand from the girl he duped, and then made one of his phony phone calls to transfer funds. They ended up in Daytona, at the club the band was playing. He actually lived the lost life of Randy Bachman, having his way with everyone he met, and got everything he wanted by merely playing the part and asking for it. In his right, he almost commanded it. And he never laid down a dime for any of it. He was bad, but he was good at it.

Everyone was questioned, and Dolphin was forced to give back the guitar. It was worth at least twenty-five-hundred dollars. The poor girl the felon had picked-up in Tampa was completely blown away, distressed and emotionally devastated. She could hardly function, and she needed comforting. Naturally, she stayed with the band a while. The band and crew took good care of her. The limo driver had a big laugh over the whole thing, and simply drove the large automobile back to Tampa as soon as the police gave him the go ahead to do so. They all had to visit the county courthouse to answer questions many times over the next two weeks.

So, Tony, at the insistence of Gene, asked Gregory Lamar Allman for his ID before allowing him onstage. Allman was a little put-off by the incident, but said he understood and he did indeed showed Tony his Florida driver's license. He said, "Come on, man. You don't wait for me, I don't wait for you. Let's go!"

He joined us onstage for *Have You Ever Loved a Woman.* He knew the song from when his late brother, Duane, played with Clapton on the Derek and the Dominoes "Layla" Album. The whole Allman Brothers Band had been invited to the studio for those sessions, and Gregg knew the song well. Gregg knew hundreds of blues songs. It was a good warm up tune. Then they jammed on *Statesboro Blues* and *Stormy Monday*. It was an interlude I'll remember for the rest of my life.

*

The house gig at The Porthole was a blessing for the group. The venue was a mere three miles from the apartments, if that, and the crowd there was cowboy Rock and Roll. They requested original tunes as well as the selection of covers that we did. The gig afforded the band the comfort level to record regularly in their home spun studio, rehearse literally at will, in house or out, and the chance to try to meld with mainstream society for the first time in their lives.

For all of the good things about The Porthole, one of the downfalls of that job was that it made most of the band drunkenly fat and somewhat lazy. They still rehearsed a couple days a week, and still managed to record, but the musicians individually did not practice, and performances began to suffer. Even though their chemical intake had all but disappeared, Dolphin, Gene and Dee were drinking more than ever. If anything will hurt a performance, it's alcohol. Under the influence of alcohol, one simply cannot hit the notes or play to the count.

Dee and Allen were smoking more pot than

ever, but Allen wasn't drinking heavily on a nightly basis. Tony was straighter – more sober than he had ever been in his adult life, the sight of his fellow musicians, sloppy and haphazard, night after night was sickening. Presh was proud of Tony. She also noticed the change in the band.

"I feel like they are each caught in a tube," he explains to Presh one night before bed. "Oblivious to what's going on around us."

Dolphin worked solo early in his career, performing in what he always considered disgusting playing situations: fronting agency-built bands. He was always the undisputed, up-front star of the show, but deep inside he always wanted a real rock band, more a brotherhood. Dolphin was an extremely talented singer, songwriter and guitarist. He eventually taught himself keyboards, as well. Everyone that sees him knows his enormous talent right away. If he had just one fault, it may be that he had a tendency to stretch solos a dite too long – sometimes missing the sweet (ending/return) spot.

He would set out to form that real rock band by recruiting his two best friends and his brother. One friend, Dee, knew a little guitar, but Dolphin taught him how to play the bass. Allen knew a little trumpet and keyboards, and Dolphin taught him how to play better keyboards. Gene always wanted to play guitar (like his younger brother), but never had the time. He actually played the drums a little bit. He, years ago, knocked up a neighboring service brat and married her, like the good ol' boy he was. So Dolphin trained his older brother Gene how to hold a guitar.

That was their existence for a good three years. Dolphin would learn each and every part, instrumental and vocal, and then teach the part to the respective player, note-by-note, and chord-by-chord. They would eventually memorize it, then play it all together a number of times, and voila! They had a new tune on the repertoire. Eventually, and finally, by force of habit and progressive nature, each player learned enough to be able to pick up most song parts on their own, but Dolphin was never really off the hook, especially over his brother's dependencies.

Gene never caught on, nor did he care to. He could never get up with another band to jam, because he had no idea what to do. At least Dee had learned his craft well enough to be able to jam a little bit, but not Gene and not Allen. Without Dolphin, they were a lost soul's cause in the music world. Mind you, the rest of the world never would have guessed, because the band, as a whole, sounded great. Part of the reason why, might probably be that they were all so married to their parts. And they played their parts so well. Remember: Tight.

As the band developed and grew, and traveled more and more, Dolphin was in his glory, so happy. When Tony joined the band, it made it all complete. Dolphin was overjoyed to have a real, honest-to-goodness fellow musician, a real musician, along with him for the ride, and to help support the others. Tony had been playing professionally two or three years longer than Dolphin, but they had full and unconditional respect for each other and their respective backgrounds. After all, it's not the age, it's the mileage. They would room together on the road, and once there, in Tampa, cumulatively for over ten years.

*

Existence in Tampa did them well for a while, but offered no genuine exposure. After repeated failures, Tony tried repeatedly to push the band into relocating. He thought and conveyed they could do much better for themselves in New York, Los Angeles, Austin or Nashville. It wasn't uncommon for bands to get signed right out of a showcase bar, but Tony thought it would be a lot easier to do business in the city. He thought they were ready for that then. They were perfectly rehearsed. Tony knew it, and Tony had to swallow it.

By then, a couple of the band members had married and established roots in Tampa, and refused to leave. Tony and Pression viewed this as a major flaw in the design of things, and admittedly, took it quite personally that the group would not follow his direction. Some of the group grew too comfortable in the house gig situation. All things considered, they upset Tony by shunning his ideas, his own growth and experimentation, and even began to shun

Pression because she, of course, woman that she is, backed her man up one-hundred percent. She was very influential over the other girls, who were not subservient enough to keep it to themselves. It drove the boys mad, too.

Almost everything the band did (individually and as a group) began to upset Tony. He felt he was choking. Ever since moving to Tampa and settling into the house gig at The Porthole, Tony was the only one who had managed to remain sober. Since recognizing, realizing and facing the truth before him, he started smoking coke again and staying high all night after show.

Now, he was looking at a wasted one in his own mirror. Even then, as has always been the case, Tony could still perform. Gene was the man that does not move. No showmanship at all. Tony tried teaching the entire band simple concepts around performance and playing with each other – on accents and crescendos - everything, but it all fell on deaf ears and lazy bodies. Except for Allen.

*

Staying high was good for Tony. That was all that calmed the noises he constantly heard in his head. Self-medication, or masking, kept him arrested and comfortably happy (numb). He not only heard voices, he heard noises. His head was so busy; he heard sounds and noise forever, clattering through his brain. Never was there a quiet, somber moment in time. Even when the voices were silent, he heard pops and chirps, and pink and white noise, and snippets of rhythms and beats looping endlessly. It was enough to drive a man insane.

…if I had not already arrived.

Pression had been completely clean and sober her entire adult life and she finally sobered and straightened Tony out by handing him an ultimatum: He clean-up too, or she goes. He cleaned-up. No question. Presh is his princess.

Tony has a problem, however. The straighter he got, the more depressed he got. If not for Pression by his side, he never would have been able to stand the tension and anxiety. Depression finally surfaced the realities in a clearly defined way for him, and they together made the gargantuan decision to leave Florida, with or without the rest of the group. Pression and Tony decided they would split for New York themselves if the band decided not to come. The band refused to move, so Tony and Pression decided to leave the band. There's been no band like the Fool Star's since, no matter what the signs may say.

The end came slow. They did not share their decision with the group for almost a year.

Tony did maintain to all that he thought a move to the city was the best idea for the group. That year provided a buffer period, just in case things turned around a bit between the band and him. Moreover, it gave Tony and Presh time to make in advance the necessary arrangements for the move, which did seem inevitable.

After a time, Tony knew he'd never get the group out of Tampa. It had become very obvious. The time thereafter became tense and dark, because Tony ended up, in essence, bullshitting the group along, virtually all of the time. It was hard, the photo shoots, videos, recording and playing, living behind the fronted schemer. Meanwhile, the voices were loud and clear, so unless he was completely occupied, depression set-in darker and deeper, and everyone else in the group played The Porthole drunken and high all of the time.

CHAPTER NINETEEN

The Ghost Farm was a very special place. It was for Tony everything, from a great place to meditate, to a great place to ride a dirt bike. Aside from birds and squirrels, he would often see different animals, such as deer, fox and ground hogs during his visits there. Whether a weekend gathering or a daily stop, the old farmland offered its power to all in a way that made it easy to use. Journeying there became habitual, as did the naked, midnight romps through the fields. One thing that the farm never offered him was a warning.

*

Tony felt no different in the classroom on that day, but as soon as he saw Sister Anastasia call Sister Honora from the room, he just knew. Just like that time in New York.

I know it is for me.

Just like the time on Governor's Island, New York, when he saw the ambulance pull up at the party across the street, he knew it came for him - Dad. Sister Honora didn't even have to say, although she did, "Anthony, Sister Anastasia would like to see you outside, please."

The rest of the class gasped externally and pitied internally, for what had Anthony done to cause Anastasia herself to come over from her office across the way and pick him out personally?! Their emotions were well intended, but all for the wrong reasons, and children they were, the feelings passed over them quickly. When Sister Honora shared the news with them they went through it all over again, but this time the feelings did not pass. For some, like for Tony, they never would. Neither would the tears.

I walked with Sister Anastasia back to the main school building away from the junior high annex. Both of us treaded, dreaded and remained shrouded in silence. She held my hand. She needn't talk, nor I. I knew. She knew I knew. I was a boiling pit of disillusioned emotion by the time we reached her office. She visibly slowed as we approached, in a way that suggested she, herself, did not want to finish the trip.

Father Kelly had been in with Sister Anastasia trying to brew up the courage to tell Tony, and the strength to lead him.

Sensing the reality of this situation and having seen them approach through a shadowed ray through Anastasia's translucent window pane, Father Kelly emerged from the office. Anthony still held up, even though he knew he knew. It wasn't until Father Kelly said, with his arm wrapped tight around Tony's shoulders that he had terrible news for him – his father had died in the night – that Tony broke down and sobbed out loud and uncontrollably.

Father Kelly planned on staying in that office space until they could both recover, but recover Tony never did. The good Father led Tony along as he cried, almost hurriedly out the door and past the varsity classrooms in the annex. Tony could see some of the others inside watching as they went, his own face twisted in degeneration and sadness, but did not acknowledge them. Some of them were still crying, and upon seeing Anthony trudging along in tears with the priest in black, others began crying too. Sister Honora let them let it out.

Father Kelly leads Anthony to the church next door, and on the kneeler before the great alter, in the Church of the Immaculate Conception, he suggested prayer together. And they did it for what seemed hours. They prayed to the point where Tony was almost taken by it. He felt light-headed, but exhausted and tired. With Tony's crying finally subsided, and after an overdose of prayer, he asks Father Kelly how his mother is.

The wasted priest walked out to his car and drove Tony home in silence, holding his hand. In the house waited a brokenhearted mother and Tony's two sisters. They were silent and red eyed until little Tony walked in and eyes met. Then, all broke out in tears and shared the longest, hardest hugs ever. That's the last thing Tony remembers, until the end of the wake. He somehow lost three days to trauma, depression and shock. He developed walking pneumonia.

The clergyman and the funeral director had given the family the last few moments alone in the vestibule with their dead, boxed loved one. When they returned to tell them that it was over and that it was time to close the casket, mom shrieked. Tony thought he was in the middle of a movie as she repeatedly screamed, "No! Norman, I love you!"

She tried to climb into the coffin with him, grabbing at his big shoulders and arms, wanting to hug him, and perhaps retire there with him. It was a grotesque sight, and although he is compelled to turn away, Anthony couldn't. Something instead told him to go and help her out. Two administrators and Tony coaxed her, quite physically and vocally, out of the box and back down onto the floor. Everyone else in the room sobbed and moaned uncontrollably, making recovery appear long away yet.

The funeral is held at Saint James church, the church where Anthony had been baptized. Father Kilcoyne said the Mass and offered a Eulogy in his strong Irish dialect. Through it all, most of the family was weeping, and most everyone else wept along or remained dead silent. The big Irish priest commanded that from most witnesses. Father Kilcoyne took the gathering through everyone in the immediate family, one by one, praising God for their strength and courage.

When finally he said "And then there is little Anthony..." the whole place fell apart. Throughout the day Tony could feel all their eyes upon him; in the church, at the cemetery. The United States Coast Guard, ARMY, Marines and Navy supplied a color guard, Taps, and twenty-one gun salute for my father and the family at the burial service. For the Navy, it was a small price to pay for killing him. The flag over the coffin was ornamentally folded and a soldier in strict steps brought it to my mother. She motioned for him to hand it to me. I still have it. Even the following September, back at St. Patrick's School, they still looked upon Tony as the small victim cheated.

*

There had been an enormous turn out for the wake and funeral. Mr. James had been Recreation Director, Founder of Jubilee Week — or Market Square Day as it is called now — and the County Commissioner. He also owned his own public relations/ad firm, and had a lot of connections throughout the entertainment and sports world. The city named the local gymnasium at the community center after him - The Norman R. James Gymnasium - the sign under his picture reads.

Anthony's mother received visits of condolence and follow up letters offering help and sympathy from everywhere. The state house, the white house, city hall, Hollywood, and friends of the family all said they would be there. The nights back then were filled with sorrow and tears. Tony remembers his mother, night after night, literally crying herself to sleep. He could easily hear it through his bedroom wall. It was sickening, but there was nothing he could do. He would often get up to hug her, and she would stop crying for the moment. She did not like to cry in front of him. A whole day's worth of tears saved-up till late night. Then, after Tony left, it would start all over again and wouldn't stop, she then crying him to sleep, as well.

After the nights like that, the days following could only be filled with sleepless, mixed-up confusion. Nothing made sense. Tony went into a state of shock, through which he developed double pneumonia. It was a long recovery for the young boy. His condition probably helped his mother somewhat, as she was forced to tend to him and take care of him through the entire time he would remain so sick - weeks. It seemed to place her disparately from the weepy woes of the widow.

*

June 8, 1970 turned out to be a pivotal date for Tony. Through that summer he became more and more aloof and carefree. He would drink and smoke for the first time, get high for the first time, and turn fully from sports to music for his own salvation. He had begun playing drums when he was six years old and took formal lessons for the next seven, but that summer he would quit the classical lessons and start jamming with local musicians, and playing out as often as he could. Even at that age, he was in-demand.

"Our parting need not be classified
as a beginning or an end.

Consider it more an event of continuity."

PART IIX

CHAPTER TWENTY

Breaking the news to the band that he and Pression were leaving was a hard thing for Tony to do. Thoughts reeled of having been through so much together in the decade-plus they had lived, traveled and played together. They had history and investment. As much as it hurt Tony to leave, it hurt them more to lose their drummer, but they never offered an alternative either. There was bitterness, revulsion, ignorance and attacks between them after the announcement until the day Tony and Presh left. By then, it had become so intense and insane and unreasonable that Tony was relieved and <u>happy</u> to leave. Every reason he had for leaving had been multiplied and replicated during that intermittent time between telling them and driving away in the U-Haul truck.

Shortly before leaving north, Pression and Tony married in the New Port Richey Courthouse. With nothing more than a secretary to stand as a witness, they made the bare bones vows and it was done. The facts that their parents, let alone the band were against it made them want to do it all the more. The decision to marry was to display defiance, and prove support for one another even though they were going through such a difficult time with the group.

Night after night, Tony and Pression watched with sadness, as the band, night by night, auditioned and played with a series of shitty drummers. How do they ever make a decision on a replacement? Because they never heard a one they would have hired. But alas, the band was forced by desperation of time to settle on one, considering they had work Tony had pre-booked for them for months to come. I knew well the drummer they hired. We were friends and had met in New Port Richey.

Before leaving the band, Tony was stripped of everything except what he had left home with eleven years earlier in the first place; his clothes, his records and his drums. Oh yeah… and Pression, of course. Several years earlier, Dolphin had given Tony a guitar, but he decided to take it back from him because he was leaving the group. There were many incidents of the same low-handed, despicable caliber; Tony would almost have paid them to let him leave in peace at that point! He felt like a really tired bride whore. There was one other thing Tony left with, something that no one knew he had, except for Pression.

"Thanks, babe," Tony said. "...for keeping my secret, even though I kept it from you for so long."

Very early on, as has much been the case from day to day since birth, we can imagine so, Tony has listened and learned. He may have chosen not to see, some may say, in defense he'll plead he did not demand to be heard. It was he, who formed the legal partnership eleven years ago. It was he who was licensed and able to sign and seal legally on behalf of the group and his self. Gene merely thought he was giving him, or rather, them, a way out of paying individual and band business taxes. It really was quite easy. All Tony needed was one day with an attorney, and a signature from a witness, and he got it.

The CPA came in on behalf of Gene and Dolphin's mama, no less, so touché again, old boys. True-CHÉ! I'm sorry to have to tell you this, but feel the time is right you know that I made money off of almost everything we ever did.

Pression and Tone loaded up the U-Haul themselves and made a four day trip to New York. They slept at rest stops, making love in the truck along the way. They kept the Certified Check from the Bank of America in the underside of her pillowcase. The $250,000.00 – which coincidentally comedic – works out roughly to one dollar per mile, kept the trip exciting, but as trips go, it was uneventful. Uneventful it was, save for one incident in New Jersey. Fucking Jersey.

They hit Jersey and started up the Parkway in the middle of a strong rainstorm during the late morning. Tony saw the signs that read "No Trucks in Left Lane." They'd never encountered one of these signs before, thought it a bit queer, and assumed they were addressing tractor-trailers, not vans, of any size, including the U-Haul they were driving, and the like. Directly out of the first toll booth, they were stopped, as Tony had passed someone on the left. The truck had been in the left lane for all of thirty or forty seconds. The trooper was right there, and he pulled Tony over. That assumption about tractor trailers was wrong, but Tony's intuition, fortunately, rarely lets him down.

The officer was a young, butch, white man. He got out of his car with his rain gear on and circled the U-Haul, climbing up on the running boards on both sides. When he finally came around to the driver's side, he asked Tony for the usual; license, registration and insurance. He had everything he needed and gave it to him. The State Trooper took another walk back through the rain to his car. Pression was crying. Whether she was upset, or she cried for effect, Tony let her sit there and do it.

The driver's license and the plates were from Florida. That instantly sent up a flag before the determined patrolman. He noticed both the older gentleman, taking issue in Anthony's hippy look, and that Pression, looked underage. This lawman smelled trouble, as his mind wandered over the sit-scape:

This is an older hippy, perhaps a dealer, taking a minor over state lines... could have abducted her, could be armed, and probably has a truck load of dopy Florida Skunk-Weed, or fucking Cocaine in the back. Shit!

Upon his return, the thumb safety strap over his handgun unsnapped, he ordered Pression to wait in the truck. He asked Mr. James to step out. He had nothing on Tony, as his record was clean, except for a couple old aggravation charges. Unfortunately, one was for assaulting an officer. Therein lay the challenge. He searched Tony first, out there in the pouring rain, then, took a quick, yet fairly thorough look around the driver's side of the cab. He found nothing, but noted Tony's look of distaste for getting soaked.

Once they were nose to nose again – the officer bending at the waist and neck to force his six foot stature in boots to reach Tony's own – the state trooper announced, loudly and clearly, that he would like to see what was in the back of the truck.

Oh shit!

…again!

Soaked completely, thrice by now, Tony opens the back of the truck and begins unloading, removing and opening virtually every capsule in transport. He also has to produce a Marriage License for the young officer, because he did not believe that Pression was Anthony's wife. For, she looks so young and pert to want to be with one older looking and seasoned as Tony.

Tony unpacked all his hard drum cases. That was two full sets of drums, along with outboard gear, cymbals and hardware. Shielded minimally from the rain, he did this, both wondering when and how it all would end. It took between ninety minutes and two hours for Tony to tear through their stuff enough to satisfy the trooper. Then, and only after the very last encasement was checked, without even a tone of apologetic inflection for the trouble, he handed Tony a citation for driving the truck in the left lane. And then, he pivoted about face, and simply walked away. Snapping up his holster, he ignored the pleas with him to drop the matter, repeating he was not familiar with the law – pleading ignorance. But asshole officer friendly wouldn't hear of it.

*

Tony and Pression reached their destination early that evening. Sister Jean's home was in a quiet suburb, a private community in Northeast New Jersey called Free Acres, in Berkeley Heights. There, she lived divorced from her children's father with her kids. Jean had taken in a freeloading boyfriend named Thad, and was living a life somewhere between a whore of sunset and The Great Gatsby, living that singleton life. Right away, discomfort rose between them, as his sister acted all too happy to let them stay, that staying up on the second floor, was certainly okay. It was Thad's unofficial getaway site, but really, he won't mind. Thad went along, had to, but the resentment was deep set in the shallow man. Boiling blood.

Tony spent the evening unpacking the truck, and Pression swept and cleaned it, readying it for return due the following day. Everything but the clothes went down to Jean's basement. It was hot and uncomfortable, a Jersey June climate. The stairs leading down to the cellar were spiraled, with very poor lighting, and they were getting little help from Thad. Tony was complaining underneath, but Thad vocally complained about near everything.

He didn't really count, Tony kept telling himself, as blood is thicker than water and she and her children were very happy to have Uncle Tony and Presh lay over there. Little Tara was a young grade school child who grew much attached to Tony in a short time. She could sense there was finally a good man in the house (for a change), and she wanted to be part of it. Shannon was a trendy high school girl, nice and polite, who remains cool and a little distant, as adolescents will with grownups. Or just too busy, with just so many friends!

Tony and Pression planned to return the truck and collect their deposit the following morning. Pression wanted to go out on night one, however, while Tony was ready to stay with Jean for a good home cooked meal. After a short argument, they went out. Pression tended to get what she asks for; always-of course.

*

Rusty didn't know where to turn without the band to blame and hassle over his problems. Sally took a house in Orlando and remained friends with many of the fans that Tony the Fool Star had introduced to her there. While the band was busy working on their own lives, Rusty went on to hassle those others, remaining much too close to Sally and their son, for comfort. Rusty, one day working his evil MoJo morbidly too far, abducted the child of an Orlando couple Fool Star Tony knew well, in fact the parents of that child were two of his dearest friends. The child, who was named after one of the group crew members, was recovered unharmed eventually, but it took time, and that crime put Rusty behind bars for several hard years.

"The city was wide and open,

Tall and just big as hell.

The ride in that yellow taxi cab

Like a high speed, mobile confessional."

CHAPTER TWENTY-ONE

It became dreadfully obvious that Tony had been the glue holding that band together for the decade plus that band existed. Within a few months of his leaving the group, Dee the bass player quit. He had been one of the most irrational upon Tony's leaving, and had been the only one to actually physically altercate, charge and attack over the incident. As it turns out, Tony had committed to a move that Dee wanted to make for years. But he never had the courage to go through with it. Now, he did, because someone did it ahead of him. Following came easier than leading for Dee, and that had always been his way.

Poor Dee had always followed whatever the Robinsons said and did, mostly for lack of confidence in his own ideas, but also over fear of the ugly face that consequence will usually bring from the brothers. There was a certain maturation that had yet to take hold, but leaving the band was Dee's first step in that movement.

Soon after Dee departed, Allen digressed, as well. He, quite simply, could not see the potential anymore. He was tired, as they all became, of the brothers' bigoted, irrational, self-centered and one-sided ideas. Dolphin and Gene, in a sort of crude underground duo-dictatorship had been running with the innards of the show, too much of the time, too much their own way. Allen's announcement came with a certain amount of twisted glee, as he had a little bit of a bone to burn with the group.

A few years prior, Allen announced his intentions to leave the group. The brothers would have you believe that Allen had been asked to leave the band. It was a well-known fact that he and Gene were the weak points in the unit, and significantly weak they were, especially when placed in a solo playing situation. But Allen quickly broke out and developed into a spectacular player and performer. Through complicated negotiations, Allen decided to remain in the group after all, but he had been scarred for ever after. The underlying sentiment that revolved around his teetering position within the group, contrasted with Dolphin's brother Gene's, further comforted him in his decision to depart. Beside all that, without his roommate and his best friend, Dee, and without Tony and Presh there to carry the torch, Allen actually found it easy and attractive to leave once he decided it would be so.

They already lost their soundman by the time Tony left, and had promoted lighting technician Droid to the open position. Everyone in the crew moved up a notch, and they hired another fellow to take the slack at the back end. Merely weeks after Allen's departure, as if disbanding wasn't enough, the road crew dismembered next. Droid, the sound technician, and Hogweed, the lighting technician, decided to relocate back to New Hampshire. They needed to find Tony, with hopes for something brighter there. They too lost their desire to work for the 'band', for the band as they chose to know it, ceased to exist.

Once Stump left, there was virtually nothing left.

Once thinking early on in his deliberations, that he will have flushed ten years and two-hundred-fifty-thousand miles right down the brown pipe was surprisingly unregretful.

Non-regretful, all that time had been, however what a waste, and what a waste it was not, both! The end of a promising run could have been avoided entirely, if the brothers would have lightened up and played fair with the rest of the crew, not to mention with the guys in the band. All they needed was to grow up together, in mutual respect and fairness, but those brothers couldn't make that graduating step. The word is EGO.

The band ended up a trio, with brother Gene, one of the original guitarists, taking up the bass. Between the two of them, Dolphin and Gene would pick-up drummers, ad hoc. Another touring dead-celeb in the South was all they would become. Eventually, they slowed down, but to this day — sadly on one hand and honorably on the other — the two brothers continued to perform under the same group name. They clearly are not the same band, and certainly not resourceful enough to pull it off, but for their own pathetic reasons, continued to exploit the once revered name. The fans resented that and blew them off.

*

Pression and Tony stayed with his sister Jean in Berkeley Heights until they found an apartment. It only took about three weeks, but it was three weeks too many if one were to ask Thad. Pression and Anthony took a place in the Crescent Historic District of North Plainfield, New Jersey. It was a one bedroom apartment that had a decent kitchen, with small, old utilities, and a larger, warmer living room. The one bedroom was the best room in the flat, with all the nice, original, over-sized windows in Victorian alcoves, behind lace-curtained, French style doors. The house was one of many enveloped within the three square blocks of very old, converted Victorian homes in the Crescent district.

Almost immediately, Tony hooked up with The Isley Brothers, who also lived in North Plainfield. They wanted him to play and record samples on a drum pad for their new and upcoming album. Tony was excited! He took them all the way through their demo.

Tony received a call from an agent he had been talking to. The band "Tokyo Rose" needed a drummer to take them through rehearsals, because their drummer had fallen ill recently and is out indefinitely. They had the old armory in Rahway, New Jersey. The rehearsals are being held on the second floor. I stayed until their drummer returned, and fortunately for them, he did.

There lived a large Puerto Rican family downstairs. A dozen people typically shacked out in the two bedroom apartment, but the worse part about it was that they controlled the thermostat for the entire building from a lock-box on their living room wall. They broke into the box our first winter there, and kept the heat turned way up past eighty degrees. The heat rising up to the upper flats made it feel like ninety in the upstairs apartments, and caused Pression and Tony daily distress. It wasn't long before Tony broke into their apartment, fixed the thermostat and left a threatening letter, posing and writing as the landlord dunning them for their actions.

On the floor across from Pression and Tony, there lived an elderly, retired woman with a cat named "Lady." The woman still had her wits about her, but she was a sad case; hair forever a nest, in slippers and robe all the day long. Her apartment smelled of cat food, cat urine, cat shit and Camels: a hint of coffee and booze over all. Many a night Tony sat at Marge's table, sharing Camels, shots and complaints.

While living off the residual money he legitimately earned even if underhandedly made with the group, Tony continued to jam, rehearse and audition with different bands and artists in the New York - New Jersey area. Trying to make the real money last, he took on a paper route in sister Jean's gourmet section of Berkeley Heights. He had one-hundred-fifty high-income, upper-class customers, and the tips were excellent. His hours were 4:00 AM until around 6:00 AM, except on Saturdays and Sundays, when he delivered the payment envelopes and collected the payments, respectively, staying out till nine-thirty or ten. The money was great, but the work was tedious. He had to start putting the Sunday paper together on Wednesdays, and then complete it on Sunday morning just before delivery, upon receiving the news section. He made a little over $300 dollars a week.

Luckily, wherever he happened to be

performing, he could usually make it back to do the paper route on time. Preparing and delivering the papers, and managing collection. Additionally, playing around free-lance, he made about two-hundred and fifty dollars a night on weekends. Most of the money he made was tax-free, of course. He made sure of that. The two-thousand dollars a month was supposed to provide a cushion, so that the other money could remain, for the most part, untouched. That was the plan. Two thousand a month was enough to survive with a rent of $350.00 a month, including utilities. Isn't it?!

Renting in Northeast New Jersey and commuting to New York studios and rehearsal halls became an easy trek for Tony. To help escape the paper route, he tried taking a traveling gig with a Top Forty Rock Band, just for the money, but it sucked. Purist that he is, completely out of his element, he couldn't stand or stomach doing the clumsy covers and dance music. Not even (hardly) the bucks they made. He soon left that group and went back to performing free-lance.

The closest he came to making it back into the business at a level at which he could be satisfied, was when he earned an audition spot with the San Francisco based band "Journey." They were looking for a drummer to do their "Radio Free" tour with them, and Tony had a chance to fill that seat. All the arrangements had been made, but then, just before he was due to fly to San Francisco to meet with the band, Benny Collins and Bill Graham, to discuss matters, and set up the audition, "Journey" ran out of time. They had to choose from the drummers that had already played for them, and they did, of course, choose Mike Baird. Mike is an excellent drummer, who Tony was glad to see get the seat, as long as it could not have been himself. Tony wasn't entirely hurt, because although he recognized the tremendous talent in Journey, their music is often times a bit too sappy. The selling point was the drum parts he'd get to play. Beside a good mark on the resume, it was the dynamite drum parts Steve Smith had lay down in the studio that held for Tony the real attraction factor.

The stage right video cameraman hired for the tour happened to be the photographer/videographer that had produced most of the Fool Star's band photography and video shoots. What a small universe it is. During the following summer, the Bill Graham invited Tony to their Philadelphia appearance to see their show and say hello. Tony felt nice receiving invitations from his old friend, the group, and Benny, to meet them and visit, before and after the show. He was recognized by everyone backstage! They remembered him from the media kit he sent them many months ago.

*

Constant conflict brews between Pression and Tony. She decided, soon after they moved into their apartment, that she wanted to sing and play bass guitar. It was a secret, life-long dream of hers, she declared. Tony expressed his thought that she should let him first try and continue planning and developing, if not revitalizing his own career, and that she should consider supporting that by finding a job, working for a while. After all, Tony feels he is the experienced one, hanging out there, with nowhere to go, still professionally relevant at that moment, and it hurt, gwod-damnit.

Her claim of desire could never have gone unfulfilled: They did enroll her in professional singing lessons, and Tony bought her a bass guitar and amplifier. (Did we happen to read already that Pression always got what she wanted?) Wrapped up in the excitement of living so near the big city, Pression wanted to shop every day and go out every night.

Day after day, and night after night, she would plead or demand to go, no matter Tony's reservations or rationale behind his reluctance, or the simple idea of relaxing at home. She spent nearly all her days shopping in those shops about which until this point she had only read. They spent virtually all their nights together driving all over the city checking out different bands, going to shows, and eating at the finest delis and restaurants. Ultimately, Tony could just not keep up anymore. When he refused to go out, she would go out alone, and this became more the norm than the exception. Meanwhile, Pression could not keep a job down. She skipped from place to place, come what may, and hadn't held any one job for more than five or six weeks at the most, at a time.

Their credit cards were maxed, and their bank account was always overdrawn.

Tony began dipping into the reserves to bail them out, promising himself he'd put it all back, and that he'd never do it again. He inevitably could never keep those promises, and repeated the desperate acts at least thrice quarterly, if not more, for a year.

"Tony, I can tell you when you changed; when you developed depression and seemed to be able to ignore significant events. It was the day Floyd took you to Rob and Deb's house to show you the execution scene."

It wasn't long before the end of a two year period that they simply ran out of money. Pression was constantly overdrawing the checking account, and running up the credit cards over the limit. Tony tried to talk her down – this is *PRESSION* – but to no avail. The more Tony tried to explain the implications, the more pissed-off she got and the further into her own dream she slid. She placed all blame and onus upon Tony, and it went on and on like that, until finally, he relented.

Tony searched for a full time job to help them financially recover. Within two weeks he found himself up for two very different kinds of jobs. One was a position as an assistant in a nursery, tending to, and arranging the plants, shrubs and flowers. Maintaining the greenhouses. The other was a job as a second shift mail boy at a corporate credit management and reporting company named Dun & Bradstreet. All he really wanted was to get back to the garden, but he also needed a job with decent benefits, just in case, so he accepted the corporate fulfillment position at D&B instead of the lower key job at the local greenhouse.

From the start, he regarded the new job as temporary. Once he did start, however, receiving a steady check every other Thursday by each, his eyes came opened to a new and different world. The everyman world so many men take for granted, though not near as much fun, 'working' felt much, much easier than performing. He opted for health, life and disability insurance, and shortly became eligible for other benefits, such as pension, profit sharing and 401k. The best part was that real, honest-to-goodness paychecks came biweekly – steadily – all the time, without fail, without negotiation, contracts, agency fees or beating streets.

Tony remembers back when he developed that case of double pneumonia in nineteen-eighty, while playing New Year's Eve in Lynn Haven. Gene had secretly subscribed to health insurance for Dolphin and himself, but none for Tony or the others. He had said when Tony specified that they should all have insurance if they are to be accountable in business to its employees, and so forth. They would go, so far as believed, for a time without, until the outfit had the funds to support a plan they had yet to shop. For some unannounced reason, Gene had piloted the plan himself, using in hand his younger brother, deceptively skimming for it every quarter. Tony's fifteen-day hospital stay cost the group over $21,000.00 cash.

After a few months at Dun & Bradstreet, Tony managed to get Pression an interview with the company, and she was hired, too. Tony is taking things in stride, though anxious for the day when he would once again produce and play his drums for a living. Pression was taking things extremely hard and heartfelt. She still wanted to go out nightly, hitting the clubs, and true to form, she soon quit the very job Tony arranged for her at D&B.

She kept spending and spending; the madness

never stopped. Tony had no idea where his Pression is or where she's going. After two years of struggling, he gave up on Pression, and was close to giving up his relationship with her. Not knowing what else to do, he began to run. They began arguing constantly about matters, sometimes turning to dubious and violent reactions. She has a way of pushing him to his boiling point with the mouth she has on her. However, it was she who began taking on the more violently physical temperament. Man, the girl could be cruel. In the physical sense, mind games too, lashing out blasts with the most hurtful things to say to Tony.

*

Undoubtedly, Pression would leave Tony to chase her own career. They were already thinking divorce. Then, Tony thought of what may follow. What Pression had done to him thus far was outrageous. Tony felt lost without his drums and gear. To know she pawned-off the equipment for a fraction of the worth, for quick cash, saddened him and hurt in every sense of the word. Enraged, it ate away at him until he could stand it no longer.

The nerve of that little bitch!

Taking all that he had ever cared about.

*

Pression copped-out by expressing that she was very unhappy with Tony in New Jersey, the way things had turned out, and that she wanted to go back to Florida. There was nothing and no one in Florida for Tony, but she had extended relatives who lived there, and, like he, left behind the many friends they had made together during the last ten years together down there.

Pression finally gave Tony the flooring

ultimatum that specified she would be going back to Florida, period, with, or without him. Tony was angered, and they fought. In an ensuing argument to end all others, she, at point blank range, threw her massive key ring full force into his face. The keys and other implements on the large ring hit just below the left eye. The gash spouted blood on impact. Tony had to leave the room immediately, because he caught the thought for a moment that he might turn to kill her. He therefore went outside, trembling in pain, with adrenalin-fueled tension and paced around the house.

After walking, with his face profusely bleeding, half-a-dozen, eight times around the yard, Tony went back up to the apartment door. He ran stupidly and tragically into the door, as he realized a tad late she had locked him out. He stood there yelling out her name, alternating fists pounding the wood panels like Fred fucking Flintstone and demanding she open up the door. His first cohesive thought was to try the back door, so he ran quickly to it. He arrived there just in time to see Pression turn the dead bolt to the right. Tony bolted back to the front door and started shoulder ramming it, screaming out her name.

"Presh!"

"Presh!"

"Fuck!"

"Pression!"

Our elderly neighbor threatened to call the police, but Tony was able to calm her down, and she relented. He tried reasoning with Pression, pathetically begging her from out in the hall to open the door and let him in. He felt like Jack fucking Nicholson in The Shining.

"Come on Presh, I'm not gonna hurt you...

"I'm not gonna <u>hurt</u> you... I swear...

"Just open the door...

"Just OPEN THE FUCKING DOOR! Please."

Finally, she came to the door and opened it a crack, against the brass security chain. All Tony had to do was give it one good, strong push and he was in there. She grabbed him by the shoulders and kneed him hard to the balls. He doubled down immediately, like a folded duck, and involuntarily gasped for air his lungs could not find. She was backing away from him diagonally across the living room, toward the wall just off the kitchen. His groin ached and he felt as though he had swallowed a bowling pin. There was no room for breath, and his muscles felt shutdown. The seconds are monumental.

Pression backed-up in disgust at the sight.

This was obviously the first time she had ever kicked a man in the nuts, for she was equally horrified and incredulous. On one knee, still struggling for air, Tony could feel himself coming back around a little. Hissing and bleeding, he reached an arm and hand out toward her. Tony thought strong to muster up all the strength he could, and using every bit of it all at once, he suddenly charged. He lunged straight at her, full weighted force. Her knee went up again, but Tony was ready for it, knocking it to the side with a kick from his left boot in step. He had her shoulders in a squeeze, edging his hands toward her neck, and they are both flying comically–she backward, he forward–toward the wall. She is trying desperately with both her hands to pry his fingers from her collar, attempting to scream.

Tony saw it coming, but Presh had no idea the tall, living room window was immediately behind her. It shattered easily, like sugar glass, but the shards were treacherous. She crashed through the window and snapped backward, and downward, until her back, and then the back of her head whipped under, and hit the wall full force with two boney, thudded smacks. She was upside down, hanging out of the window, three and a half stories up, by the skin between her calves and her knees. A slender shard of glass impaled her abdomen. Tony had a hold on her, but not a good one, as his hands had broken from her neck, down to her shoulders, and had slid further to her belt, where he accidentally – or instinctively, don't know which – negotiated a fair hold on her. Tony was leaning out the window, bent over front way, still bleeding and heaving, like a downed and beaten middleweight in the fifteenth round.

At that moment, he was tempted to let go. He would simply flip her legs up so she fell out of the opening. Even though they were little more than three floors up, there was a nice cement-paved driveway directly below.

Did she really mellow me out? Maybe once, it seems like long ago. No, not lately. No, not anymore. Have I let her yank me out of my favorite stance of poetic trooper and troubadour coveted so? As I lean forward in body, and back in mind, contemplating again another defining moment, administering my own form of poetic justice, I must ask, "Must it always come to this?"

"This is Presh!

"Presh lies before me.

"Maybe I'll write a book and call it Justice Mine."

*

Kenny B sits alone in jail, fallen, teeth rotting out, suffering from hemorrhoids.

Rusty served his time, had enough Christian-like wherewithal to find the band in Tampa one Friday, share a smoke and to apologize for all he had ever done.

Floyd died of a heart attack two weeks before he was due for the last time before the judge. He would have died in prison regardless, so he got off easy in the end. Floyd won the game. Roy went back to the stables, and kept his eyes wide open. Vonegan went to Key West and became a male prostitute. It was easy money. He kept his eyes closed.

Dambert remains in Nashville, finally having found his calling. A full-time radio talent and personality, he peddles his songs street to street in the music capital, and occasionally hobnobs with real talent.

Scar disappeared without a trace, until eighteen months later, when his naked, shredded body washed up on a beach in Key

Largo, a trio of nondescript canister tins twisted around his neck and bent about his head. The tins were labeled TFSB #! - #2 - #3.

Is there anyone left about whom I care? Is there anyone left about me, who cares? Pression is the only one – beside Mom. She could never be jiving me, too, thank God.

For some unknown reason, possibly the fear that she would not die, Tony considered pulling, instead of pushing.

I would get her back in the room without a lot of trouble.

The police would be at our door within minutes and would have plenty of questions. Since the male was the one bleeding and swollen, no one would go to jail.

…But Presh was knocked-out cold…

Let her go.

Push her out.

Figuratively, it would be more like letting *Tony* go, and he thought it profound. Literally, of course, it was physically she, and the moment he thought it so easy. Too easy, in turn he thought, and easy to swallow the idea.

How would I ever be able to live without Pression?

Moreover, why would I ever allow Pression to live without me, or worse, with another?

See?

Easy.

Yes.

Easy.

Tony stood there looking, without seeing, hearing without listening, her belt slipping slowly to the ends of his fingers, and out of his grip. She was unconscious, so she'd never know. Would he remember?

Pression's belt slips slowly to the ends of his fingers, and out of his grip. She is unconscious, so she'd never know, right? Tony remembers pondering for a second, asking himself, if he believes it, is it not the truth? Does he have the strength to deny the act for the rest of his life?

Woven through it all - the chirps, the pops, the buzzing, the waves, the laughter, coughing and cries, the noise and the clatter - with those fucking voices railroading through his busy head like cold, dull, blue steel blades, *The Clash* thundered on in a loop:

"Should I Stay or Should I Go?"

Tony remembers the love he shared with Pression for so many years. He remembers the devotion and care they bestowed upon each other by the day and by the years. In the end, he remained enslaved by it, and by her, and he knew it. So, he dropped her, and he ran. With the clothes on his back, and his denim jacket tucked under his arm, he grabbed the bloody key ring off the floor and ran out the fucking door.

Neighbor Marge's radio played polka music across the hall. She is no doubt oblivious, sitting at her kitchen table, as usual, with her bottle of scotch and carton of Camels. He took three stairs at a time, bounding to the first floor in a second. He clamored out the big, Victorian doors, leaping once down the five cement steps in the front. Around the apartment and up the driveway, he ran. He ran right past Pression, jumping over her as though she were a fleshy hurdle.

In fact, she had become a hurdle of sorts.

Not a thought spared as he backed down

the driveway faster than most people would have driven it forward. Not one thought, as Pression's limp body thumped beneath him. The little Ford Escort could never have cleared her if he had been going any slower.

He drove straight to Metro Park, a ratty train station near the ghettos of Iselin, parked the car outside the remote lot, and bought a one-way ticket to Ft. Lauderdale.

There is a cop down there, owes me a favor.

THE END